Glossy Black Cockatoos

Dan Guenther

2009

Redburn Press, Inc.

ISBN 1-933704-04-7

ISBN 978-1993704047

Printed in the United States of America
Cover design by Ingrid Guenther

Acknowledgments

I would like to thank Dow Mossman, Steve Kennedy, Ed Gorman, and Colonel Bob Fischer, USMC (Ret.) for their help with this book. As well, thanks to my daughter, Ingrid, and Dave Scott, for their ongoing design and photography work.

I would like to acknowledge my subject master at Woolooware High School, John Riley, for his coaching when I taught Ancient History. I still have the copy of *Ancient History, Book II, Romans*, Department of Education, NSW, that John gave me back in 1975, a resource I drew upon when writing this novel. To George Twogood, my headmaster at Woolooware High School, and a former prisoner of war in Singapore's Changi Prison, I owe thanks for his mentoring and encouragement of my writing.

A thanks goes to Jerry Downey, my life-long friend and fellow veteran, who served with the Special Forces and Team 30 in Laos from 1959 to 1960, for his insights and cultural perspectives.

And finally, I thank my wife, Cheryl, for her ongoing support of my writing.

Table of Contents

Author's Note

While writing *Glossy Black Cockatoos* I drew upon the input of two fellow veterans. One is a Marine who served in Vietnam, and has since returned there, also traveling extensively through China. He is active with the Hmong community in Denver, Colorado. The other is a member of the Hmong tribe who was a lieutenant with the SGU (Special Guerrilla Unit). Because they still travel back to Southeast Asia, they asked that their names not be mentioned in this author's note. However, their insights with regard to Laos and the history of the Hmong people were invaluable to me.

In addition, in the back of this book readers will find an historical note on the role of the Hmong during the Vietnam War written by Colonel Bob Fischer, USMC (Ret) former Lecturer on Strategy and Tactics of the Insurgent, Naval War College.

Also, some readers may make comparisons between *Glossy Black Cockatoos* and the 2001 arrest and outrageous incarceration of an Australian couple in Laos. No comparison is intended. That outrage takes place years after the events portrayed in this novel. Yet, that brutality is consistent with past and current treatment of the Hmong in Laos, which many in the international community look upon as a crime against humanity.

Chapter One: Long Daddy Green

Sam Gatlin and I paddled our canoe out onto the vast East Alligator Lagoon, looking for the semi-albino crocodile called Long Daddy Green, a strange and spectacular creature mottled with white spots and striking patches of a brilliant, almost luminescent yellow. This sanctuary was soon to be declared the Kakadu National Park, and we had talked to several rangers about this unique reptile. Since Long Daddy Green was said to be a relatively small salt-water croc, and others had taken photos of him, we didn't feel in any particular danger.

"We're almost out of beer," Sam said to me, waving to Celia and Maggie.

Sam, Maggie, Celia, and I were on holiday; a treat paid for by Colin, with he and his wife, Naomi, acting as our guides. This gift was in return for Sam's ongoing support of Colin's various projects with Southeast Asia Company; and, despite the rain, we were in awe of the extensive spans of water lilies and the multitudes of bird life.

Maggie and Celia huddled together, protected from the drizzle by a big umbrella. The wholesome and fetching Maggie, tall and slim, could have been the singer Joni Mitchell's twin, only with shorter, curly blonde hair. She was very unhappy with Sam. In part, her unhappiness was due to Sam's excessive drinking, but she also had a great fear of the *salties*, as she called the crocs, repeatedly cautioning us to keep our distance. And Sam, always the risk-taker, ignored her warnings.

"That ranger said Long Daddy Green stays up in the backwaters," I said, draining my Flag Ale.

"Roger that," Sam replied. "I wish we didn't have this drizzle. Not enough light for good pictures. Too bad Colin and Naomi are still passed out. They could tell us where to go. As long as we keep out of the main river channel we should be fine. The current in the main channel is way too fast for this canoe."

"I'll take another Flag Ale," I said.

"Don't have any left. All we have are bottles of Export Pilsner. I left some cans of KB back in the big cooler for Colin when he wakes up."

"Sam, Export Pilsner will do me just fine. But Colin doesn't like KB. He's got to have Flag Ale."

"Hey, where the hell do you think you're going with my canoe?" Colin yelled, stumbling out of his tent, Naomi peering out after him, her wide-eyed expression like that of a started Ring Tail Possum.

"You've taken all the beer!" Colin said.

"Colin, check out my tent. You'll find some KB Lager in the big cooler," Sam said.

* * *

Our first day in the area, Colin had taken us to see the Ubirr Site. One of the paintings at that site depicted the *Namarrgarn Sisters*. These sisters played tricks on each other until one day they realized that if they changed into crocodiles permanently they could eat anything or anybody they liked. An old man heard of their intention to become crocodiles and chased after them to stop them, but was too late.

"The painting represents the sisters as crocodiles, and the story of the sisters is told to Aboriginal children to warn them about crocodiles, part of longer set of stories told to them," Colin said, draining the first of many Flag Ales.

"I'm probably the only bitch on Ozone Street who has sipped Jean Grivot Grand Cru Clos de Vougeot Pinot from Burgundy, one of the great Pinot Noirs of the world, and still drinks KB Lager," Naomi said, pulling up her loose-fitting top.

Naomi was a Natalie Wood look-alike, but taller and leggy, and much more voluptuous.

"You got that bitch part right, Naomi," Sam said, jokingly.

"Oh Sam, you are such a fabulous cut of Yank beef. I could eat you if Maggie would let me."

Naomi's retort left Sam speechless, and we settled in to listen while Colin rambled on about a creation ancestor called the Rainbow Serpent.

"There are many creation stories concerning mythical serpents. One tells of an Emu-Man who transformed himself into an all-powerful being called the Rainbow Serpent. This being dislikes loud noises. If irritated, it is capable of causing great harm. The Rainbow Serpent will eat anything except flying foxes," Colin continued.

"Naomi, would you eat a flying fox?" Sam asked, with a smirk.

"Colin, give it a rest, we've heard enough of your bloody Rainbow Serpent. Here! This is Eristoff Premium Vodka based on Prince Eristoff's original recipe from 1806," Naomi said, leaning forward, her long chestnut hair screening her décolletage. "This bottle came all the way from Beaucaire, France. I think the wolf howling at the moon logo is particularly appropriate for Colin's campfire lectures. Sam, this is one of the very few types of vodka worthy of drinking at room temperature. Sip it, and it's easy to think you're back in Europe."

"I've never been to Europe," Sam said winking at me, weary of Naomi's drunken pretensions.

"I didn't think so," Naomi said, smiling.

"I propose a toast," Colin interrupted. "To living the good life! And fear not the lurking serpents!"

The toasts continued well into the early morning, with Colin and Naomi draining their bottle of Prince Eristoff's original recipe. I turned in just after midnight, wondering if we were disturbing the Rainbow Serpent.

At the Ubirr Site that day we learned that the spiritual life as well as the ancient laws that governed the Aboriginal people are captured in those rock paintings. But that next morning in 1976, out looking for Long Daddy Green in Colin's old fourteen-foot fiberglass canoe, Sam and I were oblivious to such laws. Looking back, I wonder what we were thinking.

* * *

The drizzle soon turned to a warm rain, and as Sam and I moved up further into a backwater, Colin faded in the distance, drinking his can of KB. Our canoe sat low in the water, not much distance between a big crocodile and us. The same ranger who had told us about Long Daddy Green had also warned us about a couple of big crocs that hung out in the main river channel. But that didn't seem to bother Sam. After an hour of searching the maze of channels, we realized we were lost, and we pulled our canoe over to a sandy bank to rest.

"Let's explore that channel to see where it leads," Sam said, pointing to what appeared to be no more than a tunnel overhung with brush. It should take us back closer to the river. "We're lost."

The rain continued, and at times we had to pull our canoe through sandy shallows. But our tunnel eventually opened up into more of a channel where the going got easier. Steep mud banks rose on each side of us and we found our way blocked by a fallen tree. We looked around carefully before getting out to pull our canoe up the bank. We would be safe from crocodiles in the canoe, but standing or wading in the water was risky.

"Oh shit," Sam said, in a whisper.

"What's the matter?" I asked.

"I'm spooked. Let's find a way out of here."

We pulled our canoe up the bank to find that we were on a sandy island, the broad muddy waters of the East Alligator River flowing swiftly only 200 yards away. Our tunnel had taken us back toward the main river. Across the river the branches of the paperbarks hung heavy in the wet. A dramatic escarpment rose behind the thick stand of trees.

"I think I know where we are. I remember some of those rock paintings over by those cliffs. Shit, we got a long way to go to get back," Sam said.

"Back the way we came?"

"Not a chance. We'd get lost again. We got to do the main channel. Our camp should be right around that big bend. I figure that's maybe five hundred yards or so. We should be able to make it. We will stay in the middle of the river."

"Let's do it," I said, trying to sound confident.

We paddled hard out to mid-river without any problems. Then, rounding the bend, we saw in midstream what appeared to be a floating log, barely awash. We grew closer and saw that it was a big croc, an eighteen-footer, and it seemed that our paths were converging.

"My God! Paddle for that backwater," Sam said, pointing to a waterway overhung with brush, similar to that tunnel where we had lost our way.

"Do you see him?" Sam asked.

"I think we lost him. Well, at least we were on the right side of the river. Let's follow this backwater and find a spot to pull the canoe out."

"Roger that, Dai 'ui. I'll never go anywhere around here again without an automatic weapon," Sam said, laughing nervously.

We continued a good fifty yards further into the calm backwater, and the water grew increasingly shallow, the banks on either side of us steep faces of slippery mud. We were in only about two feet of water and were totally surprised when something struck the canoe from behind. It struck again, the flimsy fiberglass side shuddering, and in the swirl of the water I saw the white mottled snout and luminescent yellow head of Long Daddy Green.

"That can only be Long Daddy Green," Sam said, paddling toward the bank.

"I thought you said Long Daddy Green wasn't that big. He's got to be ten feet long," I said

"Grab that tree!" Sam yelled, nodding at a nearby tree limb hanging down from the bank wall. I grabbed the limb and steadied the canoe as Sam leaped onto the lower branches, climbing to safety. At the same time, the croc glided up alongside the canoe. Without thinking I jumped for the tree and Sam grabbed my arm as I pulled myself up onto a tree branch. Out of the corner of my eye I caught the blur of Long Daddy Green's huge, toothed jaws bursting upward from the water, seizing my dangling left leg in his jaws and whirling in midair.

But Long Daddy Green's grip slipped, stripping off my pant leg and my left tennis shoe in the process. In that instant Sam and I were up and onto the bank.

"Thank you God," Sam said, breathlessly.

As if Long Daddy Green had heard Sam, he surfaced, hovering in the shallow water, his hide mottled with white spots and laced with a curious mix of brilliant yellows and greens, some shades of which appeared almost chartreuse.

"I wonder if he's been hanging out with those Namarrgarn Sisters," I said, backing away.

"That might be funny in another time and place. I can't believe that ranger called Long Daddy Green a photo opportunity. This photo opportunity will take you to your dream place, big time."

Long Daddy turned in the water and made a coughing sound, spitting out my tennis shoe.

"That could have been your nuts," Sam said, watching my tennis shoe sink in the dark water.

Sam tore up his shirt and bound the small wound on my leg. I could still walk so we struggled back along the bank until we got to our camp. Maggie wept after she heard about our close call. Celia simply sat in stunned silence. Colin gave us each a cold can of KB. We both felt foolish, having risked our lives to find Long Daddy Green. For once the gorgeous Naomi had little to say.

"I don't want to disturb Colin's Rainbow Serpent," she said, trying to make a joke, clearly still hung over from last night.

So we all sat quietly, careful not to disturb the Rainbow Serpent in the gathering dusk, listening to twilight calls of the various birds in the dense crowns of the trees, and gazing up at the emerging celestial gallery above our heads. At one point I heard Sam whisper, "Maggie, we will have a great story to tell the crowd down at the Hotel Cecil."

"Sam, I don't want to hear it."

"We were just trying to find Long Daddy Green," Sam said.

"Sam, you seem to go about the business of life as if there were no consequences for your actions. My God! That's the key, isn't it?"

"The key to what?" Sam asked.

"The key to understanding you, that's what! You avoid taking personal responsibility. That's why you haven't been able to make any commitment to me," Maggie replied.

The birds stopped calling the trees, and for a long time we remained quiet, gazing up at the stars. Then Maggie broke the silence.

"Sam, do you see that dark spot in the Milky Way, just above our heads? Aborigines call that spot Namondjok. He's one of the creation ancestors, like the Emu-Man Colin talked so much about, the being that became a Rainbow Serpent. The story goes that Namondjok broke the kinship laws with his sister, and was banished by his clan. Now Namondjok must live in eternal darkness, never to be in that common dream place where all our creation ancestors meet."

*   *   *

Chapter Two: Unfinished Business

A squall was blowing in off the Tasman Sea, making landfall just before midnight, bringing high winds and rain. Disturbed by the sound of the winds buffeting our building, I find myself awake. Our apartment is high enough so that at times it feels as if our high-rise is swaying. Maybe it is.

I was having a bad dream, walking an old trail along a high ridgeline near the Laotian Border. It was May 1969 during Operation Oklahoma Hills. In my dream it was early morning, and very still. The smoke from my first cigarette hung in the humid air of the jungle. Below me, fog had pooled in the lower elevations, filling the valley with a white blanket. I must have taken the dream as a sign, sensing an unknown in that ghostly, hanging cloud; and I broke out in a sweat from some unreasoning fear. Lately, I've been slipping back again, crossing that wine-dark ocean of my dreams, where the story is always left unfinished.

The streetlights cast surreal shadows down in Cronulla Park as the wind tosses the thick, heavy tops of Washingtonian Palms. A family of Ring Tail Possums lives in the park. One night my wife, Celia, spotted a curious male possum, peering down at her. The fact that a family of Ring Tail Possums has chosen to live on Ozone Street is an event that all the families in our building find exciting. But Celia is the most excited. The possum family brings back memories of her childhood in Iowa.

Celia is seven months pregnant, and that's one of the things keeping me up at night. She wants to raise our child in the States. Her sister arrived yesterday for a two-month visit, and plans to stay until after the baby is born. From the way her sister talks, it is clear that Celia's family wants her back home. In these last few weeks Celia has been homesick. So I'm grateful that her sister's here. It takes considerable pressure off me.

Woolooware High School is on a two-week break, and lately I've been thinking about giving up my teaching job to do something else before we move back to Iowa. The tedium of preparing daily lessons and correcting papers is wearing me out, and I long for the excitement of my past life.

The storm grows more intense, heavy drops of rain beating hard on the windows. Outside lightning flashes, illuminating the slanting sheets of rain. Cool air streams through the half open window. The curtains billow out in wave-like motions. The Washingtonian Palms continue to roll in the gusting wind. For a long time I watch the rain. Then the storm finally moves south and the night sky clears. At one in the morning there is a knock on my door.

"Dai 'ui! Open up. It's Sam."

My buddy, Sam Gatlin is at the door, calling me by my Vietnamese nickname. He sounds totally pissed, as my Aussie friends say.

"Hey Sam, What's going on? You have another late night at the rugby league club? Maggie will be upset if you don't get home."

"She threw me out. She doesn't like my new friend," Sam said.

"Who's that?"

"Jack Daniels. He's a great listener, only he never has anything to say," Sam said.

"Jack Daniels is hard on your liver," I reply.

"My liver will go sooner or later, and Jack is the perfect companion, good to have in the dark of the night. I'm sure Maggie wouldn't agree with that."

"Maggie needs her sleep. She's working hard to finish up her Master's degree. That has it's own way of wearing you out. Believe me, I know."

"I need to talk."

"Its one o'clock in the morning."

"I know. And I got a big dick that I can't get hard anymore. Maggie's not happy about that either. Maybe you can give me some advice," Sam said with a smart-ass grin.

"Happens when you drink too much," I reply.

"Well, I got all kinds of stuff we can talk about. Nam. Or what happens after you die? Will someone be there to bury me when I fucking die?"

Sam had a habit of pondering the inexplicable when he had too much to drink. After a few beers, the taciturn Sam Gatlin would open up, telling story after story, often wearing out his listeners. He was my friend and fellow brother-in-arms, but at times his long yarning wore me out. He was a man suspended between the past and the present, forever stranded between a home back in the Midwest and those faraway places that lingered in his memory. Like he said to me more than once, he had a lot of unfinished business.

"Come on in. We can sit out on the balcony and watch the stars. But you're not going to go to heaven because there is no heaven. And if there was, you wouldn't be allowed in, not after killing those Thai pirates," I reply, trying to make a joke.

While serving in Vietnam, I was exposed to Buddhist thought. That exposure had an impact on me, and even today my belief system draws from that experience. There is no creator in Buddhist cosmology, and no higher plane of meaning than the here and now. I don't believe in either a heaven or a hell. But I do believe in evil, and have experienced it first hand, watching the actions of some create a living hell for others.

As for a higher power, sometimes I think that there may be a singular force of creation, but it appears to have many faces. My travels have taught me to respect the diversity I've found, and I suppose that each fragment of creation can be viewed as part of one design that extends unbroken, connecting all life. Yet, it is also clear to me that each of us must find our own way. It is a difficult thing to explain to others, including my wife. Due to her upbringing, she is very sensitive about certain religious issues, and has a strong belief in the soul.

"Fuck you, Dai 'ui. There is a hell, and you will be wallowing in there with me, burning in the fire."

Before I can answer, a single streak of intense light shoots across the western sky over Ozone Street, a dazzling shooting star. Another brilliant streak parallels the first. The second meteor is followed by several more, smaller than the previous two. They enter the atmosphere in rapid succession, a sudden wave of stellar particles and dust burning up in a burst of energy.

Sam is awestruck. The wonder of the event calms him. Like Sam, watching the brief meteor shower, I am transfixed, and my problems seem small in relation to the beauty and excitement of the sudden shower. For a moment, I am again part of the natural order, just hanging out.

"Dai 'ui, why does a decorated captain leave the Marines to teach history in faraway Australia?" Sam asked, taking a pull on his beer.

"Oh, that's easy to answer. With the Marine Corps I found myself in a rut. There was nothing to look forward to. Teaching these Aussie kids is all about the future. And Celia wanted to see The

Outback, and the Never Never. And she has."

"Teaching history is about the future! Ha! That's a good one, Dai 'ui."

For a long time we watch the Southern Cross in the great bowl of the night sky, and I wonder how much of what affects me I bring upon myself. There is a part of me that I have never shared, a part that I have been carrying with me since my Vietnam experience. It isn't that I don't trust others enough to share that experience. Rather, it's that what I would share is so revelatory and violent in nature that they might become fearful of me, especially Celia, afraid for herself and our unborn child.

Across Ozone Street, the last drunks are stumbling out of the Hotel Cecil, a place Naomi and Colin Musto like to call a den of iniquitous pleasures. While the pretensions of the self-absorbed Colin and Naomi set them apart from the local crowd at the Hotel Cecil, Sam and I seem to fit right in. Even though the crowd is a clannish lot, united by a belief in the superiority of the Cronulla Sharks, our Yank differences in background and education don't seem to matter to the rank and file down at the Hotel Cecil. We are accepted as kindred spirits, fellow lovers of rugby league football and possessed of a confidence that can only come from having filled your gut with piss among your mates in accordance with the tribal code.

"Do you want to make some big money?"

"Doing what?" I ask.

"Helping Colin and me in Laos. The job sure beats teaching for a living. I see all the work Maggie brings home, papers to check, lessons to prepare, if you call that a living," Sam said.

"You bad-mouthing my profession?"

"Why do you want to work so hard when there are other opportunities?

"I like being a teacher, Sam. When done right, teaching is more than simply imparting knowledge. Good teachers command the respect of students and fellow teachers. And one is part of a community."

"I had a high school football coach everyone adored. Then his team stopped winning, and he eventually lost his mind to booze," Sam said.

"At one point he must have had the gift," I reply.

"What gift?"

"The gift to inspire people, not everyone can do that. The gift is about heightening awareness, to inspire students to learning in all dimensions."

"How do you do that, Dai 'ui?"

"By emphasis on the positive, and recognizing their individual differences. One has to use methods that explore those individual interests. That's how. And like I said. It's hard work.

"Sounds complicated."

"Believe it or not, Naomi Musto had the gift when we taught together. It was clear that her students adored her. She just got crossed up with her fellow teachers. It was a jealousy thing."

"Colin told me about it. You know Dai 'ui, Naomi says that we will be remembered on the wrong side of history. Because we lost the war."

"Yeah, I've heard her opinions," I reply.

"Those fucking pirates got what they deserved," Sam says out of the blue.

During the Fall of Saigon in April 1975, Sam was involved with the rescue of several boatloads of Vietnamese refugees adrift on the South China Sea. His employer at the time was Independent Dutch Petroleum. Later, in the same ship, with the help of two Dutch Marines, he took on some Thai pirates, taking out their speedboat before they could escape.

"You don't have to defend your actions with me. I'm your friend."

"According to witnesses that scum tossed little kids to the sharks following their boat," Sam said, opening another beer.

"Don't you think you've had enough to drink?"

"Dai 'ui, you sound like that controlling bitch, Maggie, or maybe Miss Swan. Miss Swan said she was afraid of me when I drank."

"I understand your history with Maggie. She likes you to show up sober at dinnertime, after she's had a long day. But you never told me the whole story about that Miss Swan," I said, pulling the bag of beer away from Sam.

"Oh, it was Miss Swan that she went by. No first name, just Miss Swan. I met her on my second tour while in Da Nang. She was working for the Musee' de Cham. You know that museum, the one with the old Cham sculptures?"

"Yeah, the place near The White Lotus with all the big stone heads out front. The White Lotus! What a great place that was! Those women! Wow!"

"Well, none of them could hold a candle to Miss Swan. It was strange how I bumped into her again after Da Nang. I was working for Independent Dutch Petroleum, providing security for one of their seismic survey boats, the ones they do oil exploration with. We pulled into Saigon for some liberty. Our captain was a Dutch guy named Van Der Molen. We had a crew of four, including myself for security, and then these two Dutch Marines," Sam continued, now into his story.

"Dutch Marines are tough dudes," I said.

"*The Korps Mariniers*! Those guys are professionals. They know their business."

"They were on active duty?"

"Absolutely. The Dutch don't mess around when it comes to security on the high seas. They've been known to put Marines on merchantmen flying the Dutch flag, depending upon the need."

"I can't imagine our country doing that with our merchant fleet," I said.

"There is always a need in the South China Sea, and on into Indonesian waters. The guys we had with us were from the Maritime Special Operations Forces, called MARSOF. Anyway, we were all sitting out on the veranda of the Hotel Continental, drinking when Captain Van Der Molen directs our attention to this beautiful Eurasian woman walking into the bar. It was Miss Swan, and they shit when they saw me get up to greet her."

"I can imagine. I bet you had them guessing."

"Na. These Dutch didn't poke their noses into other folks' business. I liked working with them. And there was no bullshit if you thought there was a threat. It was all lock and load. Captain Van Der Molen told us this terrible story about an Australian family he knew. Pirates in the Sulu Sea kidnapped them. The guy was sailing with his wife and two teen-age daughters out of Darwin. He had a schooner with a Bermuda rig and couldn't outrun the pirates. They took his wife and daughters and left him adrift in a dingy."

"Where was the Australian Navy?"

"Good question. There's a lot of blue water out there, and the guy may have actually been in Indonesian waters. Anyway, Captain Van Der Molen picked him up and was later involved with paying the ransom."

"So they recovered the wife and daughters…"

"They did. But they had been raped. The Aussies protested to the Indonesians, but nothing ever happened. No justice. Fuckers got away with it. The pirates bribed the Indonesians."

"That's an outrage! What happened to justice?"

"When Van Der Molen told the story he'd get tears in his eyes."

"Roger that."

"When Saigon was falling in April of '75 we were finishing up some oil exploration off Phu Quoc Island. About that time we got a call for help on the radio from some British and Chinese folks stranded on Phu Quoc. They had fled Saigon a couple days before and were holed up on the island. In the confusion they missed their pick-up."

"There was a lot of that. I've heard stories."

"So on our way to get the Brits we come upon a speedboat full of pirates in the process of working over some boat people. We caught them red-handed, raping a couple of the women.

"You never told me this part of the story."

"No. Some things are best left untold. I dropped two of them with my Remington. Then the captain fired our fifty-caliber into their engine. They were dead in the water and we had them outgunned. They were in a hurt and tried to surrender."

"You said, 'tried to surrender'?"

"After we took the Vietnamese refugees on board, we wasted the scum."

"That's murder."

"That's justice. A captain's word is law on the high seas."

"Sam, that's true, a captain's word is law. But was that justice? I'm not so sure."

"Yeah, well, it did bother me some. From time to time I can still see their faces. After a few drinks, I could tell that the captain regretted what had gone down. He was a former prisoner of war in Singapore's infamous Changi Prison, and he told me that when you fight monsters, you become one yourself. Then he rambled on, trying to justify why he couldn't have carried any of them back to Thailand. There were too many to take on board, too risky. But the other thing had to do with the Thai authorities. It was only a matter of time before the son of bitches bribed the Thai authorities and bought their way to freedom."

"Bribes are the way business is done in Southeast Asia. I bet you see that all the time with Colin's business," I added.

"For sure, especially in Laos."

Through Durham, Durham, Perry, & Musto, Colin provided legal services for clients who traveled through Southeast Asia. The Southeast Asia Company, a separate and specially chartered company under Colin's oversight, provided contract security services to the same clients. Those clients included the World Bank and two development agencies with the United Nations. However, through a former client and current Laotian Politburo member, Colin linked to a shadowy power broker in the new Laotian regime, a French-educated intellectual called KV.

KV was one of the few open to dealing with the decadent capitalists. Colin acted as his intermediary and legal advisor, providing him with contacts to such organizations as the World Bank and the UN. Colin was unique in his ability to access the high-ranking members of the new Laotian regime. Apparently Colin's ties with KV went back to the days when he was a student at the London School of Economics and traveled through France on a frequent basis.

"What was it that they called the Mekong, the river of evil memory?" I asked.

"I don't know, something like that. You know, Dai 'ui, it was out of my hands. Those Dutch Marines didn't hesitate when Captain Van Der Molen gave the order."

"If the captain perceived a threat, he had to do what he thought best at the time."

"When we got to Phu Quoc, the place was in chaos. We picked up the Brits and a couple of Aussies. Miss Swan was among the Chinese refugees, the *Hoa*, as they call themselves. Then we took them all to Thailand. Everything would have been cool, but some of the boat people talked too much, and the story leaked to the press."

"And now I know for sure that you're not going to heaven."

"Don't say that shit, Dai 'ui."

"So what happened to your Miss Swan?"

"Lost touch. We had cultural differences, she being high class, me being a dirt hauler from Iowa. Last I heard she went to work for some French museum. Let's change the subject. Some day I'll tell you the whole story about her," Sam said, sadly.

We had talked a long time, and the sun was coming up. Down in Cronulla Park a Sulfur-Crested Cockatoo screeched in the thick palms, greeting the new day. It occurred to me how similar Sam and I were in so many respects, both from Iowa, both Marine officers who served in Quang Nam Province; and we both had our unfinished business so-to-speak; only Sam's currents ran deeper than mine. From time to time I've seen Sam's unfinished business explode, and he has been known to do wild and self-destructive things at rugby parties, like eating glass.

"Sam, forget about those pirates. Ask yourself what you are looking for. That's the question."

"No, that's not the question. The question is how do you live with yourself after two tours in the Nam and the Fall of Saigon?" Sam replied. "And Dai 'ui, one night I made the mistake of telling Maggie about those pirates. She asked me if I believed in the sacredness of human life."

"Well, do you?" I asked.

"Yeah, now I do. I didn't then, but now I do."

Things left undone have driven more than one person crazy. But this thing, whatever it was needing resolution within Sam, was as elusive as one of those rare Glossy Black Cockatoos his Maggie raved on and on about, the birds that were the subject of her ongoing Master's degree.

"After the pirate incident I went on a two week drunk down in King's Cross. The binge, and what the Sydney Morning Herald called rash actions on the high seas by Captain Van Der Molen cost both of us our jobs. But for the intervention of Captain Graham, I'd have been tossed out of Australia," Sam said.

Captain John Graham, late of the SAS, and Sam's former comrade-in arms in Vietnam, had linked him up with Colin Musto. Colin Musto was quick to sense that Sam was different and he gave him a chance to redeem himself.

People didn't go to Cronulla for intellectual stimulation. They went there for the beach, with its bonzer surfing, casual sex, wild parties, and Cronulla Shark football. Watching Sam play rugby, Colin understood that Sam's deep melancholy masked a fearless and sanguinary temperament, a character hardened in dangerous third-world landscapes, some wet, dark and tropical, others bright and waterless, plains swept by hot winds, and ready to ignite. Colin needed Sam's experience to fill a specialized role within his firm's expanding business in Asia and Africa. It was a highly lucrative business, and Sam would be a perfect fit. Sam's proficiency with the Remington 700 BDL 308 sniper rifle was just one more added benefit to what Colin called a diverse skill set. Thus began a tale that took Sam back to Southeast Asia.

* * *

Chapter Three: Glossy Black Cockatoos

Dinner was on our eccentric neighbor from Ozone Street, Colin Musto. As usual, he was dominating the conversation, sitting across from me with his wife, Naomi, lecturing his sister Maggie about why this restaurant, adjacent to the Sydney Hilton, was the rage. As he spoke, he checked the glasses and place settings in his fastidious way.

"The menu here is short and simple. But the wine list is comprehensive. If you're feeling adventurous, try the deep-fried skate knobs with lemons and capers aioli for appetizers. Naomi and I highly recommend them," Colin said, inspecting what appeared to be a water spot on his wine glass.

The occasion was to celebrate Colin's promotion to full partner in the law firm of Dunham, Dunham, Perry, & Musto. That promotion came as a result of Colin forming the highly successful Southeast Asia Company, a unique business, with offices in Hong Kong, Johannesburg, and Sydney, that provided both legal and security services to clients in both Asia and Africa.

But to all four couples seated around the table, this was a kick-off dinner to what would be a long holiday weekend. Captain John Graham and his wife, Julia, Colin's business associates, sat to my left. Sam sat to my right, and was already loaded. Maggie, sitting by herself at the end of the table, gave him a disgusted look as he ordered another Foster's. My wife Celia, pregnant with our first daughter Inga, was having no alcohol. I was pacing myself, still on my second beer.

Colin was doing his utmost to ensure that John Graham and his wife, Julia, were entertained.

Captain Graham owned a small fleet of planes that he contracted out to Southwest Asia Company. In return, Colin facilitated an arrangement whereby Graham could now fly his cargo planes into Laos. Sam had worked with Graham in Vietnam, and then later in Angola, where Graham met Julia, and had built up a successful security consulting business to corporations doing business in Africa.

Julia, a darkly beautiful Portuguese woman, was also a resource for Colin with her network of contacts throughout Africa. She had been raised in Angola, her father an engineer who was killed in that country's civil war.

A waiter filled our wine glasses with Cotes de Provence Rose, and Colin proposed a toast.

"To eating and drinking in good company!"

The long narrow room had high, cathedral-like windows on one side, and pale, blue-green wallpaper with small, gilt-edge framed pictures on the other. Our table, lit by small, angled lights from Doric columns on either side of us, seated eight comfortably beneath a frosted lamp that sported a huge, round baroque lampshade. The white, ornate service cupboards looked French, and the whole atmosphere was warm, cozy, and, as Naomi was quick to point out, very European.

"There is an upstairs backroom along the same theme as this room. But there they have these glorious freestanding lamps. Everything fits marvelously. Colin, tell them about our last experience here." Naomi said, waving her Gaulois about as if it were a magic wand.

"Ah," Colin continued, "Truly dream entrees. Naomi had the marinated trout with zucchini flowers. I had a spiced squid with sweet paprika mayonnaise. Both dishes totally exceeded our expectations. My only criticism would be to use Gould's squid, which has bigger and thicker flesh, than the more dainty Loligo squid from the Hawkesbury. And the Loligo was slightly chewy."

"Another time, for lunch, we both ordered the beer-battered flathead with chips, and it was quite sensational, as good as Bistro Guillaumes's fish and chips in Melbourne, only simpler in presentation," Naomi said, leaning forward so that we all could admire her cleavage.

Maggie noticed how long Sam's eyes lingered on Naomi, and she was not pleased. Colin and Naomi were unique among our Australian friends. Celia and I had met them soon after arriving in Australia. Naomi was a teacher at Wollooware High School where I taught higher certificate courses in English and Ancient History. Their condo was right above ours at 21/26 Ozone Street in Cronulla, a trendy beachfront high-rise complex.

An Art teacher with a radical pedagogy, Naomi soon ran into conflicts with her department head, and left teaching after only a year. When South Vietnam was falling, she and I had endless conversations over the nature of that war. While Sam and I were serving as Marines in Vietnam, she had been a student at the University of Sydney, protesting the war. In hindsight, I now realize her objections to the war made a great deal of sense. At the time I couldn't admit that to myself.

"Naomi, it appears your husband is becoming a connoisseur of the finer restaurants in Sydney. I didn't expect that of a former standout in rugby league," Graham said smiling.

"Colin takes everything he does so seriously. Now that I'm not teaching, I've taken it upon myself to lighten his burdens by organizing his dinner events," Naomi said with a smirk, and then added, "But actually, he would probably refer to himself as a *gastronome*. When he's not researching the law, his nose is always into a book on wine or the rituals of *haute cuisine*. That study has taken a place in his life once reserved for the Cronulla Sharks."

"My dear, you are too kind. I rank myself among the amateurs," Colin replied, with false modesty.

"So what does that make you?" Sam asked Naomi with a contemptuous tone, clearly up to some mischief.

"Good question. I am best described as an *epicure*," Naomi replied, giving Maggie a sly wink.

"What is this epicure?" Julia asked.

"An epicure is one with sensitive and discriminating tastes, who is devoted to sensual pleasure," Naomi responded, studying Sam as if she were sizing up his insulting manner.

"And what does that make me?" Sam asked, his ornery streak now showing after a few beers.

"Well, my big Yank friend. To me you are a *bon vivant* for all seasons, one who enjoys fine eating and drinking in good company, as well as ridicule."

The loquacious Naomi was well educated, highly articulate, and usually a lot of fun with her twisted sense of humor. But after a few drinks her dark side could come out. With Naomi, one had to choose one's words carefully.

"Colin tells us that you met Germaine Greer at Cambridge," Graham said, trying to divert the conversation in a more positive direction.

"Yes, at Newnham College, where I studied art history," Naomi said coolly, now on guard.

"Careful, Captain," Colin said nervously, "She can quote verbatim from *The Female Eunuch*, and she is more than willing to share her perspectives on the worldwide oppression of women."

"I haven't a clue about that," the Captain said.

"I heard Greer was arrested in New Zealand for promoting the book and her ideology," Sam said, not realizing he had just stumbled into an ambush.

"Ideology? My friend would say that word is a synonym for lies," Naomi said with an unrestrained intensity. "She is an anarchist, and she also once said that reality comes first, ideology second."

"Well, I suppose there are any number of academics and scholars who call themselves anarchists, living in their ivory towers. Probably never played football, and clearly not in touch with my reality. And I certainly agree that reality should come before ideology" the Captain said, stepping into the line of fire.

"At Wollooware High School I made the mistake of once telling my students that a constant process of renewal is needed," Naomi replied. "That they should remember to question all things, and to challenge whatever oligarchy is in power, whether that be the Khmer Rouge or some American puppet dancing to *Yankee Doodle Dandy*."

"Careful! You speak of those two things as if they were one and the same. Khmer Rouge are about genocide," Sam said, rising out of his chair.

"Your American puppet or your Khmer Rouge, both have a hierarchy of power that oppresses people," Naomi said, sensing the upper hand.

"That's an oversimplification," Captain Graham said, now on the offensive.

"That's reality," Naomi replied, confidently.

"Did you find such oversimplifications in Greer's book?" Graham asked.

"*The Female Eunuch* is about how women have become separated from their libido, like a Devon ox that's been cut in order to be made docile."

"You can't castrate a woman!" Sam said, laughing.

"It's a metaphor, my dark Yank. When you cut off a woman from her capacity for action, the effect is the same. The hierarchy confines women, demeans and subjugates them through stereotypes and insipid rules that repress them. Keeps them from having real fun."

"Naomi, some women want a strong man, especially out in the country," Julia said, trying to track with the conversation.

"Julia, that's probably why I love the big cities, the masses of people rushing hither and thither, their faces lit by the flicker of headlights and neon signs, the dense, blurred crowd so anonymous, full of erotic possibilities…"

"Oh my, Naomi, that's poetic," Maggie said.

"That's un-Australian," Graham said.

"Maggie," Sam muttered, "Don't be seduced by all this shit."

"Naomi, I don't hear much about family values in your ideas. I would venture to guess that Colin doesn't repress you in any way," Graham said. "I'm sure that he gives you everything you want."

"Captain, Colin is not capable of repressing me; nor for that matter are you or any other man at this table," Naomi snapped curtly.

"Maybe you will feel differently after you have children," Julia said quietly.

Naomi was a beautiful woman who at times came across as an intellectual snob. Flamboyant, with an exhibitionistic streak, her intellect could wreak havoc at the dinner parties and other social events that she always seemed to be planning. How she and the scholarly Colin came to be a pair was a mystery. Colin was bottom heavy and bald but for a fringe of wispy red hair. With his receding chin and narrow beak of a nose, he seemed more like the Emu-Man of Aboriginal myth than a former athlete who was now a highly successful attorney.

"I think that it is time for some fine drinking," Colin said with enthusiasm. "I took the liberty of ordering us all a carafe of Rimauresq Cru Classe to accompany our food. However, you will all find this Cotes de Provence Rose is fantastic. It is a complex wine, named after the river, Real Mauresque, which flows through the Cotes de Provence district," he added, looking around the table to make sure everyone was listening.

Naomi added smugly. "It is made from Tibouren, Grenache, and Cinsault grapes. You will find that it has herbaceous undertones, and a long dry finish."

"Captain Graham, where did you say you're from?" I asked, weary of the wine lesson.

Colin answered, "Captain Graham comes from one of the oldest families in New South Wales. His family's station, Gamoowea, is east of Walgett, along the south bank of the Barwon River. Sam has been there to hunt feral pigs."

"Yeah, Maggie and I went up there," Sam said. "It's situated in a remnant patch of Pilliga Scrub, near the terminus of the Pokataroo Railway line. There are a few Glossy Black Cockatoos there that Maggie wanted to see. Only saw one. But we shot over twenty wild pigs while we were out looking. Then, gazing past Colin and out the window, he added, "You'd like it up there, Dai 'ui," Sam said, calling me by my nickname.

"What did you call your friend?" Julia asked.

"Dai 'ui. That's captain in Vietnamese," Sam replied, draining his beer. "It's kind of like a term of affection. I never made captain."

"Julia, how do you like Australia?" I asked.

"I feel quite at home out in Gamoowea," She said, a distant look in her eye.

"Ah yes, the wonderful, semi-arid rangelands of eastern Australia, home to several varieties of highly venomous snakes and herds of feral pigs that prey upon newborn lambs," Colin said.

"I like to watch the wildlife in the open woodlands. The trees remind me of those in Angola, and I have seen a flock of Maggie's Glossy Black Cockatoos, screaming through the trees," Julia said.

"Do you suppose those cockatoos were taking a dead person to the Aboriginal dream place where all the departed gather?" Colin asked, smiling.

"What was that?" I asked.

"Aboriginals believe that the spirit of a newly dead person stays near the grave for a time, until the proper completion of the burial rituals," Maggie said. "Then it sets out on the long flight to a dream place accompanied by a flock of screaming Glossy Black Cockatoos, a sign of the spirit's final passing.

"Maggie, I couldn't have explained that better myself," Colin said.

"I'm feeling a bit nauseous. I need to find a restroom," Julia said, excusing herself.

Julia was two months pregnant, and Celia went along to help her. Naomi leaned over to me and whispered, "It seems that Colin and I have been unable to have children. Pity." She then chattered on, claiming that Gamoowea had little to attract one from Sydney save for fossicking for a rare variety of petrified wood of gemstone quality. Of course, the possibility of finding her own gemstones had an enormous appeal to Naomi. Everyone tuned into Naomi at this point. Naomi pressed an increasingly inebriated Colin. By the end of the meal, we were going on a gem hunt. The Captain would fly Sam, Maggie, Colin, Naomi, and me out to Gamoowea in the Pilatus Porter plane he had recently purchased at auction from an old Air America contact. Julia would spend the weekend shopping in Sydney and hanging out with Celia.

* * *

Graham flew the five of us up to Wingham that next morning. Naomi turned out to be a pilot, and helped fly the Pilatus Porter. Colin and Maggie had an uncle living just outside of Wingham who was an active promoter of the town's Beef Days. Colin arranged for his Uncle Clive to prepare a meal of locally produced Waghu beef. Captain Graham and Colin had a mutual interest in the Japanese Waghu beef breed of cattle.

By the time we landed and secured the plane, it was late afternoon. On the drive out to Uncle Clive's we passed the Murray Road Public School where Maggie had had her first teaching job. Along the Manning River Colin pointed out Wingham Brush, and we stopped to take some pictures.

Wingham Brush is a breath-taking grove of Moreton Bay Figs that provides shelter for a colony of giant bats called flying foxes. The trunks of the trees are like gigantic pillars, sometimes reaching a diameter of eight feet. One can walk with ease among the massive trees. There is little underbrush. High up in the canopy, hundreds of giant flying foxes hang suspended from the branches, strangely silent in the gloom. For the better part of an hour we followed a trail that took us through the grove, and we worked our way up to a high point overlooking the area. Once there, we rested, just outside the grove, waiting for the sun to set.

"I don't know about you, Sam, but I've seen about all the bats I care to," Naomi said, lighting up a cigarette.

"I need a cold beer," Sam replied, sitting down next to Naomi.

Naomi was wearing cut-off jeans and a knit tube top, with one of Colin's old white oxford cloth dress shirts over the top. Now, she shed the shirt, rolled it up and set it down, her damp shoulders glistening.

"I'm bored," She said, winking at Sam.

Naomi tapped her cigarette so that the ash fell in Sam's direction. She moistened her lips with her tongue, all the while gazing at Sam.

Maggie noticed Naomi's wink and the curious mouth action, and looked over at me. I caught the green flicker of jealousy in her eyes.

"We'll be off soon. The bats are about to move out for the night," Maggie said, dressed in a light khaki safari shirt and shorts, her tall, slim form contrasting with Naomi's voluptuousness.

"About time," Naomi said, carelessly flicking her cigarette butt.

"Careful there! Pick that up before we have a bush fire," Graham commanded.

Naomi looked up as if she had been slapped. The imposing Captain Graham stood over her, tall and imperious, his cold blue eyes watching, waiting for her to recover the butt. Naomi meekly stamped out the smoking butt in the dirt. All the while Colin was watching the bats, clearly oblivious to what had happened. I could tell that our Naomi was both shaken and insulted by Graham's harsh manner. Maggie simply smiled.

"They're starting to leave their roosts," Colin said, peering out at the grove with his binoculars.

One by one the flying foxes began to rise above their sanctuary, circling the grove with a slow flapping that makes one wonder how they stayed aloft. The mass of awakened bats formed up into one huge ascending spiral, an undulating shadow in the gathering dusk. Then, quite abruptly, at first like a thin trail of smoke rising, a line of bats broke off. They headed slowly eastward, out over a vast landscape broken by occasional rocky outcrops. Soon an opaque, wavy line of flying foxes stretched away as far as we could see, tumbling down onto rolling hills and secondary forest. They melted away into the hazy, immeasurable distance. For a moment we all sat in silence, overwhelmed by the scale of what we had witnessed.

* * *

Uncle Clive had dinner ready when we arrived. Like Colin, he loved eating and drinking with others. We started off with a plate of fried Spanish green peppers and Flag Ale.

"How did you find the peppers?" Clive asked those gathered around the table.

Naomi jumped in, "I've had these in Spain, only more deeply charred and salted. I found these a little undercooked and bland."

Uncle Clive looked dejected, for he was clearly out to please. Maggie was quick to salvage Naomi's not so subtle insult. "I think you will find the main course more to your liking Naomi. Uncle

Clive has prepared deep-fried kipfler potatoes with lots of smoky paprika. And the Wagyu beef will have a surprise glaze, especially imaginative." Maggie patted Uncle Clive on the shoulder.

Colin started the conversation by telling us that Uncle Clive had been a coast watcher in the Solomon Islands during World War Two. That set in motion a series of war stories, followed by Captain Graham and Sam telling all of us how they had met in Vietnam. I hung back and observed, relishing my dinner ale.

The Wagyu beef was served in two forms, wonderfully marbled cuts of prime filet and small meatballs covered with a peach glaze, Uncle Clive's original recipe. The wine was unknown to me. All through the dinner, the war talk continued, and Naomi looked sullen and bored.

"Interesting wine," Captain Graham said.

"Martin Codax Albarino. Matches the food," Colin said, slowly, having already drunk too much.

"Well, Colin, you look as if you're ready to nod off. You should pace yourself," Naomi said sharply.

"My dear," Colin sniffed. "Did the dinner meet your high standard?" Colin replied with a smirk.

"I loved the potatoes despite the fact that they were not peeled, but the meatballs were dry and a total waste of good Wagyu," she replied. "The peach glaze did not appeal to my palate."

Hoping to deflect Naomi's slam Maggie turned to Graham. "Captain Graham, before we turn in, we should take a look at Uncle Clive's prize bull. It's red in color. Quite striking. Most Wagyu we see in these parts are black," Maggie said.

"My God, Maggie, I would think all of us have been exposed to enough bull for one night. I don't want to wade through a snake-ridden paddock of shit to see some insipid beast," Naomi snapped.

Naomi's comment left all at the table, even Colin, speechless. In an attempt to change the topic of conversation, I refreshed Naomi's wine glass and asked. "Naomi, I was wondering. Where are you from originally?"

Before she could reply, Colin spouted off. "Ah, Naomi comes from a very old and distinguished Australian family, one with lots of money. She will be more than happy to tell you about her illustrious ancestors. Her family's original vineyard goes back to the 1890's," he continued.

"Colin, spare us your fractured history," Naomi said, clearly irritated by Colin's intrusion.

"I was raised in the Sevenhill District of the Clare Valley. My people have been making wine for several generations. My great-grandfather built a winery in the 1890's that has become a Clare Valley institution. With the exception of my father and one worthless cousin, all of my great-grandfather's male line has been killed in these boring wars you all carry on about. But we have endured many changes in our economic fortunes to survive as a respected family of winemakers. Unfortunately, my father has a heart problem," Naomi sighed and continued. "My older sister Nadia helps him run the winery now. She and I are kind of like those Glossy Black Cockatoos Maggie studies - rare in New South Wales. She comes up to Sydney for a visit from time to time. Last time she came up I introduced her to Germaine Greer, who happened to be in town," Naomi said with a condescending tone.

"Well, Naomi, I hope our tales have been told in the spirit of remembering those who have been lost," Graham said. "And there's nothing glorious about war, that's for sure. At any rate, I thought you were from a citified place. I'm surprised to find that you're from the Clare Valley. I apologize if we bored you with our tales. I shared considerable hardship with my American mates here, both in Asia and in Africa."

"I heard that you and Sam were in Angola. I'm not surprised. I once read that Americans are particularly prone to self-deception as they go about whatever it is that they are doing. Who knows what they will destroy in the process? But there is a curious single-mindedness that I admire in the way Americans go about doing things, much like the Germans in World War Two, only not quite as sophisticated. Americans also seem more gullible to what their politicians ask them to swallow than the Germans. The only greater fools I know are those Australians who tag along with the Americans in the pursuit of their folly."

Graham boomed, "Naomi, have you no shame? Your disrespect for our allies embarrasses me! What would have happened to Australia without their support in World War Two? I can't handle your company any longer. Come on, Maggie, let's all go see what's so special about this red bull."

Naomi sat back in her chair, realizing that once again she had gone too far. Before she could respond, Captain Graham was out the door into the buzzing and clicking Australian night, followed by Uncle Clive and Maggie, Colin stumbling along slowly behind the rest. Finishing my beer, I decided to trail along after them.

"You go ahead, if you want. Sam and I are staying put," Naomi said taking out a Gaulois, and turning to Sam, insolence flashing in her eyes.

"You need a light?" Sam asked.

* * *

Gamoowea is not a large cattle station by Australian standards, and is juxtaposed between varied terrain features. At the heart of the station is a gilgais, an ephemeral lake, dry most of the year. It supports a wide, yellow, grassy plain. To the south, this grassy plain merges into a patch of semi-arid woodland dominated by cypress-pine and ironwoods, with occasional casuarinas and tall eucalypts. A small remnant population of Glossy Black Cockatoos can be found there among the casuarinas. As a biology teacher currently getting her masters degree, Maggie's thought was that these birds were a true breeding population and not a flock straggling down from nearby Queensland.

The boundary to the west of this forest is marked by an alluvial dry creek bed Graham calls a sand monkey. To the north, along the Barwon River, the terrain changes to a less forested outwash area with a creek that is no more than a trickling flow, although at times, according to the Captain, it can become a gusher.

A curious sandstone ridge capped by basalt marks the east boundary. Years ago, Graham's father dynamited that rock shelf, opening a seep that drained the higher ground. That water source proved to be a lure for feral pigs, considered by all to be a threat to the fragile ecology. It was on the ridge one could find pieces of a beautiful and rare petrified wood said to be unique to Gamoowea.

Captain Graham said, "Colin and I will go north with my dogs in the Land Rover. We will turn them loose and work our way to the south. All you and

Sam need to do is wait along that tiny stream that flows out of the seep. The dogs will drive the hogs right to you. Maggie can look for her birds and Naomi can fossick for stones on top of the cliff while you two wait below. This should be an interesting day." He then handed Sam and me each an old bolt-action Enfield.

"What war did this come from?" I asked.

"I'm not sure. But that rifle will knock down all but the really big ones," Graham added.

"How big are the really big ones?" I asked.

"Most feral pigs in Australia are small, wormy, disease-ridden vermin. They transmit leptospirosis to wildlife and livestock. The pigs we have here in Gamoowea are different. In the early days of artificial insemination, we had a crazy German neighbor, Heinz, now departed, God rest his troubled soul, who imported Russian Boar semen for one of his prize Yorkshire sows. He had visions of creating his own private hunting reserve. What he created succeeded beyond his wildest dreams, his hybrids favoring the Russian Boar, but with added bulk and hybrid vigor from the input of big-boned, Yorkshire blood. Although he kept his exotics penned up, he released them occasionally for special hunts. Several large mature boars eventually managed to escape, mixing their blood with that of the local feral swine. That was twenty years ago."

"I'll ask my question again. How big is big?"

"Boars over three hundred pounds are not unusual," Captain Graham said, chambering a round in his ancient Enfield.

* * *

Sam, Maggie, Naomi, and I packed into a vintage Willy's jeep and followed a track to the sandstone ridge that marked the east boundary. Sam drove. I opened the first of many beers.

Naomi nudged Maggie. "Here Maggie, take one of these little tabs. My sister calls these her current indulgence, a very weak hit of blotter acid. This will make our little jaunt much more interesting." And then she said with a wicked smile, "Maybe you will have one of those mystical Aboriginal experiences."

"I'll try one if Sam takes one," Maggie said.

"Good on ya, Maggie! Don't be so restrained. Be a self-actualizer. Come on! Let's shed our shallow bourgeois conventions," Naomi said.

"Yes. I am too repressed. Maybe I need to break out of my restraints," Maggie replied.

"Sure, I'll take one. What's a self-actualizer?" Sam asked, washing the tab down with beer.

"Being a self-actualizer is about freedom and seeing through bourgeois fairy tales," Naomi said.

"And you? You want a tab?" Naomi asked me.

"I'll pass, Naomi," I said, opening another beer. "I'll be bourgeois and keep my self-actualization to a few beers. I never mix drugs with good beer."

We all had a good buzz on by the time we arrived at the seep, which turned out to be an inviting deep pool at the base of a sandstone cliff. Overheated, we chugged down more cold beers, and soon everyone was splashing in the cool water.

Concerned about the time, I got out and dried off. I needed to be out watching the woods for wild pigs; but before I knew it, Naomi, Maggie, and Sam, were stripped down and skinny-dipping.

Much to normally shy Maggie's embarrassment, Sam called out to me that I should come observe that she was, indeed, a true natural blond. At that point Naomi was laughing wildly, grabbing Sam from behind and trying to dunk him, pushing her big boobs against his back, and calling to Maggie for help. Maggie, a wild look in her eye that I had never seen before, grabbed Sam from the front, wrapping her legs around his waist while Naomi still wrestled Sam from behind in a kind of press, all the while still laughing hysterically.

I yelled, "Hey, I thought this was a pig hunt. We need to get into position. Captain Graham and Colin are counting on us."

"Oh Please!" Naomi said with a hiss. "Did you hear that? Sam's in a splendid position, you fool! Ignore him, Sam. He's not half the man you are. You're enough for both Maggie and me."

"You go ahead, Dai 'ui," Sam shouted. "Just leave me one of the rifles. I'll catch up with you later. I'm having too much fun!"

"Suit yourself," I said, and I followed the watercourse downstream.

I looked back to see Sam still wrestling with Maggie. Then he stood up at the edge of the pool, his arms raised above his head while he let out a Tarzan-like call. Naomi lay on a broad, flat rock next to them, fully exposed, spreading and waving her legs in crazy figure eights, reaching up to pull both Maggie and Sam down toward her. I stared dumbfounded while the Tarzan yells and groping continued. As I headed off there was another wild shriek of laughter, as if a Glossy Black Cockatoo were calling from deep in the tangle of casuarinas along the base of Gamoowea's sandstone cliffs.

* * *

I heard the dogs in the distance and walked toward the sound. It seemed that the dogs were moving back and forth along a line to my front. So I moved across the tiny trickle that emanated from the seep, heading out into the open woodland toward the direction of the baying dogs.

I had gone about five hundred yards or so north of the seep, keeping the sandstone ridge to my right, walking parallel to the cliff face so that I wouldn't get lost. The baying grew faint, and before long stopped entirely. I leaned against an ironwood and listened while the intrepid bush flies climbed all over my face. For a time all was silent, except for the squawk and whistle of what I imagined was a Rainbow Lorakeet, or even a Crimson Rosella.

When I turned toward the dense thicket at the base of the cliff there was a sudden rustling. I took another step forward and a squealing herd of wild pigs burst from the dense thicket to scatter through the woodland, the explosive sound of their hooves lingering in my memory. There were at least thirty of various ages and sizes. The lead boar was all thick shoulders and head. Strangely, he trotted away slowly, as if he were unconcerned by my presence. Startled, but with a clear head, I took aim at a point behind his front leg. From about twenty yards, I squeezed off a round. He dropped like a stone, coughing up a vivid red fountain as he rolled on his side. Piece of cake, I thought.

Quickly I chambered another round and took aim. Click. Nothing. I pulled the bolt back, re-chambering the round as the pigs disappeared into the bush. Again nothing. I checked the bolt, holding my finger on its face while I pulled the trigger. Nothing. It appeared the firing pin had snapped.

It was then that I heard the dogs coming my way, and the sound of someone thumping on a log. I instantly realized the drumming was the sound of hooves, lots of them. A plume of dust rose up through the woodland. A dark line of what must have been a hundred wild pigs appeared through the trees. I dropped the Enfield and scrambled up the nearest ironwood tree that looked like it could bear my weight.

* * *

The great flow of wild pigs passed beneath me, trampling the sparse grass and sending up a cloud of choking dust. Off to the west I could hear someone shooting, too far away for anyone to hear my shouts for help. Only once did I see a dog off through the trees, a gray, wire-haired loping thing snapping after the heels of the smaller wild pigs.

I waited for a good five minutes before I began my descent. As soon as my feet touched the ground I heard a deep grunt to my left. I turned to see three massive feral boars heading toward me, carefully picking their steps. Once again I climbed the ironwood, cutting my bare forearms in the process. The Wily Three, as I called them, circled the tree several times, gazing up at me with longing, hungry eyes, their narrow, tusked snouts dripping. The largest began eating the body of the old boar I had shot, starting with the guts. The other two soon joined him in his cannibalistic feast.

* * *

The Wily Three kept me in the tree while they proceeded to devour their brother. Others began to drift in, wary of the bigger boars. They approached the carcass only after the Wily Three had eaten their fill and had settled into a post-meal nap at the base of my tree. Then I smelled the first wood smoke.

The line of fire must have been a good four hundred yards off, but the smoke crept ahead of the fire, pooling in the low places, random wisps trailing among the branches above my head. I noticed the wind began to pick up speed.

A small flock of Glossy Black Cockatoos came screaming through the trees, flashes of red on their tails. The line of flames headed my way through the sparse grass. I wondered if some aborigines had set the fire. The fire was a mere hundred yards off before the Wily Three finally stirred from their slumber at the base of my tree. They ambled off together, not the least bit spooked by the fire.

I dropped to the ground, and ran for the cliff face, hurling myself through the thicket of casuarinas. The broken ledges of the cliff made for easy climbing. When I reached the top I was engulfed in a dark plume of smoke from the flames passing below me. Looking down, I could see the bush fire had flashed by, consuming the yellow grasses. A great spiral of ash swirled skyward through the smoky haze, reminding me of the flying foxes at Wingham Brush, a multitude of distant specs disappearing into the gathering dusk.

"Hey, here he is! Where have you been? We've been looking all over for you," Maggie said, walking over and handing me a Flag Ale.

* * *

"So, Naomi! How did this goddamn fire start? It's clear that you, Sam, and Maggie are drunk,"

Colin was screaming, his face a vivid red both from anger and a day out in the Australian sun.

"Stop screaming, Colin," Naomi slurred. "It's not your style. And don't accuse me, or I'll walk away and you will never see me again. Nor will you see any of my family's money, which is all you really care about. And you call yourself a solicitor, you sorry ass. I have no idea how the fire started." Naomi was trying to maintain her composure, but was clearly in the process of losing it.

Ignoring Naomi, Colin zeroed in on Maggie. "How about you? What happened? Captain Graham has gone back to the seep to see if he can find some evidence of what happened there."

"I was exploring my possibilities," Maggie said, giggling, feeling the mix of drugs and alcohol.

"I've never seen you so drunk," Colin said.

"Or as unrestrained," Naomi giggled.

"All I know is that we were lucky not to be consumed by the fire," Maggie said, sheepishly.

"I feel as if I've been consumed by fire," Naomi said, grinning and winking at Maggie.

"We climbed the cliff to get away," Maggie said.

"That's all bullshit," Sam said, his head in his hands. "Tell the truth Maggie! Take some personal responsibility. Isn't that what you once told me? So much for my recklessness."

"What?" Colin asked, his fingers shaking.

"Maggie and Naomi are lying, bitches that they are. Different bitches, but each is a bitch in her own unique way. Naomi is a transparent, pretentious bitch. But Maggie is much more complex. She is a self-righteous, hypocritical bitch," Sam said.

"How did you all get so drunk?"

Sam lurched forward and took Colin's arm. "Yes, I am really drunk, but Colin, I am not a liar like your wife, Naomi; or your sister, Maggie, for that matter. Naomi flipped a butt into the brush to start the fire. Ask her again. This time she may tell you the truth," Sam said, turning to Naomi just as she cold-cocked him with a bottle of Flag Ale.

* * *

When he came back from the seep, Captain Graham seemed as if he knew the entire story of what had transpired. He was an experienced tracker who could read the signs left on the ground. I could tell by the way Graham looked at me that he had put together the pieces of the puzzle.

Maybe Graham thought it was best that the entire story be left incomplete, as in the unfinished tales Colin liked to tell of the creation ancestors. Colin claimed those stories grew out of the collective cultural memory, and that with the telling of each story there arose a socially redemptive power, like in the lesson of Namondjok, who broke the kinship laws with his sister, and was banished by his clan.

"I wonder," Graham said, "If the Glossy Black Cockatoos could talk, what would they tell us?

* * *

Chapter Four: Finding Jock

Sam, Colin Musto, and I were sitting on the patio of the fashionable Café Ritz, part of Cronulla's Hotel Cecil. We were admiring the longhaired bikini-clad beachgoers passing along the esplanade. The Café Ritz was a great place to dine and fast becoming a watering hole for American expatriates. In addition to the Café Ritz, with its patio facing Ozone Street, the Hotel Cecil had a men's only pub, and a bottle shop on the opposite side of the hotel. Lured by the beach, vacationing Aussies from across Australia usually filled the available rooms by late afternoon.

The name Cronulla is derived from the word *kurranulla*, meaning "place of the pink seashells" in the dialect of the Aboriginal inhabitants, the Gweagal, traditional custodians of the southern geographic areas of Sydney. That morning I noticed those tiny pink shells scattered along the beachfront were the same color as Colin's florid cheeks.

"I think today's poison will be Toohey's Flag Ale. How about I order a round for the three of us? Haven't had any of that since our little debacle up in Gamoowea," Colin said, opening up a folder of what appeared to be legal correspondence.

Colin was a very generous person. Whenever possible, it seemed that he liked to pick up the tab, and he often went out of his way to do favors for people. Of course, that was his method, to make you feel as if you were obliged to him as a result of his generosity. He used that same approach with his clients in Southeast Asia Company. The more I came to know Colin, the more I appreciated him.

Since the Gamoowea trip Sam had once again split up with Maggie. That however, didn't keep Colin and Sam from continuing their curious business relationship. Maggie and Sam usually reconciled after a few weeks. Maggie was drawn to Sam, whom Naomi liked to call "that big, dark Yank," for a number of reasons. She loved to watch him play rugby league, at which he excelled. Both Sam and Maggie also loved the great outdoors; they tracked wildlife. And at almost six feet, Maggie towered over most men. Maggie liked the way the rugged, broad-shouldered Sam could literally pick her up off her feet, and thus she overlooked a number of Sam's rough edges.

"Colin, did Naomi ever admit to you that she started that bush fire, flipped her cigarette butt into some bushes?" Sam asked in his off-handed way.

"Oh, no. She hasn't confessed to that yet. But she will. Give her time. One night, after too much to drink, it will all come spilling out of her. She will be weeping in her drug-induced hysterics, begging me not to leave her. It's all happened before. Nothing to get all excited about at this point," Colin said, absent-mindedly.

"I see," Sam said, looking confused.

The waitress arrived with our ale, and a plate of fish and chips. I noticed she winked at Sam.

"The Café Ritz has the best chips around. They may be the best in Sydney," Sam said, digging in.

"The best chips I've ever had was at The Hind's Head in Bray, about an hour west of London, just across the road from The Fat Duck. Those chips were triple-cooked and well-salted, super crispy on the outside," Colin said. "As pubs go, I would rate it second in London. It has a fine restaurant that does all the British classics such as ham and leek pie with pork sausages. Never tasted onion gravy so good."

"So what was number one on your list?" I asked.

"It's probably gone now. But when I went to the London School of Economics I belonged to an eating club. We called ourselves the Rascals and met at a small place near the Old Westminster Library. I still dream about their potted shrimp served with a peppery watercress salad, with a caramelized onion and goat cheese tart, simply heavenly. Even back then I was recognized by my mates as a connoisseur of sorts," Colin mused.

"How does a poor kid from Newscastle, who plays rugby league, attend both law school and the London School of Economics?" I asked.

"One word, imagination! My father was a squatty, bottom-heavy coal miner who could play rugby and had a vivid imagination. He was good at seeing the possibilities when it came to rising above his humble origins, and he was a dreamer. I seem to have inherited all his faculties," Colin said.

"Colin, Sam and I are out of your league. Was that Westminster place where you took Naomi when you were dating?" I asked.

"Absolutely not! Too rough a crowd. Naomi is a culinary and intellectual snob. Her favorite place was in the Dorchester Hotel, a Michelin two-starred hideaway that had a balance of formality and a knack for making each guest feel comfortable."

"You can stuff the formality, Colin. Just bring on the tucker. You and I make an odd pair, you a solicitor with a graduate degree from the London School of Economics, me so much Iowa trailer trash who barely graduated from college, " Sam said, licking his fingers.

"Nonsense. We have complementary qualities

and skills, you the intrepid, former Marine, me the opportunist trying to make the most of his old school connections. We pair well together," Colin replied. "I recall that Naomi liked the Dorchester's tiny deep-fried spinach and cheese stuffed ravioli. I preferred their Scottish black bream. It was served in a creamy, tomato-based Kerala curry sauce. Those were good times," Colin added, looking off in the distance. Then Colin proposed a toast.

"Here's to seeing all the possibilities!"

"Roger that. You're kind of quiet, Dai 'ui," Sam said, lighting up a Lucky Strike.

"Waiting to hear more of what Colin's new project is all about," I said.

Colin had asked me to attend this meeting due to a new project. He and Sam were expanding the scope of Southeast Asia Company beyond their core business of providing security services for Colin's legal clients. Their business opportunities appeared to be growing, along with Colin's vision.

"Ah, here it is," Colin, said, producing what appeared to be a letter. "Do you recall when we were eating dinner at my Uncle Clive's and Naomi mentioned her long-lost cousin?"

"I remember her being raised in the Sevenhill District of the Clare Valley. Her people made wine for generations. Something like that," I replied, sipping on my Flag Ale.

"Yes, Naomi likes to call herself a Clare Valley patrician. With the exception of what Naomi and her sister call their worthless cousin Ian, all of that great-grandfather's male line is gone but her father. Her father, increasingly frail, has left the running of the winery to Naomi's older sister."

"Naomi compared her and her sister to Glossy Black Cockatoos," I said, smiling.

"Hah! Funny what we remember. Decadent Black Cockatoos is more like it. Anyway, Ian is dying of hepatitis in Laos. This letter is a plea from his divorced wife here in Sydney. She wants our assistance to recover her four-year old son. Legally she has custody. Two months ago Ian took the boy on a vacation to Vang Vieng in Laos, promising to return him," Colin added, shaking his head.

"Vang Vieng is a nasty place. I've been there," Sam said.

"I remembered you mentioning that. That's why I thought this project might be of interest to you. The mother wants her son back. Should be an easy snatch, as you like to call it. And we know Ian's whereabouts. He's either in his big house in Vientiane, or at Vang Vieng. He's trying to open a bar in Vang Vieng, believe it or not," Colin said, twisting a lock of his thinning red hair.

"Well I know Vang Vieng, a small town along the Nam Song River. Hippies and backpackers hang out there and smoke dope. They like to float down the river in inner tubes," Sam said.

"I'm out of shape or I would go with you on this one," Colin said, smiling.

Colin had just turned thirty-five, five years older than Sam and me. Just under six feet, he had once been quite a rugby player. Now his rugged physique was going soft. His long hours of legal research left him little time for exercise, and with his large appetite for fine cuisine, he had ballooned to two hundred and fifty pounds.

In contrast, both Sam and I were tall, each over six feet, still lean and hard in every respect. I kept fit running a couple of miles every day on the beach. Sam had a black belt earned in Okinawa and he worked out regularly in a local dojo.

"Like I said, Colin. Vang Vieng is a dirty little backwater town. No telling what you will find with the locals. Even if it's just to snatch some Aussie kid, any work in Vang Vieng and we will need to be real careful," Sam said.

"I remember Laos as being beautiful. Those towering limestone karsts still loom in my memory. I spent time around Luang Prabang in the early sixties, when I was still a law student. I loved that Laotian dish they called *laap*. They could make that with either pork or fish," Colin continued.

"I never got into eating noodles," Sam said, gazing off at the young girls on Cronulla Beach.

"Well, I need to know by tomorrow what your decision is. Graham will fly you up to Thailand in his Pilatus Porter. Take a day to stage at his place in Gamoowea. Then up to Thailand. Figure a week or so, he thinks," Colin said.

"He's in charge?" Sam asked.

"Yes, and he's already done reconnaissance in the area. He still travels there on occasion. He has a contract with a museum in Paris and at the University of Sydney to guide scholars in the area," Colin continued.

"Scholars my ass," Sam said. "But the fact that Graham's involved changes things. You say that Graham has already located this guy Ian?"

"Yes. Our firm has retained him to develop a plan and guide the whole project," Colin said, leaning back in his chair.

"Okay. Count me in. What do you think, Dai 'ui?" Sam asked me.

"Is that a job offer?"

"I thought Colin gave you the skinny over the phone. I asked him to invite you. You're not teaching for a while. I figured you could use some easy money, and I need someone with me I can trust. One guy can't do this on his own," Sam said.

"I see. Well, Celia's sister is here visiting. And I could use some quick cash. What did you say the little boy's name was?"

"His name is Jock. This project is all about finding Jock," Colin said, draining his glass and beckoning to the waitress.

* * *

Julia had dinner ready when we dropped out of the sky. We got off the plane in Gamoowea to find a little old man was waiting with Julia.

"Who's the old guy?" I asked Sam.

"I don't know. But he looks familiar," Sam replied, squinting and brushing away the flies, a constant nuisance this time of year.

"Let me introduce you to my primary client these days, Dr. Jean de Fillio. He's a distinguished scholar of Asian antiquities," Captain Graham said, doffing his hat.

"Dr. de Fillio, I want you to meet the rest of my crew, a couple of Yanks who served in Vietnam with me," Captain Graham said.

Dr. Jean de Fillio was old enough to be my grandfather, and, as I was to learn, a relic from French colonial days. He was the Director of the famous Musee' de Cham, in Da Nang, and had recently attended a conference in Sydney. He had hired Captain Graham to take him back to Da Nang by way of Laos, a perfect cover for our little project.

"Have we met before?" the old man asked Sam, leaning forward to study him, his eyes magnified by thick, Coke-bottle-like glasses.

"Yes, Dr. de Fillio. It was some years ago in Da Nang. Miss Swan introduced us. The heavy rains of the monsoon had just started. As Miss Swan liked to say, Indra the rain god was weeping. You took us on a tour of the Musee' de Cham, explaining pieces of Cham statuary that represented the various gods and goddesses worshipped by the Chams."

I could see the light of recognition in the old man's eyes.

"Ah yes, yes! I remember now. Our Miss Swan. The beautiful Miss Swan, always so cool and relaxed. She still works with me, you know. Perhaps we may even see her again this trip."

"It would be very interesting to see her again," Sam said very quietly.

As we walked to the house I noticed a change in Sam's manner. The usually laid back Sam was suddenly very intense. I pulled Sam to the side.

"Is this Miss Swan the old squeeze you met up with in Saigon?" I asked jokingly.

Sam turned to me with a strange, faraway look in his eyes that I had never seen before. The no-nonsense Sam seemed shaken. He was tearing up.

"She's a beautiful woman, Dai 'ui, a regular dragon lady with a red and black Yin and Yang tattoo on her right shoulder."

"Are you going to tell me the whole story?"

"What's there to tell? I guess I fancied myself a cocksman. But she seduced me in that museum. We were on a tour of the Cham divinities. First she showed me Brahma, the Creator, with his four faces; and then dark Shiva, the Destroyer, with his third eye. I'll never forget how she laughed when we found Kama, the god of love, in the act of mounting the celestial dancer Apsara from behind."

"Ha! And she broke your heart," I smirked.

"Roger that, Dai 'ui. I suppose that's easier to do than you think. Interesting that her name should come up just as Maggie dumps me. Maybe it's some kind of sign."

"Sam, I'm not so sure I believe in signs. Clear out your brain-housing group."

Suddenly the old man spun around.

"Were you the one who returned the Devi that was looted from the museum? I must know. A source, an Ani Bui, once told me that she thought a Marine officer returned the statue," the old man said, his fingers trembling.

"Yes, Dr. de Fillio, I'm the one who set the Devi on the stairs in front of the Musee' de Cham, that day. You were standing at the top of the stairs of the Musee' de Cham, poking at the Devi with a long thin stick of bamboo. I was observing you through field glasses from the balcony outside my room on the third floor of the White Lotus. You must have assumed that someone was watching you, for you waved at the empty street. Then you picked up the Devi and were gone," Sam said calmly.

"My God!" The tiny old man yelled, wrapping his skinny arms around Sam. "You saved a national treasure. I owe you a great debt."

* * *

We started off with a plate of lightly fried Spanish green peppers and the customary Flag Ale, followed by prime cuts of marbled beef grilled to medium rare. Colin would have relished the feast.

"I love Wagyu," Sam said, draining his ale.

Julia sat back in her chair and smiled. Now in the fourth month of her first pregnancy, she seemed much happier than when I had last seen her. Out beyond the screen door the Australian night buzzed and clicked.

"Sam, Captain Graham tells me you have been to Vientiane before."

"Yes, Doctor. I spent four months as an advisor in Thailand and Laos, including three weeks in Vientiane, a beautiful place with French Colonial architecture, freshly baked French bread every morning served with a bowl of noodle soup. But the nightlife is what I remember most, best in Asia. Much of my time in Vientiane was all about eating and drinking to wretched excess. But I was there long enough to find my way around, if I have to."

"You know of the *kinnari* then? They are a special interest of mine," the old man said, smiling.

"Those half-bird, half-woman creatures, right?" Sam replied.

"Exactly. The mythical *kinnaris* have the head, torso, and arms of a beautiful woman, and the wings, tail and feet of a water bird. *Kinnaris* are a traditional symbol of beauty and grace, and their bird-like parts allow them to fly between the human and mystical worlds," Dr. de Fillio said, excitedly. "They are a concept foreign to European thinking, symbols of the lover and beloved, ever-embracing, never permitting any distraction to that love."

"How romantic!" Julia said, speaking for the first time. "Sam, did you ever meet any *kinnaris* in the night clubs of Vientiane?"

"No. Not that I recall," Sam said, smiling.

"We have a good man on the ground. He's a bush pilot and Vietnam veteran who looks more like a hippie than a former Green Beret. He works out of the Hong Kong office of Colin's firm and travels to Laos on a regular basis. His name is Woodruff. We call him Woody. He thinks that Ian and Jock are most likely in Vang Vieng. In some ways that makes our job simpler," Captain Graham said.

"We simply fly into that old airfield that is parallel to the Nam Song River," Sam said.

"You know the terrain. Ian's house is right along that river, at the edge of one of those karst outcroppings. We drop in at dusk. Woody has a Toyota pickup, and he will drop you and Dai 'ui here off at Ian's place. No guns involved. Should be a piece of cake. In and out."

"Easy money," Sam said.

At that point I should have said something. The communication seemed to be going one way. I felt the need to ask some questions but held back.

"By the way, Dr. de Fillio is supporting our little project in his own way. The Laotians respect him, and he will provide us with an excellent cover story. We have to go to Vientiane first. On our way up to Vientiane we will stop at Pakse briefly, just down from the Bolovens Plateau. Close by is the town of Champasak, and the Vat Phou. Dr. de Fillio wants to visit with a colleague there."

"One of my three-day orientation patrols in Laos used Vat Phou as a rendezvous point," Sam said, casually, his former intensity having been dissipated by four Reich's Ales.

"Dr. de Fillio says that Vat Phou is older than Angkor Wat," Captain Graham said.

"Yes, it was built in the first decades of the 9th century. Like Angkor, Vat Phou was a ruin lost in the jungles for uncounted centuries, and stood unused because it had been built as a Hindu, not a Buddhist, temple." Dr. de Fillio said.

"Dr. de Fillio just attended a conference in Sydney. He is proposing to make Vat Phou a World

Heritage Site," Captain Graham said.

"Now that the war is over we have a festival there each February," Dr de Fillio added. "Sam, your friend Miss Swan is living there, and is deeply involved in the planning of that event. She is quite a scholar in her own right."

At Dr. de Fillio's comment, Sam coughed, and almost dropped his glass.

* * *

It was an unusually hot, humid night, alive with things blooming in the darkness as we crossed over the Mekong, on our way from Bangkok.

"The river of evil memory," Dr. de Fillio said.

"Say again?"

"The Lao call the Mekong the river of evil memory. To them the legacy of the Mekong is one of sorrow. Perhaps this enigmatic title is an allusion to some ancient calamity. No one knows for sure," he added staring out the window.

I didn't reply, being quite familiar with the river of evil memory. Then we were enveloped in the musky scent of the river, close enough to the ground so that the fragrance of a million night-blooming flowers rose through the window. I could see the lights of Pakse in the distance.

* * *

The next morning Miss Swan was part of the team that greeted us. When Sam stuck out his hand to greet her she was speechless. While Dr. de Fillio met with his colleague, she and Sam sat under the shade of a large Banyan tree that overlooked Vat Phou. The wind had picked up, and the temperature began to drop. The tree branches billowed out and it started to rain, occasional heavy drops hitting the foliage. Then the downpour arrived in huge sheets, and Sam and Miss Swan sought refuge in our tent.

"Indra the rain god is weeping," Miss Swan said.

"Is it the start of the wet season?" I asked.

"Too early. Let's have some tea," she said, pulling up the side of the tent to let the air flow through. The large tent had a card table surrounded by several chairs. In the middle of the table was a pot of tea, some cups, and what appeared to be a tin of butter cookies. We sat down to that simple fare and watched the rain come down. I decided to keep my mouth shut unless addressed. Then, on an impulse, Sam got up to find Dr. de Fillio.

"So you were in Vietnam with Sam?" She asked.

"Oh, yeah. Back in '68 and '69."

"You seem nervous. Relax."

"Miss Swan, I don't think I'll be relaxing much in Laos. Sam either, for that matter."

"I understand. Things are calm here for now. But that will soon change," she said, smiling.

I liked Miss Swan's smile, and the way her safari shirt fell open when she leaned forward. That shirt had the sleeves cut off at the shoulders, and I was fascinated by the red and black Yin and Yang tattoo on the smooth, almond skin of her right shoulder. She caught me staring at the tattoo.

"Yin and Yang," I said, pointing to the tattoo.

"Very good. The red is for Yang, the masculine, and the black is for Yin, the feminine. Yin and Yang are the symbols of the Tao, forces interacting with one another to create the Universe."

"I see."

"Old Chinese wisdom."

"I'll remember that. So, you're Chinese?"

"Half. My father was French, my mother, Hao. You've heard of the Hoa, of course."

"From the Cholon district in Saigon, but ethnic Chinese."

"Yes, and now bearing the brunt of the socialist transformation. An edict from the government outlawed all wholesale trade and large business activities. That one absurd act closed over thirty thousand businesses overnight. With all private trade banned, and all old and foreign currencies confiscated, I fled. I am, in fact, a refugee, forced to leave with hundreds of other Hao because of these absurdities. Some Hao resisted, and there were clashes with government troops that left the streets of Cholon full of corpses."

"I heard about this."

"At the time Saigon fell, the Hao controlled eighty per cent of the industrial trade, fifty per cent of the retail trade, and a hundred per cent of the wholesale trade. The Vietnamese accused the Hao of using their dominance in the economy to manipulate prices. We were identified as former bourgeoisie. Many found themselves in the re-education camps. As a result there has been a mass exodus, with many Hao becoming boat people, and China sending unarmed ships to help evacuate the refugees. Others fled overland to China's Guangxi province. I help those that come through here."

"You seem safe here."

"For now."

"Miss Swan, a moment ago you alluded to some changes. Anything Sam and I need to know about?"

"Vietnam's border dispute with Cambodia threatens to break out into a war. If that happens,

China will side with Cambodia, Laos will be the puppet of Vietnam, and again I will be displaced."

"Where will you go?"

"France, maybe Hong Kong. I'm lucky. I work with the Guimet Museum in Paris, founded by Emile Guimet in 1879. Have you heard of it?"

"No. I'm not familiar with it."

"The Guimet has quite a collection of Asian art."

The rain continued to pour. The wind picked up, blowing raindrops onto our table.

"So you and Sam knew each other in Da Nang."

"Yes."

"Has he changed a lot since you last saw him?"

"Some."

"What do you remember most about him?

"He always slept with his .45, loaded. He has such a big gun," Miss Swan said laughing.

I was quite taken with Miss Swan, the living embodiment of Dr. de Fillio's mythical *kinnaris*. Then Miss Swan let down her long black hair. It fell to her waist, and smelled of sandalwood.

Miss Swan had been very open with me. She was a strange and complex woman. I wondered where her *kinnaris* wings had carried her since that time she spent with Sam in Da Nang and Saigon? What worlds, human and mystical, had she visited? In many ways she reminded me of Naomi. Both had an elegant manner, a sophistication that spoke of art and love of finer things, of living a life consumed in perpetual pleasure, and they both were driven by a longing for control, including demands for uncompromising affection, the ever-embracing love of the *kinnaris*.

"Miss Swan, you have beautiful hair."

"Thank you. It requires much care out here in the jungle."

* * *

We rose into the air heading directly for Vang Vieng instead of Vientiane. I wondered about the sudden change. Dr. de Fillio's meeting had been a success, and it appeared that the application to make Vat Phou a World Heritage Site was going well. Dr. de Fillio went on about how happy he was with this team, including Miss Swan.

"Miss Swan said that we should stay out of Vientiane. She said we would attract too much attention." Sam said quietly, as we gained altitude.

"Something you haven't told me?"

"Yeah. Miss Swan is involved with some big shot in Vientiane. But she didn't go into details."

"Could it compromise our mission?"

"No. Graham and I talked it all through. But that's why we're heading right to Vang Vieng to make the snatch. By the way, I noticed that you had no problem communicating with her. What did you talk about while I was gone?" Sam asked.

"Oh nothing. She said you like to sleep with a loaded gun. And that you had a big dick."

"Dai 'ui, you're so full of shit."

* * *

"We are really on to something here. Just over this little karst outcropping you will find a wide meadow that runs along the river. It has been cleared for agriculture. Ian's plantation house is right here, between the karst and the river," Woody said, tapping his map with a bamboo stick.

“You say that there’s no sign of security,” I said.

“No. Simple snatch. I’ll be standing by along this road. Without going into great detail, I scouted out the grounds. This guy Ian is really sick, stays in bed all the time. His Khmer wife is nuts. Total lunatic from drugs, or whatever. I watched her for a while. She dances in front of this big mirror all night long, strung out on some shit,” Woody said, pushing his long gray hair out of his eyes.

“Go over the trail thing again.”

“There is a trail through the bamboo hedgerow that screens the house from the road. Oh yeah, one last thing. Here’s some shit to feed the dog.”

“Dog?” Sam asked.

“Yeah, no sweat. He’s a little fucker. He’ll come right up to you. Just pet him and feed him this dope. Puts him right to sleep.”

* * *

It was an absurdly simple mission. Sam and I knew it was absurd. We should be able to move with stealth, maneuvering close enough so that we could grab Jock and be on our way. Woody dropped us at the foot of the limestone karst outcropping and we got lucky. We found the trail, traveling parallel to the base of the karst.

As Woody had described, the bamboo hedgerow gave way to a broad meadow that had been cleared for pasture. A small group of scrawny, Brahma-like cattle grazed, occasionally lifting their heads to sniff the wind. In the middle of the clearing, surrounded on all sides by short grass pasture, stood the rambling plantation house.

We pressed forward to within fifty yards of the house. Sam motioned me to wait. For five minutes we sat there in that steamy insect-ridden night, dripping with sweat, listening to the weird voice of Ian's Khmer wife. The house was lit up by hundreds of candles. I could see her clearly, dancing in front of a full-length mirror, wild-eyed, her black hair flying like that of a sorceress, her blade-thin body glistening with sweat in the smoky haze of burning joss sticks. Then a dog started to bark.

The dog was one of those small, pointy-eared, curly-tailed mutts one sees all over Asia. He was pointing in our direction and barking with increased intensity. Sam threw the dog the doped-up meat and waited. The little dog stopped barking and gulped down the meat.

All of a sudden I was having doubts. Part of me wanted to press forward, entering the house and snatching the kid. Another part of me felt the need to withdraw, to spare the kid the trauma that was certain to follow. Maybe I was experiencing the kind of sign that Sam had talked about, a clue of things to come.

Sam knew it was time to move. Apparently he felt a greater responsibility to the boy's mother. We entered the house without resistance.

"You've come to take my boy. You've come to take my little Jock," a voice said from the shadows.

A thin and jaundiced Ian stared at us, his eyes dark hollows. In his hand was a steel Nine Millimeter Parabellum that glinted in the candlelight.

"Yes. But we are unarmed," I said quietly.

* * *

"In a previous life I believe that I once lived in Laos. So, I would like my remains left with my Khmer wife, if you don't mind. After I am cremated, she will scatter my ashes where the Mekong flows quiet and lazy, merging with this one river, maybe it's the Xe Dong, I'm not sure anymore. I have forgotten so many names. I know there are some primeval ruins looming out of the broad, flat plains there."

"I know the place. It's beautiful," Sam said.

"And when Jock gets older, have my son read this letter," Ian said, handing me the letter.

I took the letter and slipped it in my pocket. I could see Jock in another room, sleeping in a hammock. Ian's wife looked over at me. Then she continued her dance.

"She's quite mad, you know. Can't leave little Jock with her. She is very angry about Jock and very jealous of my ex. I'm afraid she might hurt our Jock after I'm gone. She has already convinced herself that I will return in the incarnation of a cat, of that she is quite confident."

"Can I go get the boy?" Sam asked.

"Don't wake him. Just carry him gently over your shoulder," Ian said almost in a whisper.

"What does your letter say if I may ask?"

"Oh, it says simply that I love him. And that all my life I believed in a Karmic chain woven intimately into everything, and that in this life beauty offers us the only path beyond the darkness. What would the human heart be if it lived only in the dark, wanting for the moon's splendors?"

A totally weird guy, I thought to myself. Clearly, Ian was spaced out on drugs.

* * *

Woody reported back to us that Ian shot himself shortly after our plane was airborne. We flew over his plantation house on our way back across the Mekong. Jock slept through the entire trip back to Thailand. When we returned to Sydney I gave her Ian's letter to Naomi, explaining the nature of its contents.

"How did Ian look?" Naomi asked.

"Like someone spaced out on drugs and about to die. He asked me the weirdest question," I said.

"And that was?"

"He asked me what would the human heart be if it lived only in the dark, wanting for the moon's splendors?" I replied.

"I understand," Naomi said, reading the letter.

Over the years I would recall Ian's question many times, and I came to believe, as Sam did, that at times we are given signs, clues of things yet to come in our lives. But for a long while my Laotian experiences remained a mystery to me like the Vat Phou, lost in the jungles for so many centuries.

Some weeks later Woody reported that Ian's Khmer wife scattered his ashes at the confluence of the Xe Dong and Mekong Rivers, near where those ancient ruins loom out of the broad, flat plains.

*   *   *

Chapter Five: In The Fullness Of Time

Naomi had organized another special event for Colin, a Sunday brunch at their condo on Ozone Street. In addition to Sam, Captain Graham, Celia, and myself, Colin had invited Jock's mother, Dr. Camille Carlton-Smythe, as well as a Dr. Conrad von Zielke, head curator of the Cologne Zoo.

The occasion was to celebrate Jock's safe return from Laos. Maggie and Sam had reconciled, but she was not attending the brunch. Maggie was caring for four-year old Jock, with his lingering equine fever, the nature of which baffled the doctors in Sydney, except for one French specialist in tropical medicine.

"Given the success of our last enterprise, Naomi and I have prepared deep fried skate knobs with lemons and capers aioli. This time we are using Gould's squid, with its thicker flesh. It should be an improvement on the dainty Loligo which we had last time we dined together," Colin said, leaning back and gazing out over Cronulla Beach.

It was one of those cloudless mornings. In one of the apartments below someone was playing a radio. *Summer Love* by the Aussie band Sherbet blared out into the courtyard. Their lead singer, Daryl Braithwaite, was a heartthrob for all the Aussie girls still addicted to the1974 hit *Silvery Moon.*

"My God! I wish those Lebanese on the second floor would turn down their radio," Naomi said.

"I thought you were a fan of Daryl Braithwaite?" Colin asked.

"Oh, please…" Naomi said, rolling her eyes.

"That's Mary Abodeely's radio," I said. "She was one of my star students," I said.

I walked over to the balcony and looked down into the courtyard. Mr. Abodeely was hosing off his Mercedes while scolding his teenage daughter, Mary, for the loud music. Mary Abodeely had been my Fourth Form history student at Woolooware High School. She was a beauty, with striking green eyes and dark, curly hair with reddish highlights, a subtle sprinkle of freckles across her high cheekbones.

"She plays the guitar, and her rendition of Joni Mitchell's *Both Sides Now* will bring tears to your eyes. She wrote about *The Tempest* for her Fourth Form essay. *The Tempest* is a difficult play. She did an excellent job," I said.

"I know *The Tempest*. With Prospero, the master illusionist and magician," Colin said.

"Colin, is there anything that you don't know?" Naomi said snidely.

"I read that play in college," Sam said. "Almost like science fiction."

"That's right, Sam. You went to college, some tiny dot in the middle of your great heartland."

"In Iowa, Naomi. I went to college in Iowa. And sometimes you are such a total bitch. Why is that?"

"But you always come back for more, don't you? *The Tempest* is both a romance and a tragedy, kind of like your life, Sam," Naomi said.

"Naomi, you know your Shakespeare, what is your favorite play?" I said, making conversation.

"Mine is *Julius Caesar*! No, wait. *MacBeth*! Yes, *MacBeth* is my favorite," Colin interrupted.

At that point Naomi looked up at Colin and sighed, shaking her head in contempt.

"Please Colin, may I answer the question without your intrusion! I've always been fond of *Romeo and Juliet*. How about you, Dai 'ui?"

"*Hamlet*."

"Of course, I should have guessed that."

I watched Mary finish washing the Mercedes. She looked up and waved at me. The other girls were jealous of Mary. One day they stole her history notebook. These notebooks were required, a kind of journal where the students outlined my lessons and added drawings and newspaper clippings. To lose one's history notebook was a major calamity.

Mary came to me in tears, telling me her story. After classes got out we walked the entire school, searching the trashcans, finally finding the lost notebook in the high weeds at the edge of the soccer field. Mary was elated, and the next day brought me a note from her mother, thanking me for all that I had done for their daughter, and inviting my wife and me to dinner.

The dinner we had with the Abodeely family was a memorable one. We dined out on their balcony, overlooking Cronulla Park, Mrs. Abodeely having prepared a wonderful rack of lamb and a number of exotic side dishes. The conversation ranged from the Egyptian-born, Greek Constantine Cavafy, to the American University of Beirut where she had met Mr. Abodeely. Mrs. Abodeely told us her father was descended from a nobleman from Venice named d'Adday who settled in Lebanon during the time of the last Crusade. Her mother was French and had once taught at the Institute du Marai. Mr. Abodeely hardly said a thing during the dinner, commenting only that his origins were much humbler than his wife's noble line.

"We just painted those new railings yesterday. The paint may still be wet," Naomi cautioned, snapping me out of my daze.

Colin's wrought-iron railings were custom-made ironwork in a tasteful grapevine pattern, crafted after a design he and Naomi had seen in Florence. They had carried the same grapevine design over to their two patio tables, which were shaded by a simple, dark green canvas awning in the Roman style. Of course, nothing about Colin or Naomi was simple. Their condo occupied the entire fourth floor of 21/23 Ozone Street, in Cronulla. Celia and I lived right below Colin and Naomi, our humble rented apartment being a third the size of theirs.

It was a bright and splendorous time to be living in that popular beachside suburb. Back then one could look west out across the town to Gunnamatta Bay. From the beachside part of Colin's balcony, there was a good view of the various beaches stretching away to the north, as well as the local rugby league football club of the Cronulla Sharks, the team that Colin had played for prior to attending law school and the London School of Economics.

The local surf culture had given unique names to various parts of the shoreline, the Alley, between Cronulla Beach proper and North Cronulla, the Wall, between North Cronulla and Elouera, Sandshoes to the south, near the mouth of the Port Hacking estuary, and finally, Shark Island and the Point, two spots just off Cronulla Beach. And there were indeed sharks there, occasionally big ones, cruising in the clear green water to the east of Shark Island, just beyond the safety of the barrier nets.

"You seem lost in your thoughts," Captain Graham said, handing me a Flag Ale.

"Yeah, a bit. I resigned my teaching job Friday," I said, watching three young surfers greeting Mary Abodeely.

"Good, does that mean you have accepted Colin's offer?"

"How could I refuse? I made as much money for that week's work in Laos as I did for three months of teaching. And this new project appeals to me."

"Sam, I have some good news to share with you," Graham called to Sam who was opening a cold beer.

"And that is," Sam asked, in his cavalier way.

"We have another Marine joining our team."

"Hey, Dai 'ui. Finally got tired of mucking around in that teaching job?"

"On the contrary, I really enjoy teaching. But I need a change, and this is such easy money. I have to do it. Celia and I will be heading back to the States in a few months.

Captain Graham was drinking Special Export Pilsner, the beer with the red lion on the label. Brewed by Tooth in Sydney, I had recently acquired a taste for it. On the other hand, both Colin and Sam were fans of Flag Ale, made by Tooheys. Surprisingly, Naomi also liked to drink beer on hot afternoons, and she usually drank lots of it, preferring KB Lager.

"This offer was too good to pass up," I said, waving at the young surfers below. "See that tall, fair kid with his arm around Mary Abodeely. His name is Reggie Dolan. He's probably on his way to ride the curl off Shark Island. He came by to thank me after his exams, gratified to be going on to the university. A year ago he almost dropped out. I talked him into sticking it out."

"Good on ya," the Captain said, clinking bottles.

Seeing Reggie brought to mind one of the conflicts I had encountered with one of my English classes at Wollooware High School. During their last year, the tradition at Wollooware was for students to write a research paper on either a poet or a novelist. I took a liberal interpretation of those traditional topic areas allowing several of my students, including Reggie, to write their papers on musicians like Bob Dylan, John Lennon, and Bob Marley, whom I considered poets. Needless to say Reggie wrote a brilliant paper on Bob Marley's two albums, *Burnin* from 1973, and *Live* from 1975. But I didn't win any points with the English faculty for my liberal approach.

"I asked him to think beyond the football and surf culture of Cronulla. I asked him what kind of future did he want to have?"

"Think beyond football! Some would call that un-Australian," Naomi said, walking over to us.

"Naomi, we agreed to have a truce. Correct?" Graham said, giving me a wink.

"Of course, a truce. And I saw that wink. Reggie may not realize it now, Dai 'ui, but he will be better off at the university, finding, as you say, his future."

"Future? What bullshit! Reggie's future is with sweet Mary, and going with the flow," Sam said.

"Sam, you're already drunk and it's not even lunch time. I worry about you," Naomi said.

"Never went to bed. Hung out at the league club all last night. So, Naomi what's the future hold for you now that you've been shit-canned from your teaching job?" Sam asked, with a smirk.

"Don't be a smart ass, Sam. You know what happens when you mess with me," Naomi said with a wicked smile.

"Roger that. My head still aches from that bottle you hit me with. But I forgive you. Who could hold a grudge against a beauty like Naomi Musto?"

"Sam, when you want to be, you are such a charming, silver-tongued devil. Come here, I want to introduce you to Dr. von Zielke. He's going to be part of my future. He needs someone fluent in French."

* * *

Dr. Conrad von Zielke seemed ordinary enough, a bald, overweight and overly polite man in his mid-fifties. He spoke with a slight German accent, but otherwise expressed himself well. The details of his story, which he promised to share with us after lunch, were tragic. After brunch we pulled the two tables together to hear his sad tale. Naomi and Dr. Carlton-Smythe excused themselves to go for a walk. Because our recovering Jock from Laos had been a success, on the recommendation of his colleague, Dr. Carlton-Smythe, Dr. von Zielke had retained Colin's firm, and thus the special services provided by Captain Graham and our team.

"My son and his wife were murdered a little over a month ago in the Bolovens Plateau. They were mapping several large Laotian caves as part of this greater Mekong survey sponsored by Dr. Carlton-Smythe and her department," Dr. von Zielke said.

"Near Pakse?" Sam asked.

"Yes. They were working north of the confluence of the Xe Dong and the Mekong. It was supposedly a safe area. There are still a few French coffee plantations there. Champasak is close by, and the Vat Phou. You know this area?"

"I do. And I don't think there is any safe place in Laos. But that is beside the point," Sam said, looking down into the courtyard where Mary and Reggie were polishing her father's Mercedes.

"Thanks to Colin, I have a letter from the authorities in Vientiane that allows me to recover the remains of my son and daughter-in-law. Colin knows a Politburo member and a French-educated intellectual who has been instrumental in resolving this tragedy. Without his support we would be nowhere. Where I'm sure I will need your help is with my two grandchildren. I have petitioned for their custody, but, as of yet have heard nothing," Dr. von Zielke said, his eyes watering.

"Their mother was Laotian," Colin said. "So, the situation is ambiguous as to their status. Although the children carry German citizenship, we can't seem to find anyone in a position of authority who is willing to act upon Dr. von Zielke's request. I contacted Woody, our man in Vientiane, to see if he could get things moving by greasing a few palms, so-to-speak. The channels are difficult to figure. The lines of authority are blurred here."

"You know that Colin has already arranged some contacts?" Captain Graham asked.

"Yes, a Miss Swan and a Dr. de Fillio," Dr. von Zielke said. "They are part of the team drawing up the application to make Vat Phou a world heritage site. Colin also has the support from this KV. It is my understanding that Dr. de Fillio went so far as to demand that the killers be brought to justice. KV told him to back off."

"Tell us what you know about the killers," Graham said, lighting a cigarette.

"I find this whole tragedy baffling. No attempt has been made to hide who killed my son and daughter-in-law. A Colonel Dub ordered them shot, execution style. The reasons are unclear, although I suspect Karl had uncovered damaging information concerning the illegal trade in endangered animals," Dr. von Zielke said.

"Like trafficking in tiger and bear parts for the Chinese market?" Graham asked.

"Yes, as well as being a supplier for the pet trade. At first I thought my son was taken as a spy. But that was not the case. He was never charged with any crime. No one knows for sure what the circumstances were. They were taken from their campsite and shot. Just like that. No explanation."

"Woody speculates this Colonel Dub was out for revenge," Colin said. "And that there may be some kind of vendetta involved here. Your daughter-in-law was from a family of the Lao-Lum aristocrats, and was educated at the Sorbonne. Her family fled to Thailand when the Lao People's Revolutionary Party took control. The Lao-Lum are the majority of the Lao population, but very few are committed communists."

"Tell us more about your grandchildren," Graham continued.

"A boy, Francois, he's ten years old. His sister, Julianne is eight. They are in the care of the Sisters of Mercy who run a small school in Champasak."

"Champasak. Good. We have worked with Dr. de Fillio and Miss Swan before. They may be a resource to us," Graham said.

Take it Easy by the Eagles was playing on Mary Abodeely's radio. Reggie Dolan had his arm around Mary's waist. They crossed the street to Cronulla Park where Naomi and Dr. Carlton-Smythe were feeding the local family of Sulfur-Crested Cockatoos.

"Where do you suppose Reggie's going?" Sam asked.

"Well, it's simple, Sam. Look at the way he's holding on to Mary. I don't think he's going to ride the curl off Shark Island," I said.

"Yeah, I call that going with the flow, and taking it easy. You know, I'm really looking forward to seeing Miss Swan again," Sam said.

* * *

Dr. von Zielke waited until Naomi and Dr. Carlton-Smythe returned from their walk before departing. A very formal man, he took particular care in thanking Naomi, talking at length in French, which I found interesting. Sam had passed out on a chaise lounge, and Colin lowered the awning to spare him from the late afternoon sun. Dr. von Zielke drove Captain Graham back to Manly where they were staying. Colin, Naomi, Dr. Carlton-Smythe, and I gathered around a table to watch the sun go down.

"Interesting guy," I said, watching Dr. von Zielke drive away in a classy BMW.

"Yes. He's a Prussian nobleman. From one of the richest families in Germany," Dr. Carlton-Smythe said, sipping her wine.

"Doctor, what was Karl von Zielke doing back in those hills?" I asked.

"Call me Camille. He was looking for spiders. In particular a species of the *Heteropoda*, a giant Huntsman Spider the size of a pie plate."

Camille was in her early forties, a handsome woman of medium height, tan, and very fit looking, with reddish-brown hair already streaking to gray. She wore little make-up, if any; and had a sober, no-nonsense manner about her. Her light blue eyes were her most striking feature. I wondered how she ever got hooked up with her ex-husband, Ian.

"Wow. They get that big. Poisonous?" I asked.

"The poison of the Huntsman depends on the sub-species actually. Some varieties appear to be more poisonous than others. And, of course, some people have more of a reaction to the venom than others. But rest assured, any bite would be a painful experience. The specimens that Karl found in these limestone caverns measure thirty centimeters across. He planned to name them *Heteropoda maxima zielkei.* Apparently, this variety of Huntsman, like members of the genus Neosparassus, can give bites that cause prolonged pain and an irregular pulse rate. Exactly how that poison works in the long term, he wasn't able to determine."

"Karl's letters are fascinating. If you like, I'll pull the file for you," Colin said.

"Not necessary. Spiders give me the creeps," I said, lighting up a Gaulois.

Since the trip to Laos I had started smoking again, much to Celia's despair. In the lull of the afternoon, without a wind to speak of, my cigarette smoke hung in the air, drifting out over Ozone Street. A Sulfur-Crested Cockatoo shrieked in one of the Washingtonian Palms in Cronulla Park. Across the street at the Hotel Cecil, young men were spilling out onto the veranda from the increasingly noisy and crowded pub. A train was pulling into Cronulla Station to pick the weekend beach crowd and carry them back to their various mundane suburbs. A number of them were carrying fish and chips wrapped in newsprint.

"Thirty centimeters! Quite a spider," I said, flicking my ash over the railing. Reggie Dolan was walking up the promenade from the Squash Club with Mary. She was resting her head on his shoulder. I heard a shout. Then someone wolf whistled at them as they passed by the Hotel Cecil.

"The locals living near these caverns tell of a hot-pink *Desmoxytes* that is deadly," Camille continued. "However, we have yet to record that species formally. It is un-described for scientific purposes."

"Desmo…?"

"A hot-pink millipede. A number of giant millipedes have glands that produce cyanide to protect them from predators. This one is hot pink. Karl saw several, which is why his documentation needs to be recovered along with the rest of his effects and specimens. We've been told that a certain Captain Katay has Karl's entire collection, as well as his notebooks. Colin's man, this Woody, is the source of that information."

"Woody is our man on the ground. You've got to have one, Captain Graham tells me. You and Sam really need to read this file that I prepared for you, especially Woody's background material," Colin said, clearly impatient with me. "Anyway, I think this Colonel Dub is waiting for us to pay him off. It's only a matter of time, and negotiating the price. Bastards," Colin said, shaking his head.

Camile sighed, shaking her head." Colin, time is on their side. And I'm not so sure that this is simply about money. Laotians are caught up in a complex social hierarchy and very sensitive to status. It's not all about Captain John Graham of the SAS storming in there. The right people have to be there to negotiate. If it wasn't for Jock, I'd be going myself."

"Naomi says that he's doing better," Colin said.

"Yes, and I can now sleep again. A French doctor here in Sydney finally figured it out. He was familiar with the symptoms. Jock has an equine fever unique to Indo-China, and will recover in the fullness of time, as the doctor put it. Or, should I say, as he explained to Naomi. His English left a lot to be desired. Naomi was invaluable to me."

"That's why I'll be going with you, Dai 'ui," said Naomi, picking up at Camille's complement. "Your team needs someone fluent in French."

"I heard you and Dr. von Zielke conversing. I wondered..."

"According to Woody, not one of the bastards speaks the Queen's English. Not one," Colin said. "This letter from the Laotian government that gives us the authority to recover Karl's remains is written in French. I had to have Naomi translate it for me."

"Ah, that expensive Cambridge education my father paid for has finally provided some benefit for my illustrious husband, former knuckle-dragger for the Cronulla Sharks," Naomi said quietly.

Colin and I laughed, stirring Sam from his stupor. Even the serious Dr. Camille Carlton-Smythe smiled. Down in Cronulla Park a second Sulfur-Crested Cockatoo shrieked from the palms.

"Wake up, Sam! We have a surprise for you," Naomi said, blowing a smoke ring.

"Surprise?" Sam asked, sitting up and blinking.

"Yes, Camille brought some absinth for Colin. A bottle of Grande Absinth, I believe. As I recall, you are familiar with absinth. " Naomi said, smugly.

"Grande is the best. Reminds me of licorice," Colin said, producing the bottle.

I watched in fascination as Colin poured the light green liquid into a highball glass over a slotted spoon topped with a lump of sugar. Once the sugar was soaked, he lit it on fire. As soon as the flame died, he mixed the remains of the liquid with water and the absinth went milky.

"Have you had this before?" Colin asked me.

"No," I said, studying the bottle.

"Well, you should be careful what you mix it with. The original absinth had just two ingredients, wormwood, and the roots of the giant anis plant. Absinth Kubler, made in the Swiss canton of Neuchhatel, has rosehip in it. It has a more oily texture than this variety, but I like the aroma it has."

"My favorite is that Absinth Mata Hari, the one from Austria. It is such a vivid green, and has the aroma of lemon and lime," Camille said, lighting her sugar cube.

"That's much too dry for my palate! Oh, a warning to all! You will find the absinth made in the Canton of Jura clear and very dry, bitter actually, but it is very strong, definitely not for first timers," Colin said, handing me the glass.

"Colin, spare us the bloody lecture. My God! Does it never end?" Naomi said, rolling her eyes.

I don't remember much after that. They tell me that I had four glasses of the stuff. Eventually Colin and Sam helped me stumble back to my place. It took me two days to recover from my episode with absinth, and Celia was not happy, to say the least. But the worst things were dreams that I had, strange hallucinogenic snap-shots from my past.

In several of the dreams my school friend Les appeared. Les was a Phantom F4 pilot who was shot down on his first mission in Laos in June 1969. He was twenty-five at the time. He didn't say anything in the dreams. He was just there. Another Marine buddy, Rick, who was lost in early 1969, also appeared. Sam told me that he had similar dreams where the dead would appear.

Absinth is made from wormwood that contains a mind-altering chemical call thujone. It occurred to me that I might be having a reaction to the high thujone content from that bottle of Grand Absinth. Obviously there was a good reason why most European governments banned it in 1915, after all the Parisian poets addicted to absinth went ape-shit.

* * *

We arrived in Thailand according to our plan, only to find inclement weather creating impossible conditions. The rain poured down in sheets, and the word came from Captain Graham that we were slipping our schedule by two days. Colin and Dr. von Zielke also found that certain arrangements previously agreed upon had not been made.

Woody decided to use this time to gather more intelligence from a unique source, his Hmong connections at the Ban Vinai Refugee Camp. Woody had an old Land Rover, and asked us if we wanted to go with him to visit the camp. I rode shotgun while Sam and Naomi jumped in the back. We were off into the pouring rain.

Many Hmong fought against the Pathet Lao as our allies during the Vietnam War. After the communist takeover in Laos in 1975, hundreds of Hmong were singled out for terrible retribution. Thousands of others fled to Thailand for asylum. Those refugees came in phases, fleeing the compulsory farm collectivization enforced by the Lao communist government. Processing and transit camps were set up in Thailand, but neither the Western governments nor their Indochina counterparts were able to reach a solution for the Hmong refugees. Things seemed in a kind of political limbo. It was that calm before the storm that Miss Swan had described for me, that brief period before the outbreak of hostilities between China and Vietnam.

"Here we are," Woody said, pulling through a simple bamboo arch.

"There's nothing here but a patch of jungle at the edge of a muddy, red field," I said, surprised.

"They don't have much of anything. No toilets. No running water. No clinic. No land to grow food. Nothing but a few plywood shacks back in the trees. Do you want to wait in the car? It's a real mud hole out there, and some of the Hmong have tuberculosis," Woody said, shaking his head.

Naomi replied, "No, I'll go,"

"So will I," Sam said, pulling on a slicker.

"I'll stay here," I said.

"Good, someone should stay with the vehicle. When the kids show up give them these," Woody said, opening a large box of Hershey chocolate bars.

Woody, Naomi and Sam disappeared into the trees and rain. When I looked back toward the muddy field a crowd of thirty or so kids had appeared out of nowhere. They descended on the Land Rover, ranging in age from three to thirteen, all barefoot, thin and glazed-eyed, many with sores on their legs and arms. I handed out the chocolate, surprised by how orderly and polite the kids were. In Vietnam I had similar experiences handing out goodies and those kids would go crazy, absolutely ape-shit, fighting each other for a mere tootsie roll. After I handed out all the candy, I broke into Woody's first aid kit. I was treating the leg ulcers on a four-year old with a tube of triple antibiotic ointment when Naomi appeared. She was crying.

"Dai 'ui, let me do that. I want to help."

"You're crying."

"The real camp is just through these trees. It must cover a hundred acres. It is a crowded filthy place, with hundreds of people, dirtier than you can possibly imagine. The conditions are sickening. It is one great open sewer. These people have to make do with one bucket of drinking water a day."

"You're really upset."

"We were walking through those trees and I witnessed a mother digging a grave for her infant, only a month old. Dau 'ui, this is the fall-out from your Vietnam War, and all of us are now complicit in this, even those of us who protested. I just feel so ashamed. Our countries have abandoned these Hmong. When I get back to Australia I'm going to do something for these people."

At that point I looked up to see Sam herding a group of Hmong children down the trail. There must have been fifteen of them.

"What's this?" I asked Sam.

"Sick kids. Naomi wants to fly them to some Buddhist monastery," Sam said, his hair catching in an overhanging branch.

Naomi flared. "It's called Wat Tham Krabok, you imbecile. Hurry! We don't have time to waste."

"Naomi, What are you doing?" I asked, baffled by the crowd of children, all seemingly less than ten years old.

"Dai 'ui, I'm flying these children to the abbot of Wat Tham Krabok to be placed under his care. In 1975 he received the Magsaysay Award."

"Can't say as I have heard of that award," I replied.

"Well, that's the equivalent in Asia of the Nobel Prize."

* * *

Thailand was providing temporary asylum for thousands of Hmong. But it had always been made clear to these refugees that permanent resettlement in Thailand was not an option. Ironically, although many of the Hmong refugees in Thailand had been accepted for resettlement in the United States, many of those at Ban Vinai, as well as other camps, were reluctant to leave Thailand. They held out hope of be able to return to Laos without suffering reprisals.

The abbot at Wat Tham Krabok was sympathetic to the plight of the Hmong. He offered his protection and an alternative to the misery in the camps. His drug rehabilitation program, making use of herbs and meditation, was a model for the world, open to anyone, including foreigners. Most importantly, his enlightened outlook offered a refuge for the sick and infirm, especially the children.

The abbot's approach flew in the face of official government policy. But the abbot had more issues. Certain Hmong living at the monastery got involved in resistance efforts in Laos. As one would expect, Woody was tuned into all the players.

"There are rumors that a mysterious Lao power broker high up in the new Laotian government is trading political favors in return for support with the production of opium," Woody said.

"Wow! Well, it seems we trade one corrupt official for another," I said, looking down as we circled the monastery.

"Roger that. This big fish is said to direct the activities of our notorious Colonel Dub. That's someone we should be meeting soon, if Colin's arrangements go as planned," Woody said.

"I already heard of this Colonel Dub," I said.

"He's an old warlord who controls much of southern Laos, a real nightmare," Woody added, circling to make his approach to what appeared more like a soccer field than an airstrip.

*   *   *

I was surprised that the abbot was there to meet us. He had ten monks with him, all with shaved heads, and dressed in those orange robes. Naomi went to greet the abbot while I off-loaded the sick kids and Woody checked the plane. Sam was huddled in the back of the plane, wrapped in a blanket. He was shaking like a leaf in the wind, and had a fever. The whole affair on the ground took about ten minutes. When Naomi returned, she seemed changed. She was definitely moved by the experience of meeting the abbot. It was as if she were glowing.

"Well, Dai 'ui, what a great man he is. You should have come with me," Naomi said.

"Nah. I felt out of place. This is your show. What did he have to say?" I asked.

"He thanked me for bringing the children, and said something that affected me more than you can imagine. It literally took my breath away. He said the road to redemption is through good works."

"That's in the Bible," I replied.

"Yes, Dai 'ui. Yes, it is indeed in the Bible."

The sun chose that moment to break through the clouds for the first time in days. As we boarded the plane the children and the monks were walking up the monastery. We could hear them singing, and for the first time I realized that they were all smiling. They waved to us as we lifted off into the twilight.

* * *

The tree frogs were calling in the moonless night. A light, drizzling rain was falling, drops drifting through the door that opened to our balcony. The air had that pervasive, musky smell that came with the rainy season in Southeast Asia. Geckos scurried across the ceiling in our spare Thai lodgings, which were functional at best. Captain Graham had selected them because they were out-of-the-way, and adjacent to a small airstrip. In the morning we were flying across the Mekong to Pakse, and then on to Champasak and Vat Phou. I was reviewing Colin's file and the notes that Woody had put together.

Based on Woody's reconnaissance, southern Laos was reeling under the impact of the Pathet Lao who took control of the country in 1975. They had abolished the monarchy and established the Lao People's Democratic Republic, installing their own hierarchy alongside the existing administration.

Colonel Dub was in charge of a liberated district called a *khana*, overseeing a number of district chiefs, or *chao muangs*. He was the equivalent of a warlord who was to implement the new policy of the party in his district. The policy of the party was to advance to socialism without going through the stages of capitalist development, a deviation from orthodox Marxism-Leninism. There was no chance of Laos having a stage of capitalist development. With ninety percent of the population working as subsistence farmers, the party now was confronting the question of what socialism meant in a country such as Laos, given the poverty, backwardness, and endemic corruption. Most of the technical professionals and educators had fled the country.

"Ready to cross the river of evil memory?" I asked Sam.

"Say again."

"The Lao call the Mekong the river of evil memory. You should take a look at Colin's file, especially Woody's report. Colin wants the file back tonight. He's flying back down to Bangkok in the morning," I added, swatting a mosquito.

Through the thin walls I could hear Naomi and Dr. von Zielke conversing in French in the next room. Woody, Colin, and Captain Graham were out on the dirt airstrip, checking out the de Havilland DHC-6 Twin Otter. The plane looked brand new. Woody's role was varied. In addition to his ground reconnaissance, he handled our logistics and was to pilot the Twin Otter into Laos.

Sam wiped sweat from his brow. "Fuck that. I don't feel so good."

"I can't believe that you are still hung over from your binge at the Cronulla League Club. You must have picked up a bug."

"Just tell me what caught your eye in the report. I'm not going to read through Colin's bullshit."

There was a knock on the door. It was Woody.

"Captain wants us all to meet in the doctor's room for a quick meeting," Woody said, pulling his wet hair back into a ponytail.

* * *

"This will be brief," I'm coming down with something," the Captain said.

"Sam's not feeling good either," I said.

"Let's get this done and get some sleep," Captain Graham said, looking bleary-eyed.

Once again Captain Graham reviewed our plan, covering each person's role and the steps in the process. There were to be two planes, Captain's Pilatus PC-6 Turbo Porter and the de Havilland, both short take-off and landing machines with versatility and maneuverability that made them popular in areas with difficult flying environments, especially the short landing fields that we encountered in Laos. The Porter could land within the length of a soccer field carrying a payload of 1500 kilograms.

After we were on the ground in Champasak, Woody, Sam, and me would load the remains of Karl von Zielke and his wife in the de Havilland. While this task was being completed, with the help of Naomi, Miss Swan was to facilitate a meeting between Dr. von Zielke and Colonel Dub's representative, a Captain Katay. If things went as Colin thought they should, Miss Swan would arrange for the grandchildren to fly back with Woody in the de Havilland. Captain Katay and Dr. von Zielke would work out the other appropriate arrangements. Miss Swan had given the indication to Colin that everything was up for negotiation, including Karl's scientific papers.

"Are there any questions?" Captain Graham asked, rubbing his eyes.

"Only one, has anybody got any cold Australian beer? This Thai stuff doesn't measure up," Sam said, gruffly.

"I've got some cold German beer in the cooler. You are welcome to join Naomi and me. We're going to sit out on the balcony and have a smoke. You're all welcome," Dr. von Zielke said.

"I'm turning in," Graham said.

"I'll pass, this time," Woody said.

"Likewise. I still have paperwork to review," Colin muttered, peering deep into a file.

* * *

The beer was Warsteiner, which I was to learn was outselling Budweiser worldwide. I downed two cold Warsteiners in a matter of minutes.

"Damn. I feel like shit. I thought a couple of cold beers would help," Sam said, leaning back.

"You'll recover. In the fullness of time, as that French doctor said," Naomi said.

"That's from *Galatians*, fourth chapter, fourth verse, a text having to do with prophetic fulfillment as I recall," Dr. von Zielke said, pulling another beer from the cooler. "Through life and our various suffering we see signs, prophecies, if you will."

"Prophecies of what?" Sam asked, suddenly interested.

"Of the coming day; or, if you prefer, the coming Apocalypse. Of course, as I also recall, there was some debate on the translation from the Greek. Greek words tend to mean many things, depending upon the context. Thus *kronos* can mean just time, or the fulfillment of time, with the notion that past is prologue."

"Past is prologue. I believe that. And you know Greek. I'm most impressed. You studied it at Heidelberg, I presume," Naomi said.

Having taught Shakespeare, I recognized the phrase from *The Tempest*, but I didn't want to interrupt the flow of the conversation. *Whereof what's past is prologue*, Antonio says in Act 2.

"No, actually, I learned Greek on the Russian Front. I was an artillery officer far behind the lines. Most of the time I was bored. When I went to the original Greek text, I found out that two different words were being used, depending upon what translation one read. In some, I found the word was not *kronos*, but *kairos*. Both words mean time. *Kronos* means chronological time. *Kairos* means fulfillment of time or the appointed time. Thus, I salute you all. Tonight we are on the eve of our appointed time in Laos."

"But how did you resolve the translation issue?" I asked, caught up in the story.

"Two ways. First, with the help of a friend I went to the Hebrew text. Then, after the war I went to the Arabic. Over time I think I came to find the right answer, at least for me. These things tend to resolve themselves over time, like when one faces the complex matters of faith. I miss my son Karl very much. We often talked about these matters. He was as much my intellectual companion as he was my son."

Naomi, her eyes tearing up, said. "Oh Dr. von Zielke, you are a beautiful man. Yes, we are on the eve of our appointed time tonight,"

"Did you know that the name, Naomi, means enjoyment, pleasure, or gratification in both Hebrew and Arabic?" Dr. von Zielke said, opening another cold beer.

Sam stood suddenly. "Shit. I got to get out of here before I drown in the bullshit. Doctor, with all due respect, you are right on with your observation about Naomi. She is all about pleasure and gratification. That's what she's about, for sure," He said, stumbling for the door.

"Sam, get out of here before I have to knock you down again," Naomi snapped.

* * *

The next morning Graham was running a fever of 103. Sam was also feeling feverish. Colin went totally ape shit. He wanted to call off the mission then and there. Naomi pulled him and Captain Graham aside, and after a fifteen-minute conversation, it was decided to proceed. Colin would get Captain Graham back to Bangkok to find medical help. Sam insisted that he could continue on. Woody would fly the de Havilland and Naomi the Pilatus. She was now in charge. The mission to cross the river of evil memory was still a go.

* * *

In spite of heavy rain and a crosswind, Woody dropped the de Havilland onto the small landing strip without problems. Naomi and Dr. von Zielke followed in the Pilatus five minutes later. By then the rain had let up and Naomi's three-point landing was textbook.

Miss Swan was waiting in her Land Rover. Behind the Land Rover was a brand new three quarter ton Mercedes truck loaded with what I assumed to be the remains we had come for.

"Miss Swan, I didn't think we would meet again so soon," I said.

Sam gave Miss Swan a big hug. His fever was still with him and he looked bleary-eyed.

"May I introduce Mrs. Naomi Musto and Dr. von Zielke. Naomi will be taking care of the details. Captain Graham was taken ill with a fever," Sam said.

"The Lao-Lum farmers say that there is a strange fever spreading throughout Laos, and that the wells are going bad. They blame all of this on the Pathet Lao and their new policy," she said convincingly.

"Miss Swan, we have followed the instructions, and in accordance with the letter, I am here to collect my son and daughter-in-law's remains. What of the status of my grandchildren?" Dr. von Zielke asked, holding a brief case in his arms.

"Captain Katay has passed on to me some things, the *Les Regles de Jeu*," Miss Swan said.

Miss Swan's hair was pulled back in a French roll. Her slim, ivory arms were bare but for a single jade bracelet, and she noticed me staring at the spiral, red and black Yin and Yang tattoo on her right shoulder. In spite of the situation, Miss Swan seemed cool and relaxed. Outside, four Laotian workers bustled about under Woody's direction, removing the remains from the back of the Mercedes.

"The what?" I asked.

"Rules of the game; or, the play of the game, depending upon the translation. Please continue," Naomi said, winking at Dr. von Zielke.

"A certain party has a favor to ask," Miss Swan said.

"And that is?" Naomi asked.

"If a certain box were to find its way back to Paris with Karl's remains, I think we might have a breakthrough, a new start at negotiations, with everything negotiable," Miss Swan said.

"Done!" Dr. von Zielke said, excitedly.

"Wait a minute. No dope!" Naomi countered.

"No dope. If you like, I will have you inspect the box…" Miss Swan said.

"Dai 'ui, go look at the bloody box and see what's in it," Sam said, still under the weather.

The rain continued to come down. I followed behind Miss Swan, watching her beautiful ass sway as she took me to the truck. The box was more like a crate. She raised the hinged lid and I peered in. Inside were a number of strange, moss-covered statues. They appeared to be made of a kind of sandstone.

"Statues, all Gods of the Hindu pantheon. The one with the four faces is *Brahma*, the Creator. Next to *Brahma* is *Vishnu* with one face and four arms. Behind *Vishnu* is dark *Shiva*, the one with a third eye in his forehead. Then there is *Ganea*, the elephant-headed god of intelligence. That one in the back is the *Devi*. Let me pull it out so that you can look at it. It is very special."

Miss Swan pulled out the Devi from the musty box. It was the armless bust and head of a beautiful young woman, maybe eighteen inches in height, mounted on a pedestal, with its tall, ornate hairstyle and ear ornaments. The features were delicate, carved in balanced proportions.

"This is a 10th Century piece from Vietnam. I appreciate your willingness to help me get this back to Paris," Miss Swan said.

"May I hold it?" I asked.

"Of course," Miss Swan replied, passing the bust. "Meet the consort of the Hindu god, *Shiva* the destroyer. She is celebrated in songs and poems, and known by a number of different names. I know her as the good *Jaganmata*, or mother of the universe, and destroyer of evil. Today she is still worshipped by millions as their primary deity, a feminine cosmic force."

Looking at the Devi, I couldn't help but think of *The White Goddess* written by Robert Graves. Graves proposed the existence of an archaic deity, a mother goddess inspired and represented by the phases of the moon. He believed that this proto-goddess was the foundation for the various goddesses found in European mythologies.

"As you can see, no dope in the box," Miss Swan said, setting the Devi back in the box.

"Miss Swan, as Sam would say, roger that. We have a deal. You tell Naomi what to do next."

I looked up to see Sam approaching. His eyes were glazed, and he appeared very tired.

"Dai 'ui, I'd like to talk to Miss Swan alone if you don't mind."

"Sure, Sam. Call me when you're ready."

It was drizzling, and I sought shelter from the rain under a tree. For the next five minutes Sam and Miss Swan stood out in the rain engaged in what appeared to be an intense conversation. At one point Sam raised his voice, but a distant clap of thunder prevented me from hearing him clearly. Then he turned away from her, leaning against a tree. She grabbed his arm just as he collapsed.

“Sam’s had a fever off and on these past two days,” I said.

“He’s burning up now. You should take him back to Woody’s plane. I have to go now. I must make some further arrangements,” Miss Swan said, her voice shaking.

Miss Swan walked off to meet with Naomi who was waiting by the Mercedes. I got Sam to his feet.

“Bitch! Where did she go?” Sam asked, shaking his head.

“She’s talking to Naomi and Dr. von Zielke, making further arrangements of some sort. I’m not sure what’s going on. You passed out, big time.”

“I told her that I wanted to take her back to the States, and that I was leaving Maggie. She said she didn’t want that. That she was staying here in this shit hole. I don’t get it, Dai ‘ui.”

“Sam, what’s there to get? Let it go. As you like to say, go with the flow.”

* * *

Miss Swan picked up the grandchildren from the Sisters of Mercy and we loaded them on the de Havilland with the remains of their parents. Sam was running a high fever again, so I strapped him in the co-pilot’s seat. He immediately fell asleep. Woody was all freaked out about the statues, but he went ahead with the plan, taking off for an old airstrip in Northern Thailand. From there it was “a piece of cake,” as he liked to say.

“So, you’re confident there was no dope in the box?” Naomi asked me.

“Just a bunch of old statues. That’s all.”

"Old statues! That doesn't sound good, disturbing actually. But we don't have much choice, do we?"

"I don't know. There's something going on here, for sure. I looked for dope, that's all. You should have checked the box yourself," I said, disgusted.

The rain continued to pour. Woody spun the de Havilland around and slid to the right, just missing a tall stand of bamboo. But he corrected, and then let loose all those powerful sky horses, waving through the open window when he touched off, his long hair flying behind him like that singer, Daryl Braithwaite. God bless him. He was flying back to Thailand alone through heavy storm conditions, taking those kids to safety. Naomi had tears in her eyes. I was beside myself with fear, and without an automatic weapon to call my own.

"Damn! Old statues. I don't like the sound of that at all. Dai 'ui, what have we stumbled into?" Naomi said, wringing her hands.

"Miss Swan said they were from Vietnam. She called one of them *Jaganmata*, the mother of the universe."

"My God! That sounds like ancient Cham sculpture. Let's hope Woody isn't flying out art treasures."

* * *

Once the storm broke, we flew up the Mekong some twenty kilometers, following the river to find Colonel Dub's headquarters, a large, sprawling plantation house formerly owned by a French coffee planter unsympathetic to the Pathet Lao. As part of the new policy, that planter suddenly disappeared. Colonel Dub then occupied his property.

It was late afternoon, and when we set down on the muddy airstrip the sun was in our eyes. Along the riverfront side of the house all the land had been cleared of brush and bamboo for a good five hundred yards. At the south end of the cleared land lay a sleepy little village. To the east, acres of coffee stretched away as the terrain rose up into the Bolovens Plateau. We landed just like that, following our map and the river. No other guide. No further instructions. No radio contact at any time. I kept waiting for some big guns on the ground to let loose and blow our little plane out of the air.

Captain Katay met us in one of those junked up Mercedes trucks. He couldn't have been much more than five feet tall. His faded uniform was somewhere between muddy-green and khaki. The captain looked like a kid right out of college. He and Naomi exchanged pleasantries in French, and we all piled in the back of the truck for the short drive up to the house.

Behind the plantation house was a long building that had once stored coffee. Several other trucks were lined up, all packed with crates of various sizes. Colonel Dub was standing outside the building to greet us.

Not much taller than Captain Katay, I guessed Colonel Dub to be in his early fifties. He had a shock of thick, white hair under his Pathet Lao style rain hat, and was wearing that ubiquitous smile all Laotians have when they greet foreigners. His sidearm looked to me like a U. S. Air Force .38 Special, probably a Smith & Wesson. I found it odd that he was wearing the blouse of the French Paras. Then I noticed his medals. Dub had a French Croix de Guerre with palm. Two nasty old men stood on either side of him, each armed with an AK-47. The two old men were also wearing the old uniform blouse of the Colonial French Paras of Indo-Chine Francais. I had seen photos of men from Dien Bien Phu wearing uniforms like these. I felt as if I had stepped back in time.

I could tell Colonel Dub liked Naomi, even though she must have been two inches taller than the Laotian. The French flowed forth, rhythmic and resonant, Naomi periodically gesturing toward von Zielke and me. The colonel was clearly fluent, and it wasn't till much later that I was to learn from Naomi that he had fought for the French in what is now called the first Indo-China War. Colonel Dub beckoned us into the warehouse.

Captain Katay motioned Naomi and von Zielke to join Colonel Dub at a long table. He put his hand up as I started to walk forward.

Naomi caught my arm and whispered. "Wait here for us. That table is only for the Colonel, the doctor and myself. Laotian protocol. It's a status thing."

I did as I was told and backed off. Waiting by the door, I was surprised to see a pretty Caucasian woman. She was in her mid-twenties, very thin, with long, unkempt, curly red hair that fell to her waist. She wore only a bandeau and a sarong, and she was holding a baby Asian Bearcat, a creature of the triple canopy jungle also called a *Binturong.* Being primarily fruit-eaters, with the exception of an occasional rodent, the Asian Bearcat is prized as a pet. They are important to the ecology because they disperse the seeds of the strangler fig. Due to the illegal pet trade, they are increasingly rare.

"Gidday," she said. "You're a Yank. Meet my little friend, Chuckles. Ever seen a baby Bearcat?"

From her accent, she was an Aussie.

"Yes, I have, in Vietnam. They are cute," I said.

"Well, I'm Red Lotus, or just Lotus, if you prefer. Do you want a cold beer while the colonel does business with your friends?"

* * *

"My boyfriend Ashton and I were heading up to a place called Vang Vieng to tube down the river, a cool thing to do. We met while I was at Lismore getting my degree. He was from the UK, and had been hanging out at Nimbin and Mullumbimby with those folk who have gone back to the land."

"Those are communes. Is Ashton a hippie?"

"No! Ashton always said he was an anarchist. He was pure, and knew Fred Robinson. When we left Nimbin, Ashton gave me the name Red Lotus. Before that I was Amy Windham. I didn't want to leave the commune but Ashton was so exciting to be with. He was never boring, and had been all through Thailand and Laos. He said the war was over, and we had nothing to worry about. There was strife with the police so we decided to leave."

I didn't know who Fred Robinson was. I would have to ask Naomi. Maybe Fred was a friend of Germane Greer. The beer was a *"33"* from Vietnam, tasted of formaldehyde, but was indeed cold, courtesy of the Vietnamese Army who still viewed Laos as their puppet state.

"So where is Ashton now?"

"The colonel's men arrested us, thought we were spies. They couldn't believe we were backpacking. They found a carton of cigarettes in Ashton's backpack, charging him with smuggling."

"Smuggling?"

"Yep. Then they shot him. Had a little talk with old Colonel Dub, and took him out and shot him, smiling their bloody smiles while they did it. Then they ransomed the remains to his mother in the UK," Lotus said, her eyes glazing over.

It was difficult to hide my anger when I heard how Ashton was shot, but I managed. The two old men with the AK-47's kept eyeballing me.

"Just like what happened to Karl von Zielke."

"No, that was different. Dr. Karl was cool about things and had the right papers. Dr. Karl found out about the Colonel's animal trafficking. I think Colonel Dub was afraid Dr. Karl was going to talk to the authorities about his activities."

"So he shot Karl and his wife."

"Yep. And then this KV shows up with an armed guard. When he heard all the details he flew into a rage. KV made the colonel crawl on his hands and knees to beg his pardon in front of all the troops. Then KV relieved the colonel of his command, although the Colonel still has his district authority. But with no troops, what can he do?"

"He has those old men. And Captain Katay..."

"Of course, those old men were with Colonel Dub when he fought with the French. Captain Katay is here to make sure Colonel Dub honors his commitments. You see, Colonel Dub took all of Dr. Karl's specimens to add to his collection. That's the colonel's trade, you know. He supplies exotic animals and their parts to the Chinese market. Everything from tiger and bear parts to live snakes and lizards, even spiders, like the big one Dr. Karl brought back from the caves. Even KV realizes that business is business. That's what I do here. Take care of the bloody collections. Once in a while I translate for our visitors."

"Lotus, are you being held here for some reason?"

"No. I've been here for almost a year and have never been charged with anything. I take care of his collections. That's what I do. You know, a few weeks ago we had a couple of Yanks here from California. They were looking for baby bearcats. There is a big demand for those because they're easy to tame. Worth quite a bit down in Bangkok."

No doubt about it. Lotus had slipped off the edge. And I needed to find some way to defend myself. The diminutive Captain Katay did not inspire my confidence.

"Lotus, have these people abused you?"

Lotus looked at me for a long moment, saying nothing, her arms folded against her sides. She did a little spin, then, facing me, brought up the index finger of her right hand to her lips as if to shush me. It was then that I first noticed that the tips of the fingers on her right hand had been burned.

"Just once. Cigarette burns. That happened just one time," Lotus said, her eyes tearing up.

* * *

I was called back to the table when Karl's papers and documents were brought out. They were stuffed in several old metal ammo boxes, the kind that you can shut air tight to keep out the moisture. One by one Dr. von Zielke looked through them, separating what he believed to be important. When he was finished the boxes were stacked to one side.

"Ask the Colonel again about Karl's specimens. I would like to see those if I could."

"He's already made it clear those are not negotiable," Naomi said.

"Try again. Tell him I have something very special to trade," von Zielke said, his voice shaking.

"All right," Naomi said, launching once more into negotiation.

It was Lotus who brought out the first box. It held about fifteen formaldehyde-filled bottles containing what appeared to be everything from spiders to snakes. The second box, carried by one of the two old men, contained several squirrel skins, striped on the back and sides.

"Colonel Dub says those are very valuable on the Chinese Market," Naomi said.

"I know their worth," von Zielke said, watching Lotus leave the room.

"Who's the girl?" von Zielke asked.

"She's an Aussie. I think she's being held against her will and is kind of crazy. Check out her fingers when she comes back," I whispered.

Something about my tone irritated Colonel Dub, and he launched into explosive French. He yelled for Captain Katay. The two old men shuffled a bit, unsettled by the colonel's change in behavior.

"Careful. Colonel Dub's impatient. He's says it is time to pay up. He says make your final selection of what documents you want, and then go home. Time to get out of Laos," Naomi said, her voice trembling.

Dr. von Zielke put his leather bag on the table and opened it. Inside was a plastic case holding six gold bars, each about four inches long. From where I was I couldn't rightly gauge their thickness, but my guess is that they were the old standard ten-ounce bars popular before and after World War Two. The day we flew out of Sydney gold was up to a thousand U.S. dollars an ounce.

At that point Lotus entered the room carrying a small bamboo cage slightly larger than a shoebox. Inside was the largest spider I'd ever seen. I knew from Dr. Camille Carlton-Smythe's description that this must be the Heteropoda, the giant Huntsman Spider the size of a pie plate that Karl von Zielke had named *Heteropoda maxima zielkei.* Naomi gasped. The two old men backed off as Lotus set the cage on the table. The huge spider, yet to be formally described to science and the object of Karl von Zielke's quest into the remote caves of eastern Laos, rose on its back legs in an aggressive display. Colonel Dub leaned forward and hissed something in French to Naomi.

"The colonel said the spider is not negotiable. He must honor a previous deal he has already made with the Chinese," Naomi said.

"Thank you, I got the gist of it. When we first began, he said all things are negotiable, did he not?" Dr. von Zielke said.

"He did. Now he seems to have changed his mind, and clearly he has withheld some things from us, not what we agreed upon with Miss Swan. He has not honored our agreement, and our commitment from KV, for that matter," Naomi said.

"Please tell him that," von Zielke said.

While Naomi engaged the colonel, Dr. von Zielke pulled his chair closer to Lotus.

"My dear, are you well?" von Zielke asked.

"No," Lotus said in a low voice.

"Are you being kept here against your will?" von Zielke continued.

"Yes. I want to go home."

"May Dr. von Zielke look at your hands please?

Lotus held up her hands and Naomi groaned. The colonel barked something to Captain Katay in

Laotian. The captain, who I thought was a kid, suddenly snapped back viciously, ordering the two men to leave the room. They lay down their rifles and left the room. Colonel Dub sat back in his chair as if struck. He took out his Smith & Wesson .38 Special and handed it to Captain Katay.

"Ask him how much for the girl? According to what KV said all things are negotiable based on the favor we did for Miss Swan. He must honor that commitment," von Zielke said.

Captain Katay interrupted. "You may take the girl with you," he said in perfect English. "She is free to go and not part of this negotiation. As a Laotian officer I regret what has happened to her. The big spider must remain here in Laos. It is still alive and thus it will be set free. Take your son's documents and dead specimens as part of the agreed upon price."

Naomi's mouth dropped open. Colonel Dub then hung his head, looking down at the floor.

"Your English is excellent, Captain," von Zielke said, clearly surprised.

"Yes, and I was given to understand from my sources that you, as a man of letters as well as science, speak fluent French."

"It is written that all things are revealed in the fullness of time," von Zielke said.

Captain Katay pondered this for a moment.

"Thus we have not withheld anything from each other, Dr. von Zielke. We have honored KV's commitments. Have we not? But for one thing."

"And that is?"

"Why justice, of course. In Laos we are not all barbarians like Colonel Dub."

Captain Katay then turned to Colonel Dub and fired a round into his right temple at a distance of about two feet. The impact spun the colonel to the left, jerking his head backwards, fluids and fragments of gore from the bullet's exit spattering across Naomi's face and hands. Lotus fell to her knees in hysterics, shaking uncontrollably.

"Just go with the flow, Dai'ui. Like Doctor von Zielke said to us, past is prologue. And this is all part of *Les Regles de Jeu*, to quote Miss Swan," Naomi said calmly, as if what had happened was all part of a previously written script.

Naomi then reached for Lotus and wrapped her arms around her, slowly rocking back and forth. Captain Katay called in the two old men and ordered them to load the boxes of documents and personal effects belonging to Karl von Zielke on the Pilatus. Dr. von Zielke left his briefcase on the table, and walked toward the plane. He paused briefly, looking back as if he were waiting for me. I was still sitting in my chair, in shock, watching a slow, but steady stream of blood drip down from the colonel's head wound, down upon his French Croix de Guerre with palm.

Chapter Six: The Wolly Man

Naomi, Sam, and I sat on her patio having a late lunch. It was a quiet Monday afternoon on Ozone Street. Naomi should have been rested from our trip. The dark circles under her eyes suggested otherwise.

"I haven't had a good night's sleep since we crossed back over the Mekong," she said, taking out a cigarette.

"Maybe you should get a prescription for some sleeping pills," I said, lighting her cigarette.

"I have a new respect for you Naomi. The Dai 'ui here said you did a real good job. From him, praise doesn't come easy," Sam said.

Below, in Cronulla Park, our new friend, Lotus, also known as Amy Windham, was feeding the Sulfur-Crested Cockatoos with Mary Abodeely. Lotus and Mary seemed to hit it off right away. I had assumed Mary was only sixteen, but I was surprised to hear from Lotus that recently she had turned eighteen. It seemed that her mother had held her back a year before starting school. I also learned that during our trip to Laos with Dr. von Zielke, there had been a big blow-up. Her father had forbidden Mary to see Reggie Dolan again, under any circumstances.

"I'm sure you heard the bad news about Reggie and Mary from Lotus," I said.

"Dai 'ui, are all Yanks as nosy as you are? You spend too much time peering into other people's business," Naomi snapped. "People's private lives should be their own. Back in the Clare Valley people respected that."

"Reggie Dolan is my former student. I've taken time to mentor him."

"I've heard that story," Naomi continued. "And I've seen the way you and Sam both eyeball sweet little Mary. Of course, if Mary continues to hang around Lotus, she may lose some of that sweetness."

"I can tell you don't like Lotus. But I find her interesting, with all that red curly hair, kind of attractive in a wild, skinny, feral sort of way," Sam said, tightening his belt.

After coming down with a rare form of equine fever, both Captain Graham and Sam had been hospitalized briefly. Graham seemed to have bounced back. Sam, however, continued to have relapses. His difficulties were not unlike those that affect victims of malaria; chills and fever, at times uncontrollable trembling. Unable to sleep and still having difficulty holding down food, he had lost twenty pounds from his rugged frame. Maggie and Sam had recently reconciled, and she worried about his sleeplessness and wild dreams.

"Feral! Oh please," Naomi said. "The woman's all skin and bones. Apart from being a hippie who's gone mental, she won't touch the food we prepare, subsists entirely on fruit, veggies, and fish. Anyway, tomorrow she'll be traveling back to Nimbin to see some healer, part of a festival or something."

"It's a harvest festival of some sort. She said it was similar to Samhain, whatever that is. I told her I'd drive her up. You want to ride along, Dai 'ui? Since your sister-in-law's here to see Celia, maybe you want to take a road trip?" Sam said.

Naomi hissed. "Samhain is a pagan festival, you fool. What you Yanks in the states call Halloween, and what my Scots Gaelic ancestors called *Oidhche*

Shamhna, the Festival of the Dead. With all the weight you've lost, you'll fit right in," Naomi said.

"Yeah, I'll go. Maybe I'll drive, more room in my Land Rover than your old Holden," I said.

"Naomi, I find it surprising that you and Lotus don't have more in common. You were both teachers. You both got shit-canned from your jobs," Sam said, smirking.

"The woman lacks intellectual rigor. A notion that I expect you would have trouble defining. And don't presume to compare us. If you really knew anything about Australia, you'd realize that she comes from a different social class than I do. And she worships at the Church of the Holy Smoke, if you get my drift. In Colin's world, cannabis use is not chic. Being a solicitor, he's not as open-minded as I am. Anyway, he'll be glad when she's gone," Naomi said.

"Naomi, you are such a hypocritical bitch, and you once told me that you were an anarchist," Sam said, relentlessly.

"I said that Germaine Greer was an anarchist. I view myself as fiscally conservative, but socially liberal. Yet, I have been known to have an occasional smoke with selected friends that I trust."

I jumped in. "Hey, when I talked to Colin, he said little Jock was up and around. That's good news," I said, changing the subject.

There never seemed to be an end to Sam and Naomi's sparring, a thing that also troubled Maggie, who admired Naomi's *chutzpa*. Over the past few months I watched Maggie and her sister-in-law become closer, spending more and more time together. That bothered Sam who viewed Naomi as a pretentious snob. No doubt Naomi could get nasty, but I found her to be a person with an inquiring mind. I found our many talks compelling.

"Yes. Colin said that Camille took Jock to an alternative healer, an Aboriginal man living down in Redfern," Naomi said. "He's some kind of bush healer, with bush medicine, if you can believe that."

"But Jock seems to be getting better," Sam said.

"She actually believes that Jock's fever may have been spiritually inspired," Naomi continued. "That his spirit was affected through some sorcery of that Khmer slut Ian was living with. Camille surprises me sometimes. A woman with all that education chasing after bush medicine."

"I believe in it. That's one of the reasons I want to drive up to Nimbin. I want to visit this one healer Lotus told me about," Sam said.

"Sam, get a grip. These hippie communes or cooperatives, or whatever, are all about drugs and sex. You'll get yourself into some cult or something worse. For all your Marine bravado, I think that down deep you are emotionally very fragile," Naomi said sincerely.

"Roger that. Maybe a big cult is what I need," Sam replied.

"Sam, cults manipulate people," Naomi replied. "Germaine Greer would tell you not to trade one social hierarchy for another. You're too smart to hang out with mindless drop-outs and their distorted realities."

"I think there are trade-offs. And sometimes we trade one set of distortions for another. Isn't that what happened to us in Laos?" Sam asked.

"A lot of things happened to us in Laos. Shit happens, as you Yanks like to say, and it happens randomly. That's why I don't paint anymore. Sometime I'll tell you the story about that, and how my attempts at being an artist turned into a fiasco. Anyway, you won't find any answers on some commune up in Nimbin."

"Naomi, you seem to have things all figured out. Well, I don't have such a fixed vision of things like you do. In fact, I don't have plans beyond trying to get over this fever. I just want to take some time off," Sam continued.

Naomi put her left hand on her slowly shaking head. "My God, talking to you makes my head hurt. It's almost the Devil's Hour. Let's go over to the Café Ritz and have a drink. The drinks will be on Colin," Naomi said, her right hand flicking her cigarette butt out towards Ozone Street.

* * *

"Here's to my wild rover Yank friends, and to the success of our last enterprise, Naomi said, leaning back in her chair.

In Cronulla Park a radio was blaring *Summer Love* by the Sherbet. Mrs. Abodeely was hanging out her sheets along her balcony railings.

"I hate looking up and seeing Mrs. Abodeely hanging out wash like some peasant." Naomi said.

"Naomi, Mrs. Abodelly is a wonderful person, as well as highly educated and cultured. She is by no means a peasant," I said.

"What rubbish. As rich as they are, you would think she would send her laundry out like we do," Naomi said, unsettled by my challenge.

"Easy, Dai 'ui. Go with the flow," Sam said.

"I didn't want to sit by silently and appear to agree with Naomi's inane and fatuous remark. Mrs. Abodeely doesn't have a mean spirit in her bones."

"Fatuous? My, my! Dai 'ui, I continue to underestimate you," Naomi replied.

"Old man Abodeely seems to be doing all right, making the big bucks," Sam said.

"He's a Maronite Christian from Beirut who came to this country without a dime ten years ago. Now he runs an import-export business, and retains Colin's firm for overseas contracts."

For a brief moment I was tempted to tell Naomi how sophisticated I thought Mrs. Abodeely was, and that Mary's grandmother was actually French, and had taught Latin at the Institute du Marais.

At the far end of the Café Ritz was a long bar, and the bartender started clinking a spoon on a glass to get everyone's attention, and as a signal for Naomi to hush. After all, it was the Devil's Hour, a time between four and five in the afternoon when someone at the bar would raise their glass and call for a toast, facing toward Western Australia. Supposedly, the same thing was happening in the bars and pubs in Western Australia, the other side toasting their Eastern brothers. It was explained to me that it was called the Devil's Hour because, instead of going home after work, everyone would stop at the pub, thus eliciting an unhappy response from spouses.

The person calling for the toast today was a sometime surfer and arm wrestler we all knew as Whizzer. Whizzer was something of an anomaly among the local surfer crowd. For one thing, he was older, close to thirty. Balding, stocky and unshaven, with his thick, dark three-day stubble, he looked more like a Newcastle coal miner than one of the slim, fair-haired Cronulla surfers. I was told that his nickname came from a wrestling move for which he was known. But the most interesting thing about him was that he had served with C Company of the 6th Battalion of the Aussie forces on its first Vietnam tour in 1966, when that unit earned the high honor of being awarded the U.S. Presidential Unit Citation.

Over a beer Whizzer had told me the story of his role in the battle of Long Tan on August 18, 1966, when C Company was on sweep operations in a French rubber plantation. Attacked by a regiment of North Vietnamese and Vietcong troops, and outnumbered by more than ten to one, C Company held its position for more than three hours until a relief force arrived. When the enemy fled, leaving 245 dead on the battlefield, the nineteen-year old Whizzer had been wounded twice. His company had seventeen killed and twenty-one wounded, he said, his eyes glazing over as he told the tale.

No sooner had Whizzer completed his toast than four rangy lads came up behind him and jumped him. I recognized three of the four who attacked Whizzer in the wild punch-up that followed. The first, trying to put a headlock on Whizzer, was Malcolm Askew, a local fisherman who surfed more than he fished. Whizzer handled him with ease, taking his legs out from under him with a neat sweep move. The second, whom Whizzer dropped with a clean shot to the jaw, was Quentin Hully, a Wollooware dropout in his early twenties. The third was Reggie Dolan, who took a straight shot from Whizzer to the nose, which knocked him to the floor. The fourth, unknown assailant, had a black beard, and was much bigger than Whizzer. He actually got in a good punch before Whizzer kicked him between the legs and put out of the fight.

"Don't even try to get up, Reggie. You're out of your league," Whizzer said, pausing to take a drink as if the punch-up were over.

Taking that sip of cold Toohey's Flag Ale proved to be a critical mistake for the over-confident Whizzer.

"The one with the bloody nose, that's Reggie Dolan, your student," Sam said.

Apparently Whizzer had not knocked all the fight out of Reggie Dolan. For Reggie grabbed Whizzer's muscled calf and bit down hard. Whizzer screamed in pain, and blasted Reggie to the side of the head with his fist. At which point Malcolm was up from the floor in time to punch Whizzer in the groin.

Whizzer fell backwards, hitting his head on the bar as Malcolm struck him a second time in the mouth. Quentin stumbled to his feet and swung wildly, just missing Whizzer. All this only served to enrage Whizzer further, and he head-butted Malcolm twice in the face, sending him to the floor, spitting teeth. By this time Quentin had recovered sufficiently to grab Whizzer from behind in a chokehold, allowing Reggie to throw a punch that caught Whizzer in the solar plexis. Reggie then began to put the boots to Whizzer's groin, with Quentin hanging on for dear life.

About that time I grabbed Reggie to restrain him, while Sam pulled Quentin off Whizzer's throat. I found it curious that all the others in the bar stood by without moving a finger to help Whizzer. If it weren't for the two Yanks having a drink with Naomi, the bystanders would have let Whizzer take a beating.

"Easy now, Reggie. Let it go. Four on one is not a fair fight. It's not Australian. It's over," I said, easily handling Reggie.

"You don't know anything about Australians. He's a bloody snitch, a police informer who rats on his mates! He's got this coming to him. Everyone here but you dumb Yanks knows that," Reggie said, twisting free and running out the door, followed by Malcolm and Quentin, dragging the unknown fourth party to his feet.

* * *

"Well, I guess a fight ain't over 'til it's over. I owe you two Yanks. Reggie would have put the boots to me. Guess my cover is blown now, for sure," Whizzer said, still breathing hard.

"You're police?" I asked, totally surprised by the turn of events.

"Yeah. Been undercover for about a year. Say, Mrs. Musto, one favor deserves another. Tell Mr. Musto I said that the red-haired lady staying with you is fooling around with Quentin Hully and his cousin, Bryan. Bryan was the big bloke with the black beard who popped me a good one. Fancies himself a cuntoisseuer, as they say, a regular lady's man. We think he's dealing heroin in Cronulla."

"You mean connoisseur?" I asked.

"No mate, in Cronulla we call a cocksman, a cuntoisseuer," Whizzer said, smiling.

"That's enough Whizzer! Shush. If you want to do me a favor, don't say the word," Naomi said, grabbing her purse and making for the door.

"Now ain't that something. Trying to do someone a favor, and they up and walk out on you."

"Maybe you are trying to tell her something that is best left unsaid. If you get my drift," I said.

* * *

The evening was unseasonably warm, and Celia, my sister-in-law, and I, sat out on our balcony to enjoy the balmy weather. Celia's potted hibiscus had a new flower blooming. The red bloom exploded with fragrance. The bright moon was not quite full, hanging over the Tasman Sea, and for a time we watched a pod of dolphins. There must have been a hundred of them, diving and surfacing in a great mass just to the east of Shark Island.

Over at the Hotel Cecil a crowd of surfers spilled into the street, tossed out of the bar for being too rowdy. Celia had just drifted off to sleep, curling next to me. Her stomach is lunar at this stage. The yelling and hooting of the crowd woke her, and when she sat-up, leaning close to me, I could feel my unborn daughter's dolphin kick.

On the promenade below, along the beachfront, Lotus was strolling with black-bearded Bryan Hully; the one who Whizzer claimed was dealing heroin in Cronulla. Earlier, along the beachfront promenade, I had watched Whizzer, Colin, and Bob, an American expatriate who had also witnessed the fight, in an intense conversation. Thus it didn't surprise me when Colin knocked on my door wanting a rundown from my perspective.

"I'm concerned. Lotus has shown little gratitude to Naomi, consorting with these hippies, Quentin and Bryan Hully. Based on my sources, this Bryan is under police scrutiny. Fortunately she'll be leaving in the morning. I've told Naomi to distance herself from Lotus. But what concerns me most is Sam's association with Lotus," Colin said.

"Sources? You mean Whizzer. He's a snitch."

"No comment. I did talk to him, as well as Bob, the Yank who works for General Tire. Bob also witnessed the punch-up. You've met him, I believe. He knows you and Sam."

"I know Bob well, played squash with him. As for Lotus, I think Sam has a thing for her. Of course, he hasn't been his old self lately. This fever has really affected him. By the way, we're driving Lotus up to Nimbin in the morning."

"Naomi told me. Maggie is quite upset by this trip to Nimbin. If she knew that Sam was infatuated with Lotus, she'd be furious."

"Yeah. I want to take my Land Rover out for a spin. I'd like to see that part of the coast. Celia has her sister staying with us, so I thought I'd take advantage of the opportunity."

"Well, I haven't talked to Sam yet, and given my priorities right now, it doesn't look like I'll be able to. So, please caution him about Lotus for me."

I found it curious that Colin had contacted Whizzer directly. Colin's motives were never clear; and he was, by nature, a paranoid person. Maybe that was the reason he sought out Whizzer. As for Bob, I heard that he was connected with the local CIA Station Chief, and had once used Captain Graham's special security services in Africa.

* * *

We were making good time, Sam helping me with the map, Lotus chatting on about the various attractions of Nimbin.

Until 1973 Nimbin was a sleeply little dairy town near Lismore. Mt. Warning is nearby, *Wollumbin* to the Bundjalung people who lived in the Big Scrub, the largest sub-tropical rain forest in Australia. Then came the Aquarius Festival, a gathering of various counterculture folks, including a wide range of artists, musicians, students, hippies, and what Naomi Musto called the great unwashed.

"I told Naomi I was there in 1973 for the festival. She was not impressed," Lotus said as we wound our way beneath the tall gum trees.

"Not surprising. Mrs. Musto is a little too snooty and citified for the great unwashed," Sam said.

"That's not entirely true, Sam," Lotus replied firmly. "I found Naomi to be a very sympathetic person. I owe her a great debt. And what kind of fool are you to criticize her?"

"Lotus, Sam is not a fool, by any means," I said. "But Naomi did call you counterculture, one of those great unwashed who worship in the Church of Holy Smoke."

Lotus paused for a moment. "Well. I'm surprised to hear that. What I find hurtful is that she would speak of me that way. I was open with her. That's why I like you Yanks. No bullshit."

"Lotus, you can't be so naïve as to assume all us Yanks are the same. Look at Sam, brute that he is, and then look at me. Everything depends on what Yank you are talking to."

"Fuck you, Dai 'ui," Sam said,

"Lighten up, Sam," I said, giving Lotus a wink.

"I don't understand. All I know is that Naomi is someone I admire. She is unique. There are not many like her in Australia. I wouldn't presume to compare myself to her. She is so high class, with all her education and money. But I wouldn't trade places with her. I am happy with who I am. You see I have found excitement and novelty in my life. Naomi is still looking for that novelty in her life. And my guess is that it has to do with her interest in German Expressionism, and that painter Kirchner, or whatever his name is. I know that she traveled outside of Australia when she studied him."

"Naomi went to Cambridge," I added.

"Yeah, and Naomi is more than happy to tell you all about it. She thinks she's better than other folks. There's still a lot of this snotty, class thing going on Down Under."

"Sam, you don't know what you are talking about," I blurted. "You've been in this country for a year or so and all of a sudden you are rendering these judgments. Try going out there and doing the tough job of teaching the Aussie kids. Go have dinner with the families who invite you in as a teacher so that their kids have a better chance. You don't know shit about the real Australia, and the aspirations of the people. You're a parasite living off a fat job. As far as I'm concerned, you haven't added a lot of value to Australia."

I could tell that I pissed Sam off. For a long moment he was silent, looking off into the swish of the wind in the eucalypts, the low keening sounds of unknown insects buzzing in the background.

"Well, Dai 'ui, my friend, and brother-in-arms, you have struck a chord. And I'm sure Maggie would agree with your assessment. I haven't added much of any value to anything, especially in Australia, a country I love. My only request is that next time you want to bash me, spare me the embarrassment of doing it in front of someone like Lotus. Please stop the car."

"Say again?"

"Stop the fucking car, Dai 'ui, now!"

When I stopped, Sam got out and stomped off into the bush. For a moment I thought Lotus was going to follow him. Then she turned and looked at me, waiting for me to say something.

"Give him a minute. He'll cool off," I said.

Lotus and I got out of the car and sat on a log until Sam returned. He stumbled out of the trees, brushing away the bush flies hovering about his face.

"Sam, did I start all this rubbish with our discussion of Naomi?" Lotus asked.

"No, Lotus. Dai 'ui is just an asshole."

"Well, I don't believe in standing in judgment of anyone in any way. I have learned to live each day for all that it is worth. I don't want to appear ungrateful for all Naomi did."

Sam snorted. "Frankly, Lotus, Naomi is a hypocrite. If she was so sympathetic to your situation, why did she toss you out? I know that occasionally she likes to have a smoke herself."

"It's Colin. Colin was freaked out by having me around," Lotus said, shaking out her thick hair.

"See Dai 'ui. Colin is a big pussy. Everything freaks him out, and there's no pleasing Naomi, unless you're one of the elite, up and coming. She and I live in different parts of the universe," Sam said, lighting up a Lucky Strike.

Lotus immediately picked up on what was happening.

"Colin and Naomi saw me talking with my old friend Bryan. I guess they didn't like his looks. But Bryan is very wise in his own way. I expect to find him celebrating. He told me he was going to be in Nimbin. When I think about Colin I remember what *Matthew* said, seventh chapter, sixth verse, 'Do not give dogs what is holy; and do not throw your pearls before swine, lest they trample them underfoot and turn to attack you."

Then Lotus got back into the car. Sam followed. I looked at Lotus in the rear view mirror, her thin face framed by an abundance of curly red hair cascading down her back and shoulders.

"I'm ready to go. How about you, Sam?" Lotus asked.

"Yeah, yeah. Lotus, I never read the Bible much, what are you attributing to this seventh chapter, sixth verse?" Sam asked.

"It means that you can't bestow wisdom upon those who are unwilling to hear it. If someone has a closed mind, why bother? As Fred Robinson says, why rile them up?"

I downshifted to make a tight turn. "Lotus, the first time we met, you mentioned Fred Robinson. Who exactly is he?" I asked.

"He's a modern day prophet. Reminds me of Moses. I first heard him in Sydney when I was still Amy Windham. He was spreading word of the Elder Brothers who will be coming to save the righteous from the world's imminent end."

"I see. Elder Brothers," I said, looking at Sam.

Lotus went on, "Beings from outer space. You must have heard of *The Urantia Book*?"

"Not really. Doesn't sound like something Marines like Sam and I would be interested in," I said, trying to be polite.

"Speak for yourself, Dai'ui," Sam said.

Lotus smiled back, knowing that she clearly had Sam under her spell.

"Good on ya, Sam! Let's get you up to see the healer. He will purge you of this fever, and whatever ails you. You'll see a change right away. Good bush medicine."

"Sam, I think you need an adjustment to your brain-housing group," I said.

"He calls himself the Wolly Man, and he lives in a humpy under a White Booyong tree way back in the woods. Right close to where we will be having the bonfire to celebrate," Lotus said, pulling out a comb and running it through her waist-length hair.

Sam didn't reply to either Lotus or me. For a long time he just stared while she continued to brush out that thick, curly red hair, watching her as if he were in awe of a divine feminine force out of ancient mythology. Lotus had become his earth mother, like the pagan, proto-deity described in the *The White Goddess*, or perhaps the embodiment of Miss Swan's *Jaganmata* from the Hindu pantheon, a cosmic spirit for good throughout the universe.

Lotus turned away from Sam, looking out the window at the passing countryside. I sensed Sam's unblinking stare made her feel uncomfortable. In Laos, Sam's old love, Miss Swan, had rejected him, and it occurred to me that he was still on the rebound, now clearly obsessed with Lotus, as if this slim and foxy free spirit were the solution to all his unfinished business. Sam's real motives for traveling to Nimbin had little to do with his fever, and I knew then that his so-called healing would be a lengthy and complex process, one driven by an infatuation with Lotus.

* * *

Nimbin sits on top of a hill. Below that hill a broad valley fell away, a river winding its way through the paddocks and clusters of trees. Across the valley we could see tents, vans, and a number of makeshift shelters.

"Turn left here and head up on the track. That's where the Wolly Man lives in his sanctuary; and he is, indeed, a holy man. Maybe he can do something about the pain in my fingertips. You never know with this bush medicine," Lotus said.

We drove up another hill into what was clearly old growth forest. Once on top, we entered a small clearing surrounded by towering trees. Several tents were pitched to one side of a stream. Opposite the tents, on the other side of the flow, was a structure that reminded me of a sweat lodge. When I opened my door I was greeted by a group of naked, deeply tanned and wild-haired children. In less than a minute they were swarming over my Land Rover, poking their noses into everything, our baggage, our food, even our beer cooler.

The oldest boy spoke. "Gidday Mate, ya looking for my old man? He's in the humpy with his new wife, Bandi. She's got a big bum on her he calls *Uluru.*"

I laughed.

"Oh yeah, why does he call it that?" Sam asked.

"Why, because it's at the center of all things."

"Hush Possum! Let the men pass now," a tall, dark-haired woman said.

I guessed her to be in her mid-thirties, and as tan as the naked kids running around the camp. She was also naked except for sandals made from old tire treads and what appeared to be necklaces of shells and pieces of bone. Possum and his mates ran off as a thin, middle-aged man emerged from what I guessed to be the humpy.

"Gidday Wolly Man," Lotus said, taking off her sarong and top.

"Red Lotus. Good to see you again. I heard the sad news about our friend Ashton. But now he is at one with all things, hanging out at that cosmic intersection he often spoke about, mingling with visitors from other galaxies."

"I miss him very much," Lotus said.

"People pass on, but the story never ends," the Wolly Man replied.

The Wolly Man was close to six feet tall but painfully thin. He was totally bald except for a white fringe of hair that grew down to his tan shoulders. He was naked except for a pair of combat boots without laces and a single bone ornament that he wore on a leather thong around his neck. A slender white Cockatoo plume was tied around his ropy penis, and it dangled freely.

"Jesus," Sam whispered.

"You wanted bush medicine," I whispered back.

"Tell me about these men. They have a dark aura. I can see one of them is very sick."

"I'll vouch for the both of them. This one is Sam. He comes to be healed," Lotus said, her red hair contrasting with her pale, alabaster-white skin.

"Well, we can begin by you telling them that in this sanctuary we are all equal. To remain here we all must be as one," the Wolly Man said.

"Lotus, what does he mean by that?" I asked, confused by the Wolly Man's language.

"He wants you all to get naked. No clothes allowed here in the sanctuary.

"The sanctuary?" I asked.

"Yes. Here we live the contemplative life," the Wolly Man said, the dangling white cockatoo feather twirling. " I call it a return to innocence and humility where we become children again. Prejudge nothing. Criticize nothing. In the sanctuary we live the life of perfect correspondence with the essence of things. In this place we aspire to unite with the whole of reality, which we feel all around us, and of which our own lives are but a part. And I am the Wolly Man, keeper of the sanctuary."

"Wolly Man, Sam may not understand what you mean by the contemplative life, and how that will help cure him, " Lotus said, watching us strip.

"I understand. Meditation. Contemplation. Call it what you will. We all choose in which realm we wish to dwell. Here I can help you let go, draw you forth from the shadow," the Wolly man said.

"Go with the flow. I believe that," Sam said.

"Excellent! Here you can find the deeper understanding you seek," the Wolly Man continued, his voice rising as the wind picked up and the white cockatoo feather continued to twirl. "Most never experience this because they do not seek it. To shed light on the dark and unknown requires going beyond conventional knowledge. There is a higher, more sacred plane of life and energy, but to reach that higher level requires leaving behind those things that hold us back. Things like guilt and shame, the anguish of lost loves."

"I have love troubles," Sam said, mesmerized.

"Our healing process can help emancipate you."

"I want to learn more. Let's do this," Sam said.

"Emancipation from what?" I asked, skeptically.

The Wolly man spun around and looked at me wild-eyed. It was immediately apparent that my question irritated him.

"Here we have forsaken the frivolous Babylon our cities have become, with their glorification of Hollywood," the Wolly man snapped.

"Hollywood. What does Hollywood have to do with emancipation?" I asked in disbelief.

"Why, the cinema, with its gangsters and chorus girls, provides the wrong entertainment. Images of impure love corrupt the soul. Wrong entertainment lowers the moral ideals of the human race," the Wolly Man continued, clearly agitated.

"Sam. Let's get out of here," I said.

"Wait! There is more! Sometimes we are deflected from our proper path by the illusions presented through the cinema. We are manipulated and become lost in our favorite movies. To be emancipated is to move beyond the corruption of the past, to stop playing those old tapes."

"Makes sense to me," Sam said.

"I will prepare the sweat lodge. But first, how much money do you have?"

"A couple of hundred," Sam replied, fishing through his pockets.

"Give it to me, all of it. Free yourself from that burden and at the same time offer support for our sanctuary. Then I will heal you."

Sam handed over the money. The Wolly Man then motioned Possum to gather up all our clothes. I noticed him peering into my pockets so I grabbed my wallet and car keys. The Wolly Man moved closer to Sam, placing his hands on his shoulders. The penis feather was spinning wildly in the wind, and I watched Possum scurry away with our clothes.

The Wolly Man raised a hand. "One caution. The potential for a more profound understanding awaits you. However, if you open yourself through the process of the sweat lodge you may become more vulnerable. The complexities of the soul rise to the surface, threatening the surface-self. At times there will be conflicts that may seem irreconcilable. Are you strong enough for that?"

"Let's get it done," Sam said quietly.

"One more thing. The average person tunes in only to the self, and not with things as they really are. You will get beyond the common consciousness and touch upon the divine that exists in each of us. You may even glimpse that grand design hidden from us by that veil of our own unknowing."

"I just want to get well. And maybe better understand some things that have been bothering me, like the Fall of Saigon," Sam said.

The Wolly Man now made a sweeping gesture with his arm. "Subject yourself to the sweat lodge, and the process of contemplation, and your fatigue will vanish. You will find that deeper understanding that you seek. It will arise from your contemplation like a flash of lightning in the dark." He began spinning in a circle and raising his arms towards the heavens, holding a big fistful of Australian dollars in each hand.

* * *

While Lotus went off with the other women and kids, Sam and I followed the Wolly Man inside the humpy he called a sweat lodge where the healing was to take place. The Wolly Man gave Sam small dried pieces of mushroom. Sam washed them down with a bottle of Flag Ale.

There was a small fire in the center of the humpy. Periodically, the Wolly Man sprinkled a dust made from what appeared to be crushed leaves on the fire. A highly aromatic smoke that was not at all unpleasant rose from this mixture. We sat around the fire, each one of us squatting at a point in an equilateral triangle drawn in the dirt.

"What's wrong with me?" Sam asked, now dripping sweat.

"The cause of your recurring fever is not due to a little mosquito," The Wolly Man said, his blue eyes staring at some fixed point above our heads. "You have fallen into that hole of being we call grief. And your soul is sick from this."

"Tell me more."

"Grief is like a stone, a weight that grows infinite upon reflection. Reflect on it too long, and before you know it, you are carrying a burden that will break you down and sicken your soul. If you are in love, there will be heartbreak."

"And the cure."

"In a moment I will try to cure you. But first you must pray to whatever higher power you believe in, at the same time remembering that life still means all that it ever meant, and that you must continue on. That is what those who you are still grieving for would want of you."

"I see."

"Do you have faith that there is an absolute unbroken continuity in all things?"

"I'm not sure."

"Then I may not be able to cure you. You must once more become the close friend of your soul. You must let your soul be the center of your life. I will guide you, and you will understand the greater consciousness that we all share."

"Guide me. I feel like I'm letting go, kind of like leaning on nothing" Sam said, adjusting his squat, and still sweating profusely.

"The mushrooms are doing their work. Tell me more about your troubles," the Wolly man said.

That the Sam Gatlin I knew, my fellow brother-in-arms from Vietnam, would undergo this process, and would submit himself to any spiritual discipline, astounded me. Sweat poured out of him, and I was afraid that he was going to get dehydrated. But I was having my own problems. I wasn't used to squatting, and before long nature began to call, my lower bowels rumbling. I had to squeeze my butt cheeks together real hard, holding back an emerging turtlehead. I didn't want to spoil Sam's healing by dumping a load on the triangle.

"The woman I've been living with keeps talking about personal responsibility. She told me that she was tired of me not being able to make a long term commitment, and that I needed to determine what was of real value in my life, and then decide what kind of life I wanted to live."

"You must begin by believing in the intrinsic value of human life. Do you believe in that?"

"I think so. But lately I've been real confused about things. Strange. Maybe it was the fever."

"As the mushrooms take effect you will go down inside yourself, clear to your center. Before the mushrooms take over, you must meditate on how you want to be when you awake. That is how you find your vision for the future. In that way the healing process takes you into a dream where that vision and you become one, unswervingly authentic and pure. The more you let go in that dream, the more open you become. The more open you become, the more the healing will move forward and you will be at peace with your grief. Sam, let go of what you have, and you may become a healthy man again," The Wolly man said, dropping more dry leaf dust on the fire.

The Wolly Man then took my arm and pushed me outside the humpy, closing the door behind him.

* * *

It was all I could do to get out of the humpy before I dropped my load, right there by the door of the humpy. Embarrassed, I then made a quick dash to the Land Rover and pulled on a pair of shorts. Lotus was nowhere to be found. Down the hill a huge bonfire was burning. And even from where I was, on my hilltop, I knew by smell that the Church of the Holy Smoke was in session. I could hear strange music and harmonious singing. The music was from another world, flutes, and what I guessed was a didgeridoo. Since Sam was in the humpy for the duration of the night, I cranked the Land Rover and headed back down the track.

The sight that greeted me was beyond my wildest expectations. There were actually two bonfires, with about a hundred naked celebrants dancing around them, in what I learned later was a ritual of purification. Lotus was there, spinning arm in arm with her friend Bryan, his member swinging semi-hard. The woman that greeted us upon entering the Wolly Man's camp sat surrounded by a circle of people, while she cast her bones on a hide, a form of divination once a common folkloric practice among the ancient Celts. When Lotus saw me she came running over, Bryan following, both of them wild-eyed and glistening with sweat in the firelight.

"Welcome to the celebration. You are welcome to worship with us," Lotus said, spinning in a slow circle, her arms outstretched.

"Who are we worshiping?" I asked, awestruck by the spectacle before me.

"Why, the source of all being, of course, the singular force of creation is represented here, among those dancing around the fires. Come. Dance. Celebrate yourself."

"I've always found that easy to do," I said, somewhat amused, but also, a bit frightened.

Then someone started beating on a kind of Polynesian log drum, a loud, staccato knocking that had everyone mingling and changing partners. Lotus grabbed my hand and Bryan took the other, and we were turning in a circle, spinning toward the fires where people were forming up into two lines.

"Come on, this is the sweet dance," Bryan said.

"The what?"

"We all dance naked," Lotus said.

Then the Wolly man shouted for all to hear: "Let us relive the moment of cosmic creation, when the primeval god of us all hung the stars upon the great celestial bowl above our heads! Let the dancers begin the ecstasies!"

To my dying day I will remember how the swaying throng crowded around the fires, the many faces glassy-eyed, the young men lean and bearded, with bushy, wild hair, dancing in a single line; and opposite them, the young womanly hips and breasts swaying back and forth in some improvised Polynesian dance, couples breaking away and running off to the trees for spontaneous love-making. The two lines merged as one, and the people, caught up in the rhythm of the drums, raised their arms above their heads, swaying back and forth, while the Wolly Man, led them in a snake dance around the fires. Lotus let go of my hand, and in the blink of an eye, she and Bryan were off toward the trees, his penis now fully erect.

I paused briefly where the Wolly Man's woman sat, casting her bones. She was no longer surrounded by people, and beckoned me to her.

"Shall we cast the bones for you, to see what path your life will take?" Wolly Man's woman asked, parting her hair to peer up at me."

"Sure. Why not?"

She gathered up the bones and held them in both hands, her arms raised above her head.

"We are but fragments of creation, but each fragment is part of one design, the pattern of being that extends, unbroken, connecting all life, and is constantly in motion. For this man I cast these bones, that he might find the voice within, and connect with the vision that awaits him."

The bones were smooth and sun-bleached white, about the size of the large marbles we used to play with as kids. I was later told they were actually knucklebones from swine. Some of them had rune-like markings. She cast the bones. Then she bent down to study them.

"What are you looking for?" I asked, curious.

"A certain configuration in the bones. Reading is only part of it. At times, I am able to see the future. The Wolly Man and I are different in this. I rely on intuition. He is integrated with the harmonic frequency of the Earth, in tune with the cosmos, so-to-speak. How he knows what he knows I can't tell you. I'm guessing it has to do with energy and electromagnetic waves."

"Oh! Oh my!" She said, hysterically.

"What is it? Is something the matter?"

"Your friend, Sam, who the Wolly Man said was born under the sign of Mars, his path portends eternal conflict! Beware his selfish, indomitable will and hotheaded actions! He is cursed to opposing paths of creation and destruction!"

"That's the Sam I know. Tell me what to do."

"Listen to your intuition, and trust that voice within. Remember. We don't know what we can do until we are called upon to play the game."

In the far distance lightning flashed a blue luminance. The Wolly Man's woman jumped up and ran into the night, never looking back. A moment later thunder rumbled, and I wondered about Sam meditating within the humpy on the glowing horizon of his memory, his past coming to life again so that he could free himself from grief.

Lightning lit up the sky a second time, followed by more thunder as rain began to fall. Then the Wolly Man was there by himself, the lone remaining dancer, dancing like a crazy, spinning dervish between the great fires.

* * *

I retreated to my Land Rover as the downpour hit, and was lulled to sleep by the falling rain. In the morning I woke to the crow-like Currawongs cawing in the trees. A heavy mist drifted across the valley, and a cow was calling to be milked. The bonfires still smoked, and bodies clustered together in the damp grass, wrapped in a rainbow of shawls and blankets. Bryan and Lotus were cuddled together in a sleeping bag at the edge of the trees, clearly living a moment of perfect correspondence with the essence of all things.

I cranked the Land Rover and drove up to the humpy. Sam was sitting outside waiting for me. Surprisingly, he looked refreshed, as if his fever was gone. I wanted to ask him if he had reached that deeper understanding he was seeking, especially with regard to the Fall of Saigon.

"You okay?" I asked,

"Yeah, I'm fine. Have you seen Lotus?"

"She went off into the woods with some friends. I don't know where she is right now," I lied.

As we started back down the track, Possum came out of nowhere yelling and pointing to where I had taken my big dump. He ran after us for quite a while screaming: "Dirty Yanks!"

Sam was very quiet as we headed down the bumpy track. I wondered if he had the opportunity to get beyond the common consciousness, and to touch upon the divine that exists in each of us. Maybe he even glimpsed that grand design, the one that is hidden from us by that veil of our own unknowing.

* * *

Chapter Seven: Favorite Movies

Sam's fever was gone and he was hungry. He opened a can of spam I had in the Land Rover and washed it down with a warm beer. Sam's fever may have been gone, but his need for alcohol was not.

Around nine in the morning we started back toward the coast, but we didn't get too far. We had gone some thirty kilometers when we stopped to buy some more beer. We found this wayside, shaded by a dense clump of trees, and decided to sit in the shade and drink a Toohey's Export Pilsner. Up to that point Sam had said little. That changed after the second beer.

"Dai 'ui, I have wasted my life."

"That's bullshit, probably some residue in your brain from the mushrooms the Wolly Man fed you."

"Naw. I got real chunderous in the middle of the night and puked. Made a mess of the humpy."

"Not to worry. I didn't chunder, but I couldn't hold back a colossal dump. Placed that colossus right outside the Wooly Man's humpy. Couldn't help myself. I'm sure the Wolly Man will think we fouled his sanctuary."

"I was wondering why that kid was running after us, yelling dirty Yanks!"

Then we laughed for a long time, letting the flies slowly crawl over us. We smelled like wood smoke, and I felt as if my head were about to crack open in the midday sun. I was opening my second beer when a canary yellow Volkswagen Bus pulled into our wayside. The bus was crammed with baggage, with Lotus in a back seat. The driver turned out to be Quentin Hully of Hotel Cecil fame. Bryan was sprawled in the front seat, passed out.

"Gidday Yanks, fancy meeting up with you. Lotus told me Sam went to visit the Wolly Man," Quentin said, opening the back door and grabbing a black Nubian milk goat from the rear of the bus.

Lotus opened the side door and rolled out of the back seat, her hair wild and unruly, eyes glazed over from the night's revelry. She was wearing an orange sarong and multi-colored tie-died cotton shirt. There was a cage of chickens crammed in the bus, as well as a small platform that Quentin pulled out for the goat. Bryan remained passed out, his mouth agape, flies crawling over his bearded face.

"Ain't she a lovely nanny goat?" Quentin asked as the goat hopped up on the table.

Quentin tied a red bandana around his head, leaned against the nanny, and began to milk her, sitting on a little three-legged stool. Sam got up and walked over to Lotus who was peering into one of the bus's mirrors, trying to manage her hair.

"Lotus! You disappeared on us. I was wondering what happened to you."

"Went down to the bonfire. Danced all night," she said, coolly.

"I was hoping to run into you again. I wanted to thank you for introducing me to the Wolly Man. My fever is gone, and the Wolly Man said I would see a sign that would foreshadow what was to come."

"I knew he could help. But be careful looking for your sign, especially astrological ones. Ashton always said that all signs have multiple meanings. Some Frenchman he studied with told him that."

"Astrology is bullshit, Lotus. The stars and planets have no influence on human affairs," I said.

Quentin laughed, and brought the pail of warm goat's milk over to Lotus. She took a drink and offered it to Sam who declined.

"Hey mate, Hitler consulted astrologers. History is full of kings and big mucky-mucks that consulted the positions of the planets, worried about their fate. What Ashton meant was that the truth is relative. All signs are given to interpretations," Quentin said.

"And all signs blur together after a little Queensland Green," Lotus said, lighting up a joint.

"We all need a reality-blurring event from time to time. By the way, Lotus, that Frenchman's name is Jean Baudrillard. He's famous, and Ashton didn't study astrology with him," Quentin said.

"I don't believe in fate, either," I said.

"Ah, but wouldn't you agree that certain quirks of character and temperament influence what we become?" Quentin asked, winking at me, and nodding toward Sam and Lotus.

Sam and Lotus walked over to the beer cooler. It was clear to me that Sam was smitten with her. I could see it in his eyes.

"I'll have to think about that one," I replied.

"So we're all off to Eden Bay for Queensland Green," Lotus said, walking back with a cold beer and handing the joint to Quentin.

"Want to take a hit?" Quentin asked me.

"I'll pass. I generally limit my reality-blurring events to beer and wine," I said.

"Well, I believe in fate. I'm a fine example of my theory. I'm now an outlaw," Quentin said, smiling.

"Over the punch-up?"

"Yeah. You know that Whizzer turned out to be a police snitch. And I'm sure someone's out there looking for me. Ah, life is so unfair," he laughed.

"I heard they were looking for you."

"Yeah. I thought so. Looks like I'll have to keep away from Cronulla for a while," Quentin said.

"I thought you were a part-time fisherman, working with Malcolm and his father."

"Changed my mind. On our last fishing trip with Malcolm I had this premonition of a drowned man."

"Strange, considering all the time you've spent surfing off Cronulla's Shark Island," I said.

"Yeah. I used to call Cronulla home. Now music and poetry are my home," he said, laughing to himself. "But I like traveling around and, as Ashton used to say, enjoying the grand spectacle."

"Lotus told me that a Laotian warlord put a bullet in the back of Ashton's head," I replied.

"I call that fate," Quentin said, winking.

"I heard Ashton's name," Lotus said, walking over and accepting the joint from Quentin. "Eden Bay awaits. Let's get on the road," she continued, giving me the distinct impression that my comment brought back something she wanted to forget.

"That one of your communes?" I asked her.

"Cooperative," she said, as if correcting me. "Low impact living. No hierarchy. No dominant males preying upon the helpless women folk," she said, looking Sam in the eye.

"Sounds like a commune to me," I said, smiling.

"Eden Bay is a place of true harmony and liberation, free of the greed and exploitation we find in our big cities, where the power is concentrated in the hands of the elites," Lotus said.

"What elites are you talking about?" I asked.

"Why people like Colin Musto, of course," Lotus replied, walking away to the bus.

* * *

After the bus drove off, we made the mistake of buying more beer and heading off to find the coastal highway that would take us back to Sydney. Sam seemed deep in thought, clearly preoccupied with Lotus.

"Funny how Lotus disappeared on us. Did you see her down by that bonfire?"

"No," I lied. "She's another rootless hippie. Give her some space. I think she's afraid of you."

"Yeah. For sure," Sam laughed. "With all that red hair, she's a wild one. I can't help it. I'm really attracted to her. After you left the humpy, the Wolly Man said I would see a sign. I asked him if it could be Lotus, and he said no, that I should look to the heavens, and by that time the mushrooms were taking effect. I kind of drifted off."

"Forget it, Sam. Lotus is nothing but trouble. You just got things back together with Maggie."

"Let's change the subject."

"Open another beer for me," I asked.

"Sure. And let's not talk about Lotus anymore."

I remembered the Wolly Man's warning to Sam, about how if he opened himself to the process of contemplation, he might become more vulnerable, and further conflicts might arise. He told Sam that to shed light on the dark and unknown required going beyond conventional knowledge. There was a higher plane of life and energy, he said, but to reach that high level required leaving behind those things that held us back, the guilt and shame, all the bad memories that kept him awake at night. Stop playing those old tapes, the Wolly man said. Sam's fever may have been gone, but now he was looking for a sign from the heavens.

About that time I missed our turn-off to the coast, keeping on what I thought was the main route. It wasn't until we were a good ten kilometers down the road before I realized our error.

"Pull over, Dai 'ui. I got to piss."

I pulled off onto a track and we got out. All around us tall trees hummed and clicked with life. Scores of flies hovered about as we peed down a slope into some thick bush.

At that point a Glossy Black Cockatoo came winging through the trees. Unlike the raucous flock I had observed in Gamoowea, this bird was quiet, perching high up in the branches, with the pointy, irregular feathers on its crest falling forward. The bird gazed down on us, flapped its wings several times, and then spread its tail into a fan, revealing vivid, orange-red tail feathers. A moment later it was gone into the dense scrub.

"Hey Sam, remember Naomi's smart-ass comment about her and her sister being Glossy Black Cockatoos? I never understood what she meant by that."

"Yeah, I didn't get it then either. But I understand it now. We were talking about movies. You can tell a lot about a person from their favorite movie. Her favorite is *Splendor in the Grass*."

"So what does that have to do with cockatoos?"

"She said it was as if the movie had a magic power over her. It held her spellbound, and she had a revelation about how she was being brought up. Actually, sublime revelation, were her words. She compared the movie to the first time she saw a Glossy Black Cockatoo in the wild. Maybe that's the kind of sign the Wolly Man was talking about."

"You're drunk," I replied.

"Maybe. That's when I do my best thinking."

"And Naomi's revelation was?"

"She said it had to do with sexual repression, and how she almost went crazy, just like Natalie Wood did in the movie. And there's that part where

Warren Beatty's father shoots himself when the Depression comes along. Naomi's mother shot herself when her father almost lost the vineyard."

"You and Naomi are tighter than I thought."

"For a while I thought she might be my sister-in-law. But now I doubt that's going to happen. We have this curious love-hate relationship. We go back and forth. I once asked her what she was looking forward to after her teaching debacle. She said she was looking to find the splendor in her life."

"Splendor, as in beyond the ordinary?" I asked.

"Yeah. Right. So, what's your favorite movie?"

"*The Searchers*, with John Wayne."

"John Wayne is a crazy Indian killer in that movie. Scalps a Comanche chief at the end."

"It's a classic film. Is John Wayne's madness an affliction of his soul, or a reflection of a mad society, frontier Texas during that transitional period after the Civil War?"

"Never thought of it that way. Is Naomi a product of her father's financial embarrassments or her mother's suicide? How about that?" Sam asked.

"Probably both. I know that at the end of *The Searchers* John Wayne finds an intellectual deliverance where he comprehends both his present circumstances and his past. It's a very powerful scene. When it happens, he just walks away. It's a great film. John Wayne is relentless."

"Dai 'ui, that movie is about a noble Comanche getting wasted. Seems strange now that I liked it."

"The film reflects attitudes at the time," I replied.

"Maybe I long for another time, Dai 'ui. Back when things were clearer to me," Sam said.

"Sounds like nostalgia for the past. That's fine as long as it isn't a falsely idealized past," I said.

"Hey, I just realized that Natalie Wood is in both your favorite movie and Naomi's."

"Yeah, you're right. Maybe that's a sign. You know, Naomi looks a lot like Natalie Wood, only with bigger tits. And Naomi has a much bigger ass."

"Oh, but you got to love that ass, Dai 'ui. I'm an ass man all the way!"

We laughed a long time over that. I picked up our trash and started the Land Rover. Sam took his time, clearly having had way too much to drink.

"Hey ass man, Lotus doesn't have any backside to speak of," I said, to get his attention.

"I thought we weren't going to talk about Lotus. Enough of this talk about women!" Sam said, his belligerent streak beginning to show.

"Ok. Let's get back on the road."

* * *

We stopped at a gas station and asked directions. The owner showed us the way to Taree, close to Uncle Clive's place, and we headed back toward the coastal highway. We met little oncoming traffic, and it appeared that we were driving through a national park. Thick gum trees lined the road, and at one point I had to swerve to avoid a big snake.

"Dai 'ui, that snake must have been six feet long. Holy shit!"

"I think that was what they call a Western Brown Snake," I replied.

"Poisonous?"

"Very. Almost as deadly as the Taipan, I'm told. The Taipan is supposed to be the worst. One of about fourteen Australian snakes that can kill you."

"Don't tell me anymore."

We started up a long grade and I downshifted. The engine began to lug, and I downshifted again to hear gears lock up. There was a sickening crunch.

"You dropped the fucking transmission," Sam said quietly. "And we're in the middle of nowhere with deadly six foot snakes crawling through the fucking woods."

"Shit. Ready to hike back to that gas station."

* * *

We had walked about a kilometer, sweating and covered with flies, when a farmer offered us a ride. At the gas station we called Colin's condo and got Naomi. Naomi said she would call Uncle Clive to come pick us up and tow my Land Rover to Taree. Captain Graham could then fly in the next morning and meet us at the Taree Airstrip.

It was dark by the time Uncle Clive showed up with his truck. We hooked up my Land Rover and began the long slow trip down to Taree. Fortunately Uncle Clive brought plenty of cold Flag Ale.

* * *

It was one in the morning when we pulled up to Uncle Clive's front porch. He immediately went to bed. Sam and I decided to finish the beer.

"Got to ask you a question, about something that's been troubling me. What is this grief thing you talked to the Wolly Man about?"

"Dai 'ui, we lost the fucking war. The Fall of Saigon keeps me up at night. Was it a big waste?"

"What?"

"Vietnam, that's what," Sam said.

"Like the Wolly Man said, you got to quit playing these old tapes," I said.

"Easy for you to say, Dai 'ui."

"Sam, I know what Captain Graham would say because he and I talked about how quickly Nam went down. The Fall of Saigon was one thing; but I don't think he would view our involvement as a waste. I don't. I'd do it all again."

After Saigon fell, Captain Graham and I agreed such an outcome was inevitable, given the U.S. withdrawal. But we also came to the conclusion that the lives lost were not a waste. For contrary to popular belief, the Domino Theory had not proved false. Rather, countries like Thailand stayed free of communism because of the U.S. commitment to Vietnam. While we taught together, Naomi and I would go at it time and again over that particular issue. Like Captain Graham, I believed that the Vietnam War was the turning point for communism. I valued his perspective as one who had served three tours in Vietnam.

"Another thing. It's these bad dreams I keep having. Seeing faces of the dead, that kind of thing. I call them my ghosts," Sam said.

"I've had the same kind of dreams," I replied. "I get visits from two old friends. One was my best childhood friend, Les, a Phantom pilot shot down in July '69 in Laos. It was his first mission. The body was never recovered. Then there was my good buddy Rick, a fellow Marine officer blown up by a huge mine. There was nothing left of him."

"I believe in ghosts. I keep seeing gooks that I wasted, and those Thai pirates. I don't know."

"You don't know what?"

"I don't know what to think anymore, like Colin arranging to have Colonel Dub wasted."

"Colonel Dub was scum. That was justice. No different than you wasting those Thai Pirates. Get your brain housing group back in shape."

"Captain Graham was blown away when he heard how Colin dealt with Colonel Dub. He didn't have a clue what was going down," Sam said.

"Neither did I, and that still bothers me."

"Well, history teacher, you and I are now signed up with Colin Musto and Southeast Asia Company. Right now, I find that depressing for some reason."

"You are depressed. For sure."

"Yeah, I am. I'm depressed. Like the Wolly Man said, I'm playing old tapes. I wish I knew what keeps them running through my head."

"Me too."

Like Sam, I longed to understand those things that kept coming back to me, late at night, things continuing to unsettle me, and at times even shake my confidence. What were the triggers that took me back down those old trails to places and past events that I wanted to forget? In that "deep infinity pool" of my memory the dead kept rising to the surface.

In Sam's case the mere mention of the Fall of Saigon proved to be a trigger. In the sorry aftermath of Saigon's collapse, of our abandonment and betrayal of our South Vietnamese allies, it was hard to know where to place the blame. When things go down like that, there is nothing left, no hope, only a crippling disillusionment where one can no longer believe nor trust in anything.

I wondered to what extent this sudden change of character on Sam's part was the aftermath of his fever. Sam also suffered a head trauma in Vietnam, and maybe his neocortex was still misfiring from the mushrooms the Wolly Man fed him.

"Well, what are you looking forward to besides your next beer?"

"I don't know. I don't think that I'm looking forward to anything. Oh, wait! Maybe I'm looking forward to seeing some good movies. But no war movies glamorizing the Nam, for sure."

"Sam, movies will always glamorize war. Think about this way. All wars are dirty business. But one serves his country when called upon. Honorable folks don't walk away from their responsibilities. They do their duty, and the Fall of Saigon doesn't change the meaning of their sacrifice, not in my eyes. And I would go to a war movie if it told the right story."

"Duty? What fucking duty? Was it our duty to be sacrificed, and for what? It was all lies."

"You did your part when called upon. Find comfort in that. Vietnam was not a waste."

"It's not that simple. In my heart I know that our cause was not just."

"You've been talking to Naomi too much. I've heard a lot from her about our not so just cause. What does the sleek and pampered Naomi know about war, having never experienced it?"

"Naomi knows about a lot of things. She compares the Fall of Saigon to the Fall of Rome."

"Which Fall of Rome is she talking about? The end of the republic was in 27 B.C. In 476 A.D. Rome fell to German barbarians," I said.

"So you know your history. Naomi said they made a movie about it. I saw it back in the Sixties. Sophia Loren was in it."

"You bet I know Roman history. I taught it at Wollooware High. The movie you're referring to was called *The Fall of the Roman Empire*, and it also starred Alec Guinness and James Mason, among others. The story is about the last days of Marcus Aurelius and his son, Commodus, who was a real asshole. The title comes from the work by the historian Edward Gibbon, who called the reign of Commodus the beginning of Rome's decline. Gibbon said a great civilization is not conquered without until it has destroyed itself within."

"That's the one, full of lies and deceptions. Colin would like it. Naomi said that our western culture is repeating the same mistakes of the Romans."

"Oversimplification! Big time! Let me tell you a story told to me by my headmaster at Woolooware High. He taught history all his life. He also was a prisoner of the Japanese during World War II, and I learned a lot from him, especially over a couple of beers at the Hotel Cecil. The story has to do with the origins of the Domino Theory.

"The Domino Theory is bullshit. Another lie."

"That's an opinion, however uninformed it may be. You've heard of Hannibal from Carthage?"

"Sure. He's the guy that took the elephants over the Alps. Kicked the Romans' ass, big time."

"Roger that. His father's name was Hamilcar, and he made a treaty with the Romans that the Ebro River would be the boundary between Rome's sphere of influence and that of Carthage. The problem was that the people of Sagunto, who were on the wrong side of the Ebro, wanted to be Roman allies. Everything was cool until Hamilcar died. Then Hannibal decided to conquer all of Spain, including Sagunto. The citizens of Sagunto appealed to Rome for help, their arguments quite similar to those we find in the Domino Theory."

“I’ve heard of Sagunto. We did an amphibious landing there during my Mediterranean cruise, working with the Spanish Marines.”

“The Senate in Rome was slow to act, but they eventually sent ambassadors to appeal to Hannibal to lift the siege on Sagunto. He declined, saying the city was south of the Ebro River, the boundary Rome and Carthage had agreed upon.”

“That makes sense. None of Rome’s business.”

“But it was Rome’s business, Sam. The issue was Hannibal’s quest for empire, and the question put to the Roman Senate was do we fight him in Spain or do we wait until he attacks Italy?”

“I get it. So what happened to Sagunto?”

“When the city was about to fall, they gathered their treasure together and burned it in front of Hannibal. Then, fearing the inevitable, the rape of their women, their children being sold into slavery, they committed mass suicide.”

“Shit,” Sam said, lighting a cigarette.

“Sam, the resulting outrage was too much for the Roman Senate. Rome declared war on Carthage once again, shamed by the perception that they had abandoned a people whose appeal for help was denied. What Rome had jeopardized was their reputation, and their moral authority. For years Roman historians wrote various explanations, expounding on the various events, trying to justify the reasons behind Rome’s reluctance to get involved. The great irony was that the Romans wanted to avoid an engagement in Spain, yet ended up fighting on their own soil when Hannibal crossed the Alps with his elephants.”

“Good story, Dai ‘ui. But I’ve also talked to Graham. He believes what moral authority we had in Nam was lost when we had Diem killed. And maybe Colin Musto lost his moral authority when he had Dub killed. I worry about our complicity with the events surrounding Dub's death."

"Colonel Dub got what he deserved," I said.

"I think your illustrious historians would call Dub's death a crime, no different than the killing of Diem, or the carpet bombing of North Vietnam. What will your historians write about My Lai, or Agent Orange?" Sam asked, cynically.

"Historians will say most of us fought well. In the Nam there was no foreordained moral clarity. But in the end I believe our cause was just." I said.

"Dai 'ui, history is nothing but a chronicle of immorality and atrocities. And peace is that brief, glorious moment in history when everybody stands around reloading," Sam said, grabbing a beer.

"Sam, wars by their very nature are immoral. Innocents get wasted along with soldiers. After the shit goes down, isn't it all a matter of one's own conscience, and how one conducts oneself? My conscience is clear."

"What if my own conscience is not clear?"

"Then I don't know what to say, other than to separate yourself and your experience from those who died serving their country honorably."

"Dai 'ui, I have come to the conclusion that you're kind of an intellectual snob. You think you have it all figured out. And maybe you do, but I'll never understand it all. Naomi is right. Enjoy the splendor while you can. If we are lucky, there are a few moments when we transcend the bullshit."

"Like the Wolly Man said, carry on. That's what those whom we left behind would want. It's those mushrooms you ate. That's what's happening to you. And don't place too much stock in what

Naomi says. She blames our country for what happened to the Hmong, that we abandoned them."

"Listen to her, Dai 'ui. We are all complicit."

"That's more Naomi bullshit. You know, Sam, I think you are obsessed with her."

"Yes, I admit it. I am drawn to her. A while back she gave me a book to read about this white goddess that folks in Europe worshiped before Christianity. But I couldn't get through it," Sam said.

"Now I know that you are obsessed. What you were reading was *The White Goddess,* by the poet Robert Graves," I said, amazed.

"That's the guy! Naomi said it explained how this single goddess was worshiped under many names. Maggie found the book and asked me where it came from. I told her Naomi gave it to me. That made Maggie jealous as shit."

"Naomi once told several faculty members at Woolooware High that she believed in something called the divine feminine, which she claimed was the one, true pre-Christian religion. And that didn't inspire the faculty's confidence. Believe me," I said.

"No one is ever bored when she's around. She can be a lot of fun if you handle her right."

"Be careful of Naomi. She was a crazy protester while we were slogging through rice paddies. Naomi doesn't seem to regret a bit of it," I said.

"I regret some things. My conscience is not clear, Dai 'ui. I don't think it will ever be."

"Sam! Enough! Whatever you did does not discredit the service of those we left behind, nor make their death any less honorable. Those who served with courage and honor did not die in vain.

They died serving with their mates, and they will be remembered that way."

"You sound so sure of yourself, Dai 'ui, the history teacher, with all your high-minded nonsense. Well, I don't have any of your profound wisdom to share. I can only tell the tale."

"Sam, when you sober up, you will see things differently. And like von Zielke said, things become clearer as we look back over the years."

"Oh yeah, in the fullness of time," Sam said, chuckling. "The Wolly Man was right about one thing. What the movies glamorize is bullshit."

"Roger that. But remember that Nam was the central event of our times, and we were both part of that experience. Be proud that you served as a Marine officer! No one can take that away."

"That's true, and for that I am proud. And Nam was the main feature, for sure. But it was a horror movie. So clean out your brain-housing group, Dai 'ui. See the world for what it is: deceptions, lies, summary executions, our former allies in Vietnam and Laos hunted down like animals."

"Let's hit the sack. I'm done in," I said.

"I won't sleep much, Dai 'ui. No sweet dreams for me. I'll be waiting for the faces of the dead."

* * *

The next morning we dropped off my Land Rover at a shop in Taree. Since they had to order the parts, it would take a couple of weeks to get it fixed. I had no choice but to leave it. We got to the airstrip about noon, just as Captain Graham touched down. His fever now gone, he looked much better.

"Gidday! Understand you blokes had a bit of trouble," Graham said.

"Captain, You don't want to know," I replied.

"Naomi was insistent that I pick up you blokes today. She said that Colin has some urgent business for you both," Captain Graham said.

We lifted off and flew over a yellow plain flecked with occasional stunted trees and clumps of tall grass. A lone vehicle was heading westward on a highway that ran in a straight line out to the horizon. In the far distance we could see one of those rotating columns of dust the Aussies call a willy willy taking shape, whirling like a phantom.

Dark thunderheads loomed up to the south, and below, a cluster of Emus scattered as we flew by.

"Emus, check them out," Sam said.

"Colin tells the story of the clever Emu-Man, Gurugadji," Graham said. "Two hunters tried to capture him, but he hid in a waterhole. There he transformed himself into the Rainbow Serpent, Mamaragan, and ambushed the hunters. Since that time Mamaragan appears in the form of a rainbow, and is feared throughout Arnhem Land."

"We heard Colin tell that story at least twice up on East Alligator Lagoon," Sam said.

"It was more like three times. Some folks have their favorite movies, others have favorite tales to tell, like Colin and his elusive Emu-Man," I said.

"Since he started Southeast Asia Company, Colin's become a kind of Emu-Man, arranging to take out Colonel Dub like he did," Graham said.

The Captain's comment left me wondering. Out of loyalty I felt compelled to defend Colin.

"After Dub's death, Colin told me that people everywhere create their own myths, just like they write their own history, but if one wants justice, they must take action to make it happen," I said.

"I don't buy that, Dai 'ui. I believe in the rule of international law, even for men like Colonel Dub.

Dub might have been scum, but what went down in Laos was wrong. If I had been there, let me assure you that events would have been much different. Things got out of control. I'm still trying to figure out how that happened," Graham said.

"Colin played at the skull game at our expense. He used us, big time. What kind of jingle-ass exposes his wife to such risks?" Sam asked.

"Sam, I honestly don't think what happened was by design; nor did Colin intend to expose Naomi like he did. He was simply out of his league. Colin unwittingly became KV's chess piece, allowing Captain Katay the opportunity to get rid of Dub and place the responsibility elsewhere," Graham said.

"Dub was a murderer. What rule of law is there in Laos? I think that sometimes things happen more by luck than design. Justice was served," I said.

Neither Sam nor Captain Graham replied to my comments, and for a time we cruised along in silence over that vast yellow plain.

"Hey, look at all the lightning in those storm clouds up ahead of us. Are you ready to meet Namarrgon himself?" Graham asked, smiling.

"Ok, who the fuck is Namarrgon?" Sam asked.

"Why, that's the Lightning Man, one of the creation ancestors Colin talks about. He splits the clouds with his great ax to make lightning, and bring down the rain," Graham replied.

* * *

Chapter Eight: Wollumbin Falls

We arrived at the Hotel Cecil just as the sun was setting. Celia, Naomi, and Dr. Camille Carlton-Smythe were enjoying a glass of wine in the patio garden. Barely visible from Ozone Street, the patio was screened by foliage made up of thick-leaved shrubby little trees, with an occasional Waratah and Banksia scattered here and there.

"Well, well, look what we have here back from a stomp out in the Bush. Tell us, Sam, are you all cured?" Naomi said.

"The Wolly Man in Nimbin gave me guidance."

Sam's response gave Naomi pause. It appeared she already had a buzz on.

"I see. Are you taking treatment for alcoholism first, or are you going directly to the asylum?" Naomi asked with a deadpan face.

Everyone laughed but Sam.

"Naomi, don't be so quick to mock bush medicine. It helped my little Jock," Camille said.

"Oh please, Camille. Don't start. I hear enough of that rubbish from Colin."

"We have been discussing Naomi's work on the German Expressionist, Ernst Ludwig Kirchner. She did her master's thesis on him when she was at Cambridge," Celia said.

"Celia, I doubt if these two would have any interest in that subject. The only German culture they understand comes in a bottle," Naomi said.

Then, leaning forward, Celia whispered to me, "We really need to talk. Naomi told me the whole story about your trip to Laos."

"Hold off Naomi, my father's German. I know something about this Kirchner through my family. He shot himself in the 1930's," I said defensively.

"My, my, I'm impressed. The date was June 15, 1938, to be exact, leaving behind more than a thousand oil paintings, several thousand more pastels, and a multitude of prints and drawings waiting to be catalogued. I spent a year in research with that archive and only scratched the surface."

I was miffed by Naomi's arrogant presumption. Being from Dresden, as a young architecture student, my grandfather had known the four members of *Die Brucke*, or The Bridge, quite well. The four – Fritz Bleyl, Erich Heckel, Ernst Ludwig Kirchner, and Karl Schmidt-Rottluff, were responsible for the emergence of German Expressionism in the 1905-1913 period before the First World War. The group intended to become a bridge between the past and the future, embracing the emerging Fauvism, but without compromising their own heritage. Many of their paintings depicted the nude form, and a more open attitude toward sexuality, a series of Kirchner's showing nudists at the lakes outside of Dresden.

"Those paintings in Naomi's living room are Kirchner's work. I love the primary colors and bold brush strokes," Celia said, enthused by the subject.

"Those paintings were executed before World War I, Berlin street scenes with cocottes on the prowl," Naomi continued, self-absorbed and clearly loaded. "His paintings are fast becoming icons of the twentieth-century metropolis with their dense, anonymous crowds, and jazzy, erotic images, the best scenes of urban decadence since the archeologists uncovered Babylon."

"Coquettes?" Sam asked.

Naomi frowned. "Prostitutes. By the way, Camille said that Dr. von Zielke help clear up a long and sordid story concerning Kirchner's most famous work. It seems this painting, entitled *Berlin Street Scene*, originally owned by a Jewish family forced to flee the Nazis, emerged in the collection of a German museum after the war. Upon discovering this, Dr. von Zielke was instrumental in returning the painting to the original owner's heirs, who eventually sold it at the Neue Galerie in New York for thirty-eight million dollars."

"I assume that Dr. von Zielke got compensation for his efforts," I said, motioning to a waiter.

"He was offered a commission, but refused it. He said that he simply wanted to do the right thing," Camille said.

"Well, roger that. Let's get a beer, Dai 'ui," Sam said, flopping down in a chair.

Naomi stood up suddenly and unsteadily. "Hold off, Colin needs to see you two right away. He's up at our place having a meeting, as I speak, with Bob and that sleeze Whizzer. Reggie Dolan has run off with Mary Abodeely to some cult. Mr. Abodeely came to Colin, retaining his firm's services to bring her back. Wants to keep things hush-hush."

Sam immediately got up and walked across the street, not waiting for any further explanation. I rose slowly next to Naomi and whispered.

"If you are talking about Bob from General Tire, the word is that he has contacts with the CIA station chief here in Sydney."

Naomi whispered back.

"You Yank fool. He *is* the CIA station chief here in Sydney. Now get your bum up there. He needs a favor, and Colin is more than willing to oblige him."

*   *   *

Colin and Bob were looking cool and composed in short sleeved white oxford cloth shirts and tan slacks. Whizzer was in a blue and white pinstripe seersucker suit that looked as if it had been tailored. Quite a change from the skuzzy t-shirts and stubbies he usually wore down at the Hotel Cecil pub. Sam and I still had on our bush gear and needed a shower. They were all drinking Bombay Sapphire gin and tonics, Colin's favorite.

"My client, Mr. Abodeely, wants his daughter back without any embarrassing exposure in the Sydney Morning Herald," Colin said, leaning back in his canvas chair.

"No biggy. If we know were she is, we just go pick her up. Right?" Sam asked, refusing the gin and tonic that Bob offered him.

"More complicated than that," Colin said.

"Sergeant Kent, that is, Whizzer here, has located them at a commune called Wollumbin Falls. He's organizing a raid on this place. Given what we know, it would be easy for Mary to get caught up in the process. Officer Kent, maybe you can walk all of us through the process," Colin said.

"Thank you, Mr. Musto. You Yanks witnessed the punch-up at the Cecil when Quentin and Malcolm jumped me with those other two blokes. Well, I'm getting ready to bust Quentin and Malcolm when I find them. Those two are the main source of cannabis here in the Sutherland Shire, supplied out of Queensland by Quentin's cousin Bryan. There's also a rumor that they now are dealing heroin. Let me walk you through the details real fast. It will be a predawn raid the day after tomorrow. We're talking a twelve hundred acre property here, and I've been coordinating with local law enforcement."

"But you will have the warrants in order, correct?" Colin asked, concerned.

"For Quentin, yes. For all the others we have yet to work out the details."

"You said getting Quentin Hully was your priority. That's one of the reasons I agreed to coordinate with you on this," Colin added.

Among the surfer crowd in Cronulla, the charismatic Quentin Hully was recognized as a rebel in the tradition of James Dean. Since I was a regular at the Café Ritz, I knew him quite well. Quentin was an accomplished surfer and sometime rock musician who had also published poetry in several small magazines. He had a con man's charm, and was one of those folk who hung on the fringes, crossing artistic boundaries, sustained by friends, and occasionally scoring some dope for certain select clients. Quentin's clients were mostly professionals, and they included Naomi's sister. I once heard Maggie tell Sam that Quentin was romantically involved with Naomi's uncontrollable and self-destructive sister, Nadia. It didn't take much for me to understand why Colin wanted Quentin out of Cronulla. At that point Bob stood up.

"Sergeant Kent, that warrant issue could be a fly in the ointment. But please, let me interject something here, staying focused on Mary for a moment. Quentin has broken the law, and that is clearly a matter for Sergeant Kent and his team. My goal is to make sure Mary gets back to her father, and is not implicated in any way," Bob said.

Bob lowered his voice and leaned toward us. "Mr. Abodeely is a leader in the Lebanese community here in Sydney, a Maronite Christian who has supported our work in the Middle East. It's simple. He doesn't want Mary fingerprinted, photographed, nor her name appearing in the Sydney Morning Herald. Find her while this raid is going down and get her out of there. Sam, do you think you can handle that?"

"Piece of cake," Sam said, now reaching for the gin and tonic Bob had offered him earlier.

"This will all go down like a military operation. Trust me. And if we don't get rid of Quentin and his mates, one day we will have rioting in the streets of Cronulla. Mark my words," Whizzer said, gulping down his gin and tonic.

Sam looked at me and rolled his eyes. He didn't have to say a word. Whizzer was out of control.

* * *

Whizzer left with Sam on their way to the Hotel Cecil. I was to rendezvous with them the next morning at nine. We would be gone for three days. Celia would not be happy to hear that. But again, this was easy money, and our future was uncertain. I hoped that she would understand.

With the wind picking up off the sea, Colin, Bob and I moved inside. Colin displayed his art in the one long room that ran the length of the beachfront side of his condo. With windows on three sides, the light was just right to display the Musto's extensive collection. There were five of Kirchner's paintings along the south wall: haunting, moody scenes of Berlin streets, nightclubs and cabarets. In one of them, two tall, slender coquettes walked arm-in-arm with each other, dressed in black but for their gaudy, red-feathered hats, and strutting down a

Berlin street like two Glossy Black Cockatoos. On the west wall there were three paintings of couples dancing and embracing, very erotic, with wild, striking brushstrokes and bold primary colors.

Colin gestured toward the west wall. “The dancers are my favorite. Naomi prefers the Berlin paintings with their brooding qualities. One can see that German tendency toward darkness in his work. These Berlin paintings are a set that he did in Leipzig. I think they reflect his growing preoccupation with a cynical here and now. Kirchner had a number of nervous breakdowns, and his career didn’t flourish during his lifetime. He fretted about becoming too bourgeois, and toward the end he was drinking a liter of absinth a day.”

“Looks like King’s Cross on Saturday night,” Bob said, easing back in his chair.

Bob Cushing was an ex-Marine with service in both China and the South Pacific. He was balding, stocky, a bit under six feet, and old enough to be my father. However, he still looked very fit, with his bull neck and broad shoulders.

“Colin,” Naomi said, leaning at the doorway. “Who are you trying to impress with your naïve clichés? Bourgeois, my ass! Bob, don’t listen to his poppycock. He knows absolutely nothing about the German expressionists.”

“Neither do I. But I do know that Abodeely does. He has quite a few paintings, some like yours. I’ve been to his place a couple times.”

“Bob, you are so observant,” Naomi said with a mocking tone.

“Naomi and I have helped Mr. Abodeely make some important investments,” Colin said.

Bob shifted in his chair, his heavy eyebrows raised. “I’d be interested in hearing more about that, actually. I'm getting ready to retire, and am looking for a hedge against inflation. You have stirred my interest in modern art."

Naomi couldn't resist the temptation. She turned and gave Colin a wink.

"Bob, you want to see a hedge against inflation? Come with me. I'll show you something in Colin's study that my father gave me."

Celia was behind her and gave me the nod that it was time to go home. But I wanted to see what Naomi was referring to. As we entered Colin's study Naomi pulled aside what I thought was a window curtain. Behind the curtain was a painting, maybe two feet by three feet, showing a small house on a landscape by the sea.

"This is the Cezanne my father left me. It's titled *Cottage Overlooking The Bay Of Marseille Seen From L'Estaque*. My grandfather brought it back after World War One, acquiring it at an estate auction. This is Colin's pride and joy."

"What a hedge against inflation!" Bob said.

"Well, Celia and I have to excuse ourselves. Her sister is staying with us. Bob, good seeing you again," I said.

"Yeah, good to see you too. Always enjoy visiting with another Marine. By the way, in case you haven't heard, there's a war brewing between Cambodia and Vietnam. I expect the shit to hit the fan in the next month or so."

"My God! Expect that to impact making Vat Phou a World Heritage Site," Colin said.

"No doubt. And I foresee that we might need you and Captain Graham to help us with another matter," Bob said.

"And that is?"

"The Hmong refugee problem. The coming war will accelerate the need to move as many of our old allies as we can out of Laos."

* * *

When we got to our condo Celia's sister was out shopping. I opened a bottle of Flag Ale and sat down. Celia was very quiet. Clearly something was on her mind.

"Colin and Naomi have acquired quite a collection of Kirchner's paintings," Celia said.

"How much would that collection be worth, I wonder?" I asked. "For that matter, how did they acquire so many of his original oils?"

"Naomi spent that year in Kirchner's archive, working to catalogue all his work. My guess is that those oil paintings are from Kirchner's early work, acquired as a result of her research," Celia replied.

"Still, seeing the extent of their collection makes me wonder. Now I understand why Colin goes to such great lengths with his security system," I said.

"Mary Abodeely called while you were gone. I told her you were out of town. She wanted to talk to you about Reggie. She was worried about him. Maggie was also very concerned and wanted you to talk to Mary," Celia said, quietly.

"When was this?"

"The day after you left for Laos."

"Reggie is working through some issues. I hope it's just a phase."

"Here is a post card that came for you yesterday from Nimbin. It's from Reggie."

"Nimbin?"

"Yes, that's the postmark."

"I'm not surprised. He took off with Mary

Abodeely. Whizzer says they are out in Nimbin."

The postcard showed a flock of Rainbow Lorikeets and read: 'good on ya for all the help you gave me. If I don't see you before you leave, congrats on the baby. We will meet again on the next round. All hail Bob Marley.'

"All kids go through phases," I said.

Celia nodded and sat down next to me, staring out at the Tasman Sea.

"Why don't you tell me what happened on this last trip to Laos."

"Something on your mind?"

"Yes, something is on my mind. Naomi got real drunk yesterday and broke down in tears. When I asked her what was wrong she told me that she actually feared for her life on that last trip to Laos."

"Naomi is overly dramatic when she drinks."

"Is that right? When I pressed her she said she didn't want to get into the gory details, for that might be violating a confidence, and that I should ask you about this Colonel Dub."

"For someone who didn't want to get into the gory details, I think that's bullshit."

Celia bored in. "Who is he?"

"It's like who was he? He's dead."

"Were you involved?"

"Interesting question. Let's say I was present when he was shot. Was I material to his manner of death? No! I feel no complicity in Dub's death.

"You must have been in danger for Naomi to be so upset."

"Danger? Yes, I felt in danger."

Celia put her hand on mine. "What is this all about?"

"Another good question. This was just about some easy money. Then things took a twist."

"You call seeing a man killed a little twist. I don't know what to say. You put yourself and the future of your family at risk, and for what? Tell me! Was this all about money?"

"Yes, and its over. Done."

"Is it? I think not. This is another one of those stupid adventures like Long Daddy Green. You and Sam are alike in this adventuring. I don't know what else to call it. I truly worry about your eternal soul," Celia said, burying her face in her hands.

Yes, it was about more than the money. Part of it was the excitement, and when done, having the tale to tell. Deep within me there was this wish to possess something beyond the commonplace, something beyond the ordinary and conventional; that I might see myself again as that young Marine officer in Vietnam.

Clearly I didn't fully understand the wild impulse that drove me to work with Southeast Asia Company. I should have realized not only the risks involved, but also my own limitations. I now understand that longing for what it was, a thing as natural as the wind for a young man when each morning is a door opening to infinite possibilities. In hindsight, I was a fool.

I once asked Reggie if he had seen any of the big ones off Shark Island while waiting for a wave. Reggie replied that a ten-footer, with a head broad as his surfboard had brushed his dangling legs, mere inches away. "But you still go back out there?" I asked. "Yeah, I do! It was a terrifying, bloody rush! But Quentin tells of a fifteen foot White Pointer he saw off North Cronulla Beach, said he could see the shark's white rimmed black eye when he turned in the clear water, peering back up at him," Reggie said. “What a story! Quentin sure had a tale to tell,” I had replied to Reggie.

“You’re crying,” I said, turning to Celia.

“Yes. You go do what you need to do. My sister is here with me. But when you get back from this next trip, I want you to promise me that you will buy our tickets back to the States. Something happens to you when you are around Sam, and it’s not good. We need to go back home.”

I wrapped an arm around Celia, leaned in close, and kissed her on the cheek. “I’ll buy the tickets. You have my promise.”

* * *

We left early the next morning, Captain Graham flying us back up the coast to Lismore, not far from where Sam met with the Wolly Man. Whizzer sat next to me during the flight. Sam sat across from us and slept through the whole flight while Naomi acted as Graham’s co-pilot, taking the controls after we lifted off. Whizzer and I had a chance to talk about our experiences in Vietnam as well as his undercover role.

“C Company was the finest outfit I ever served with. They were amazing blokes, to a man. Anyway, we were sweeping this French rubber plantation when Long Tan went down. It was August 18, 1966. We got hit and were outnumbered by more than ten to one. But we held our position, and the gooks left 245 dead. I was nineteen-years old at the time, wounded twice by shrapnel. Two of my mates in the hole next to me died. They evacuated me to Vung Tau for the rest of my tour,” Whizzer said, his eyes glazing over. I had heard the tale before.

"Vung Tau is pretty, on the South China Sea."

"You want to see something pretty. Look at this," Whizzer said, pulling a photo from his wallet.

In the photo a slender Vietnamese woman was holding a fat little baby.

"Wow!"

"That's Mai, and my little boy, Kevin. I got them out of Nam three months ago. They're waiting in Hong Kong for the papers to go through. She had an uncle who got her onto a fishing trawler."

"She's one of the Boat People?"

"In a way, I suppose she is. She didn't suffer like a lot did, drifting for days out on the open sea. Her ship made Hong Kong in three days. A priest married us a year ago. But the paperwork got hung up. Flying up there to get her after this bust. I owe a great debt to Colin Musto. He pulled some strings in the government to make everything possible."

"Whizzer, you're an interesting man."

"Like your mate Sam likes to say, roger that. I've been with the Australian Federal Narcotics Bureau for three years now, this past six months all undercover in Sutherland Shire. Mind if I smoke?"

"No. Go ahead. Sounds like that could be some dangerous work, going undercover."

"At times, depending on the blokes I was trailing. Quentin's nothing but a big poofter, plays in a rock band from time to time, mostly sponges off his friends for a living. On the other hand, I've done some research on Bryan. He's a real wanker, a petty thief with a record as long as your arm, everything from breaking and entering to shaking down school kids for change. Dealing marijuana comes naturally for him. He's been smoking since he was six."

Whizzer lit an Upman Cuban cigar.

"I thought he was just a hippie."

"Oh, he's a cocky one, he is. My jaw still aches where he punched me. But he's small change."

"And Malcolm?"

"Ah, yes, me boy, Malcolm. Let me tell you about Malcolm. His father is former IRA. The old man was born here, but with connections back to County Cork, and he did hard time in the UK for smuggling weapons. So Malcolm comes to his calling through his father. I now know that Malcolm is the main supplier for all the small time dealers in the Shire like Quentin. New information. And I believe it was Malcolm who first brought heroin into the Shire. That's what my warrant says, by the way, heroin. His nickname is 'the Pony.' I'd hear blokes refer to someone called 'the Pony,' I didn't realize for the longest time they were talking about Malcolm. I just didn't make the connection."

"Really. Why do they call him 'the Pony'?"

"Because he's hung like a horse. And they say he likes the blokes better than the girls, a habit he picked up while he was in the slammer," Whizzer said, starting to laugh.

He laughed for a long time, the smoke from his fine Cuban cigar swirling in the air.

* * *

We dropped off our gear at the Winsome Hotel about six that evening. It was overcast and rainy, with a big storm building up out on the Tasman Sea. Captain Graham's fever had returned, and he looked thin and drawn. We all waited in the lobby while Naomi freshened herself.

"I need to shove some tucker into my gob," Whizzer said.

About that time Naomi appeared. She looked stunning in a bare-shouldered, white cotton dress, contrasted against her deep tan, and long, dark hair. It was hard not to stare at her cleavage. She wasn't wearing a bra, and her firm nipples were distracting. If I looked hard, I could make out the shadowy circles of her areola through the light fabric.

Naomi nodded toward the door. "Well, follow me then. I know a daggy little café not far from here. We can walk. It's not far from a nightclub called The Unicorn. Good place to dance."

The so-called little café was called The Wine Cellar, and it turned out to be a three star temple of gastronomy. The owner, a former *chef de cuisine* from a fancy place on George Street, had fled Sydney to the north coast of New South Wales to make a new life after a nasty divorce.

We all ordered the chef's special that evening. It was fabulous - huge fresh prawns from the Clarence River Estuary marinated in a chimichurri sauce made with sweet smoked pimenton from Spain, and then grilled. The prawns were served with crushed dutch cream potatoes from the Southern Highlands, and Naomi ordered a large wedge of creamy soft cheese from Bourgogne, l'Epoisses, for dessert. We washed this feast down with five bottles of a pinot gris Naomi had heard about from a small vineyard out west of the Blue Mountains near Orange.

"Damn fine meal, Mrs. Musto," Whizzer said.

We all had a buzz on, and I could see Graham was fading fast.

Naomi scrunched up her nose. "I was a bit disappointed in the soft cheese. In France you get it unpasteurized, which is superior. Colin and I first had it at Georges Blanc, near Lyon, some years ago. Here the authorities only allow the pasteurized version into the country, which is absurd. Well, are you all ready to party? The Unicorn is right around the corner!"

"Naomi, I'll forgo any further activity. I need to get some sleep," Graham said.

"How about you, Sam? Do you like to dance?" Naomi said with a wicked smile.

"Bring it on," Sam said, draining his glass.

* * *

Northern Rivers College was once called Lismore Teachers College. It was a wonderful place to learn, and in the evening the students had a number of venues where they could let off steam. The most well known was The Unicorn.

"You know, our boy Quentin used to play in a band here. Also dealt a little pot to the students," Whizzer said, watching the crowded dance floor.

For a moment I was tempted to tell Whizzer about meeting Quentin and Lotus on our way back from Nimbin. But my intuition told me to withhold that information. I didn't want to reveal to Whizzer that I found Quentin to be interesting company, someone with whom I shared more than one conversation down at the Café Ritz.

"Quentin appears to be a man for all seasons," I said, ordering another round of Castlemaine Bitter.

We were sitting near the bar, a fair distance from the band, next to a large door that opened onto a big patio. Even with the open doors a smoky haze filled the room. Outside a light rain was falling, but the damp weather had no effect whatsoever on the wild crowd. We sat a little above the dance floor and had a good view of Naomi and Sam enjoying themselves among all the college students.

The band wasn't bad, with two lead singers, a guy and a gal. They had the place hopping, singing the latest hits. The gal sang the Rita Coolidge hit *Your Love Has Lifted Me Higher*, followed by *Dancing Queen*, Abba's hit.

"Hey mate, *Dancing Queen*, that's Malcolm's favorite tune! We better check the crowd real good. We may find him trying to get Quentin to play with his pony," Whizzer said, laughing at his own joke.

The band took a break. Sam and Naomi returned to the table, drenched with sweat. Naomi's light cotton dress was clinging to her body in a most provocative way.

"What's so funny?" Sam asked.

"You don't want to know, especially in mixed company," I said, nodding at Naomi.

"Come on, Dai 'ui. I've heard it all. What's the joke?" Naomi asked.

"Well, Whizzer said he heard Malcolm was a poofter. And he pointed out to me the song was *Dancing Queen*, and that we should be searching the crowd to see if we could find him chasing after Quentin," I explained.

At that point Whizzer began to laugh hysterically. He continued to laugh for a long time.

"I don't find that amusing," Naomi said, upset.

When Whizzer heard that, he laughed even harder, excusing himself.

"Be right back. Going the loo," Whizzer said.

"Strange man. He told me that Colin helped get his wife into Australia," I said.

"Yes. That's true. They were stuck in Hong Kong. Colin's firm was a bit upset with him over that. He has an altruistic streak. There is a lot of good in Colin Musto. I admire him for that. He's a much better human being than I am," Naomi said.

"That's a side of Colin that I didn't know about," I said, lighting Naomi's cigarette.

Whizzer stumbled back to the table and sat down. He waved at two uniformed officers walking into the club.

Sam looked hard at Naomi. "Colin didn't seem to show much charity for Lotus. He couldn't wait to have you get rid of her."

Naomi blew a perfect smoke ring as she gathered her reply.

"Sam, I feel real bad about having to send Lotus on her way. But Colin is so concerned about his image, and Lotus was associating with the likes of Fred Robinson and other members of his cult. It was really out of my hands."

"Fred Robinson!" Whizzer blurted out, his eyes glazing over. "That crazy wanker!"

Whizzer was out of control again. "Robinson is a threat to society, that's what he is! He undermines the values of our Australian youth. Just look around at all the hippies sliming around in this club."

I couldn't help but think of the comparison my headmaster at Woolooware once made between the hippie communes and the cult of the Bacchae in ancient Rome. The Roman Senate sent a spy to mix among the worshipers during their wild nocturnal bacchanalia down at the Tiber. Once the Senate heard of the sexual details of the bacchanalian frenzy, they gave the consuls authority to make arrests. They feared that the cult posed a threat to the future of the Roman Republic and undermined the values of its youth. That scenario was not unlike what Sam, Naomi, and I experienced with Whizzer, a police spy who had us involved in a drug raid on a hippie commune.

"Dai 'ui, what movie is this? What are we doing here, chasing after some runaway kids?" Sam asked, shaking his head.

"Shush!" Naomi said, putting a finger to her lips.

"How about *Romeo and Juliet*? That's about two runaway lovers. Or maybe even *One Flew over The Cuckoo's Nest*, I said, nodding at Whizzer.

"That's a good one, Mate! With Jack Nicholson and his bloody gang. They take over the fucking asylum!" Whizzer shouted, starting to laugh again.

This time everyone laughed, Whizzer's craziness was contagious. That brought the two uniformed officers over to our table. They motioned to Whizzer to join them at the bar.

"We better keep it down. Let me go see my two mates. Be right back," Whizzer whispered.

The band started up again. They played *Hotel California.* For a number of complex reasons that song always affects Sam, and he seemed to drift off, lost in his thoughts. The waitress brought us more beers and Sam chugged his down.

"What's the matter? Is something wrong?" Naomi asked, putting her hand on Sam's knee.

By that time we all had been drinking steadily and it showed. But I was surprised by Naomi's sudden familiarity, the way she touched Sam. Whizzer was still at the bar, talking to the uniformed policemen.

"It's nothing. This song brings back memories of Africa. That was a difficult period in my life," Sam said, looking directly into Naomi's eyes.

"You've never told me that story. I know that's where Graham met his wife. You should tell me the story sometime," Naomi said.

"Naomi, you don't want to hear it. Certainly not tonight," Sam said, reaching for her hand.

The next song was *Nobody Does It Better*, the Carly Simon hit, sung by the gal fittingly.

"Sam, you big dumb Yank, dance with me! This is a nice, slow dance," Naomi said.

They disappeared into the crowd. Occasionally I'd catch a glimpse of them, dancing close, arms wrapped around each other, Naomi reaching up with her hand to stroke Sam's thick neck as if he were her big pet, which I was beginning to think he was.

It was getting late and the crowd was thinning out. Whizzer came back and plopped down in his chair. He started swaying on it.

"You talked to those officers quite a while," I said, making conversation.

"Old mates of mine. Wanted to tell me things were a go for the raid. You can have my beer, mate. I don't want anymore," Whizzer said, putting his head down on the table.

A moment later Whizzer was passed out face down on the table. The band then began to play *Easy*, by the Commodores. I saw Naomi reach up and give Sam a kiss. When the waitress came over, I paid our bill and asked her to tell Sam that I was taking Whizzer back to the hotel. As I hauled Whizzer out the door, I looked back to see that Sam and Naomi were still kissing, dancing very slowly.

* * *

Whizzer was rooming with Captain Graham, and Sam was bunking with me. The captain woke up when I dragged Whizzer over to his bed. I pulled off his shoes and threw a blanket over him, to keep off the chill. Outside, the wind was picking up, and a heavy rain drummed on the roof.

"As they say at the Hotel Cecil, he's got a gutful of piss. Sam and Naomi are still raging on," I said.

"Do I hear those black cockatoos calling?" Graham said, smiling.

"What's that?"

"Like that time back at the seep in Gamoowea."

"You don't miss much, do you Captain?"

* * *

I woke just before dawn. The rain had stopped but a chill hung in the air. Sam's bed was still made up. I pulled on my boots and opened the door. Sam was walking down the hall, looking sheepish.

"Well, what do you have to say for yourself?"

"Deep down I'm just another one of Whizzer's cuntoisseurs," Sam said. "So spare me any of your high-minded judgments, Mr. Self-Righteous."

"Have you lost your mind?" I asked.

"Maybe I have lost my mind, or maybe I lost it a long time ago, that day we found those Thai pirates out in the South China Sea. So I break Naomi down like a shotgun to watch her quiver and shake. And she likes it. Shit happens."

At that moment I couldn't help but remember what Quentin had said to me about fate, and how certain quirks of character and temperament influence what we become. Perhaps he was right.

"Sam, Colin's our boss!"

"Colin's pissed me off. I have nothing but contempt for him. Because of his deceptions we all are complicit in Dub's murder. And it was murder, Dai 'ui, just like those Thai pirates. "

"Wake up Sam, Dub's death was about justice."

"You wake up, Dai 'ui! Colin ignores Naomi. His fat ass cravings are about food and the power he feels because he runs this dinky little Southeast Asia Company. Naomi said that food was Colin's fetish. That may be. But Colin's deceptions are all about power. And he's used us! Nam may have warped me, but Colin warps everyone involved with Southeast Asia Company, even Captain Graham."

"I don't know what to say."

"Roger that. Just go with the flow," Sam said.

* * *

Later Sam, Whizzer, Naomi, and I headed west on Highway 44, turning north on Nimbin Road, passing through Koonogan and Coffee Camp until we reached Nimbin. The plan was for Graham to wait in Lismore until the raid was over. Then we'd all fly back to Sydney. But the rain continued throughout the day, with high winds blowing down a few old trees. Whizzer made a few phone calls and met with several uniformed officers. We drove on through the gathering darkness, the heavy tops of the trees billowing in our headlights. Finally, as the rain changed to a drizzle, Whizzer pointed out a narrow track just outside of town.

Turning in, I could see a number of police cars pulled up in front of a rambling old house. Someone was barbecuing, the aroma drifting through the rain. More men were unloading cattle into a paddock from a big red stock truck, directed by a beefy, thick-necked uniformed officer. As soon as we got out, the officer approached.

"Come on in out of the rain and have some barbecue," the beefy one said.

"Give me a minute," Whizzer replied.

“Mrs. Musto, you’re welcome to come in and have something to eat,” Whizzer said.

“I don’t think Mrs. Musto would be very comfortable with this crowd,” I said.

“You’re right,” Whizzer said, laughing his strange little laugh. “I’ll arrange to have her taken back to the hotel,” Whizzer said.

“No sense in keeping me out here all night. I’m ready to go back to the hotel,” Naomi said.

“Roger that,” Sam said.

“Wollumbin Falls is about four kilometers west of Nimbin. My mates here have set up a command post up there to oversee the whole operation.”

“I thought we had to see someone about warrants?” I asked, repeating Colin’s concerns.

“I’ve got that covered. Photocopied enough for everyone,” Whizzer said, continuing to laugh.

He seemed to be in his element, and high on the action about to go down.

* * *

Whizzer’s radio crackled with static. “They call their cooperative an Athenian democracy. The headman is a goofy blodger named Bandicoot. There must be a hundred and fifty of them, living in little hamlets spread out across the place. We will be targeting the creamery where they process the milk from their stock. Two other teams will be hitting the other two hamlets, where they tend their big veggie gardens,” Whizzer said, his radio crackling with static.

Whizzer was carrying a Stevens pump shotgun and was dressed in old camouflage.

“What’s the cattle truck for?” I asked, hearing the diesel engine crank.

"To haul them all to Nimbin," Whizzer laughed.

* * *

The raid went off according to plan. Three teams of police stormed through the darkness at two in the morning, surrounding each hamlet with a cordon. These dwellings were primitive affairs, and when several dogs started to bark alerting the occupants, many simply ran through the makeshift shanty walls, escaping in the rainy darkness. All told, forty-two people were caught, including Mary, Reggie, and Bryan. Several women were allowed to stay with the very small children.

Sam and I spotted Reggie and Mary in the creamery, and took them into custody. Mary was terrified and in tears. Reggie acted like a smart ass and tried to make a break for it, whereupon Sam restrained him. We headed out the door to find Whizzer beating the hell out of Bryan.

"You'll wear out before I will mate. And you won't be a fancy cuntoisseur anymore by the time I'm done with your pretty nose. Better tell me where Quentin is, and I'll ease off," Whizzer said.

In less than a minute, Whizzer had managed to make a total mess of Bryan's face. It was brutal. Bryan was on his knees sobbing, with his hands cuffed behind his back, blood pouring out of a smashed nose. Whizzer was wearing leather gloves to protect his hands. To everyone's relief Bryan finally lost consciousness and fell over. At that point Whizzer spotted Reggie.

"Ah, Reggie my lad. Maybe you can be of more help than Bryan. Sam, bring him over here," Whizzer said, making a fist.

"Not a chance, Whizzer. No damaged goods, please. Not what Sam and I signed up for," I said, stepping between him and Reggie.

"He'll tell me where Quentin is, or I'll take out his pretty front teeth. His mama will cry when she sees him," Whizzer said, pushing me aside.

At that point Sam grabbed Whizzer by the throat in a crushing grip.

"Not part of the deal, Whizzer. Get the message!" Sam said, through clenched teeth.

Whizzer froze. Two officers moved to help him.

"Hold it, everyone! I know where Quentin is! All you had to do was ask me," I yelled.

"Tell your fucking goons to back off, Whizzer," Sam said, that berserk look in his eyes.

"Whizzer, I know where Quentin is. I'll tell you if you let us take Reggie back with us," I said.

Whizzer nodded, and Sam let him go, immediately taking Reggie and Mary to the van.

"Quentin is at a place in Queensland called Eden's Bay. I know that because he told me."

"When did he tell you this?" Whizzer croaked.

"Three days ago. Sam and I ran into him."

"Why didn't you tell me this before?"

"You didn't ask me Whizzer. That's why. I'm taking the van back to Lismore to drop off Reggie and Mary. Sam and I will meet you at the Winsome Hotel tomorrow. We're out of here!"

* * *

Naomi was upset when she heard the details of what had happened. At first light, she and Graham flew out to Sydney with Reggie and Mary. At about eight in the morning one of the officers who had witnessed Whizzer abusing Bryan came by the hotel and offered us an apology for Whizzer's extreme behavior. He also told us that forty-two people were herded at gunpoint into the red cattle truck and taken to Lismore where charges were filed, most of which involved alleged possession of marijuana. No heroin was ever found.

* * *

About noon, when Whizzer finally showed up, he was beaming. He had contacted the Queensland police who had important news. During the storm Malcolm Askew's boat had crashed off rocks near Coff's Harbour. Malcolm, the only survivor, was in custody. When the storm struck he was sailing with Quentin and Lotus, taking a load of Queensland Green back to Sydney. When the morning tide came in, the bodies of Quentin and Lotus had washed up on the beach.

"I'm on my way to formally charge Malcolm. You two blokes are welcome to ride with me to view the bodies," Whizzer said, as if the troubling events that had transpired had never occurred.

"Roger that. We need to make sure Lotus is identified as Amy Windham, and returned to her parents," Sam said, clearly shaken.

"Well then, let's get on down the track," Whizzer said coldly.

* * *

Chapter Nine: The Heavenly Wolf

The road ahead leveled out, clear of trees on either side for a long stretch, and offered a great view of the heavens. Away from the lights of Lismore, and without a moon, the stars were spectacular. The Milky Way rose up from the southeast, millions of stars and glowing clouds of gas light-years across. Stars were condensing out of interstellar dust, and all was quiet as we drove along the coast, each preoccupied with our own thoughts.

I had no idea where Whizzer's head was at, but I could almost read Sam's mind as he stared up at the night sky. I guessed he was reflecting on how Lotus and Quentin had met their end. I wondered if he saw their drowning as the sign, the one the Wolly Man had told him would come.

Since I was a child I have always thought that the celestial order reflected the work of an architect whose purpose was to create the grand design, as I liked to call it. As a young man, I wanted to believe that all the laws that governed the planets and stellar events reflected a single universal mind. On the other hand, my experience with so many deaths in Vietnam had shocked me to a new level of reality, leaving me forever cold when I gazed up at the heavens. For most it is a matter of faith, how each death fits into the scheme of the universe. To me, as we drove through that moonless night, the deaths of Lotus and Quentin seemed just more of those uncontrollable events that consume day-to-day existence. All I knew for certain was that life was precious, and it could slip away so suddenly.

We came upon a patch of eucalyptus trees, and I swerved to avoid a curiously spotted night creature that scurried across the road.

"Native cat," Whizzer said, breaking the silence.

Once we passed through the trees we had the Tasman Sea on one side, and a field to our west, offering us a better view of the sky.

"There's Orion, low on the horizon. See his belt," Sam said, calmly.

"Orion shit! That's the sauce pan," Whizzer said.

"Negative on your last, Whizzer. You're looking at the mighty hunter, Orion," Sam countered.

"That's where the Abo sky gods cook their tucker. Everyone knows that. When you're in Australia, it's the sauce pan," Whizzer snickered.

"Look at the bright star to the left," Sam said, ignoring Whizzer.

"That's the Dog Star. Sirius. It's in the constellation of Canis Major, and the brightest star in the sky. Sirius was also the name of a ship that sailed to Australia as part of the First Fleet," I said.

"One of these days I'm going to take time out and learn all the constellations," Sam said.

"Let's stop for beer and tucker. Next little town down the road has a bottle shop," Whizzer said.

* * *

When we got to the next town I pulled into a station for petrol. The bottle shop was across the street and Whizzer went in to buy some beer. Sam bought three orders of fish and chips at a place next to the gas station. Whizzer took us to a park about a mile down the road. The park had picnic tables, and we sat at one of them to have our dinner. Away from the lights, Sirius dominated the night sky.

"So that's the Dog Star?" Sam asked.

"Roger that. What the Chinese call the heavenly wolf, twenty-five times the size of our sun," I said.

"No shit. You know about a lot of things, Dai 'ui," Whizzer said.

"Whizzer, don't encourage him. You'll get a fucking lecture. Like Colin Musto, the Dai 'ui has it all figured out. He's thinks he's intellectually superior to you and me," Sam said, smiling.

"I make no apologies for being a man of letters; just as I don't make apologies for being a man of arms who served his country," I replied, irritated.

"Take it easy, Dai 'ui," Sam said.

"What's a man of letters? Is that like a pimp?" Whizzer asked, winking at Sam.

They both then laughed and clinked beer bottles.

"You guys are fucked up," I said.

"Roger that, Dai 'ui. But the difference between you, and Whizzer and me, is that we know we're fucked up. You don't know! You haven't figured out yet just how fucked up you really are. It's guilt by association, Dai 'ui. And it's about complicity, like Naomi says. We are all complicit."

"Sam, complicit rhymes with bullshit. I'm tired of hearing about it! It's never over with you," I said.

Sam and Whizzer cracked up at that and again clinked bottles, shaking their heads.

"Give it time, Dai 'ui. Give it time. I've already seen all the signs in you," Sam said.

"Signs of what? You need to get over it, Sam! Like I got over it. Were you listening to the Wolly Man? He told you to quit playing those old tapes. Now, do you want to hear about the heavenly wolf, or not?" I asked.

"I want to hear about the heavenly wolf," Whizzer said, child-like in his enthusiasm.

"Okay. There's lots of folklore about the Dog Star. The Dog Star was a big deal to the ancient

Egyptians. To them it heralded the rise of the Nile, and was the doorway to the afterlife." I said.

Sam leaned against a tree, mumbling just loud enough to be heard. "Afterlife. Dai 'ui, where do you get all this shit?"

"It's part of Egyptian history, Sam. All you have to do is read it. When you read that history you will find that the Dog Star was like a watchman, fixed in one place at the bridge of the Milky Way, keeping guard over what the Egyptians called the abyss. In Egyptian myth the Dog Star exemplifies the One who had succeeded in bridging the lower and higher consciousness."

"Now you're beginning to sound like the Wolly Man." Sam said. "And the heavenly wolf?"

I got up from the table and walked over to Sam. "That's a Chinese myth," I said. "The Chinese thought the heavenly wolf guarded the bridge between heaven and hell. Between each life the soul must judge its past progress and the conditions needed to aid future growth. As long as the soul attaches to desire, it takes a new body. The soul cannot pass over the bridge until it is perfected."

I paused to drain my Flag Ale. I could see Sam was tuned in, so I continued. "It is said that the fixed stars contain the essences of matter, and a living soul is a high essence of matter that when perfectly evolved may also be called a star. Like souls, stars are viewed as having divine attributes."

"That's it, Dai 'ui!" Sam exclaimed, punching my shoulder in celebration. "You answered the sixty-four thousand dollar question! That's the sign! That's the sign the Wolly Man was talking about!"

"Who's this fucking Wolly Man?" Whizzer asked.

"He's a counter culture shaman who thought he could heal Sam. He's no one you want to know, Whizzer. No one you want to know." I replied.

* * *

We drove on through the night for quite a while. When Sam and Whizzer drifted off to sleep, I pulled over into a thick stand of gums. The air smelled sweet. The flies had yet to swarm. I looked out over that dark ink of placid water that yesterday was the raging Tasman Sea. For a time Sam slept soundly, his fever gone. But later, watching him stir and call out in his dreams, I sensed that his therapeutic journey had just begun, and that he would wake at dawn, after a long night patrol through the dense thickets of his existential despair, looking back down the long valley of his past to see if any pursuers were gaining on him.

* * *

For the next two days the fallout from the Wollumbin Falls raid was considerable. The newspapers were full of editorials on the violation of civil liberties that had occurred. The papers claimed the police acted in ways that went beyond law enforcement, and showed a degree of intolerance viewed as unacceptable by their fellow professionals. The result was embarrassment for the government agencies involved.

When Colin talked with Whizzer on the phone he was livid, rebuking him for the abortive raid. By the time we got back to Cronulla, all forty-two who had been charged were bailed out of jail. Newspaper coverage continued to be very critical of the police, in particular, for the abuse of Bryan. Finally, all charges were dropped after the search warrant was successfully challenged.

To Colin, the throwing out of the warrant ended the matter. It seems that a warrant to search the Wollumbin Falls community was the equivalent of searching a village, which was not acceptable. The warrant was not specific enough in the address to be searched, and photocopies of warrants were not acceptable, a thing that Colin had specifically warned Whizzer about. The actual warrant had to be served. In addition, the warrant was to be served between sunrise and sunset, but was served before sunrise. Whizzer, of course, had all kinds of excuses, and ranted on about how we were witnessing the Fall of Rome all over again.

* * *

Three days after we returned from the raid, Bob and Colin hosted a party at Bob's high-rise penthouse to celebrate Mary's safe return to Cronulla. Bob's garish penthouse was just across Cronulla Park from our place, overlooking Ozone Street. From the west balcony one had a great view of Gunnamatta Bay, while the south and east balconies overlooked the National Park and the Tasman Sea. Bob invited a lot of different people, including Mary and Mr. Abodeely. For some reason Mrs. Abodeely chose not to attend.

Bob's wife, Lucille, who met us at the door, was related to a member of the mafia who owned the Hotel Fontainbleau in Las Vegas. When Celia and I walked in she was engaged in a verbal battle with Whizzer over Frank Sinatra. Colin and Naomi were standing to the side, looking on in disbelief. Nadia,

Naomi's sister, had also showed up. She was an older and heavier version of Naomi, an attractive woman with long, dark chestnut hair.

Whizzer had his face right in Lucille's and his voice was too loud. "Sinatra has bashed the unions in Sydney one time too many. Now the unions are calling for a boycott of Sinatra's Australian concert tour. Good on them, I say. Send the gangster back home where he belongs," Whizzer said.

Lucille stomped off in disgust, leaving Whizzer with a moronic grin on his face.

"He is such an ill-mannered thug, a thug with an exaggerated sense of his own self-importance," Colin whispered in my ear. "Whizzer doesn't realize that he just insulted his host. I'm sure he thought he was making a joke."

"Gidday Whizzer, how's your bad self?" I asked, taking a drink from a nearby tray.

"Never better, mate. We should feel proud that Malcolm and Quentin ain't around to cause trouble anymore. The rogue dope dealers are gone for now. Even young Reggie seems to have dropped out of sight," Whizzer said, alluding to the recent news that Reggie's parents had reported him missing.

So, the beachfront Esplanade was now safe for kids, as well as was Cronulla Park, where at night, the potheads hung out with the Ring Tail Possums under the Washingtonian Palms.

Naomi took an inebriated step forward and said. "Well, Whizzer, the young, beautiful, and clueless in Cronulla can now devote themselves to the simple surfer pleasures of getting high and achieving orgasm, gorgeous airheads that they are." She continued, apparently oblivious to my presence. "Cronulla is such a shallow, delusional place, one with absolutely no culture, and where surfing and football are everything."

"Why do you live here then?" Nadia asked.

"Because Bob is a silent partner to many of Colin's quixotic projects. That's why. But I find Lucille intolerable. She does her own laundry. These Americans are masquerading as if they are people of taste, when in fact, they are merely climbers." Naomi replied.

I cleared my throat to make my presence known. Naomi looked startled when she saw me.

"Terrible news about Lotus," I said. Naomi threw her arms around me and gave me a hug.

"I let that poor woman down. I should have done more to ensure her safety, kept her away from Bryan and Quentin," Naomi said.

"Quentin's demise was inevitable. It was only a matter of time. His candle burned brightly, but now he is gone. In some ways we should be relieved," Nadia said. "But then again, he had such a big candle!" She added wickedly. Nadia was witty, and cool, with a self-mocking manner about her.

"My God, didn't he though," Naomi, said, wiping a tear away. "I feel as if I've passed through a brutal initiation these past few weeks. I feel so bad about Lotus, and those Hmong children are constantly on my mind. Sometimes I get so disgusted with the wretched excess in my life. I thought I could do anything. I was deceiving myself. I wanted to do something novel upon returning to Australia. What a false notion. Then the dreary realization hit me that all I could do was teach," Naomi said.

"What's wrong with that?" I asked, insulted.

"It's boring," Naomi said.

Nadia gave Naomi a stern look and said.

"Naomi, I think that you have had too much to drink. Go freshen up a bit. Maybe lie down for a while."

"Actually, that's a good idea," Naomi said, wobbling out of the room.

I wondered about Naomi's apparent remorse for Lotus.

"Naomi seems to be taking the death of Lotus quite hard," I said.

"That so? You're a good friend and business associate of Colin, so I want to share something with you," Nadia said, looking me in the eye.

"Okay?"

"Naomi's infidelities have caught up with her. Your good friend Sam should watch himself," Nadia said, coldly.

I shot back. "I don't even know you. You lay this on me!"

"We both know Naomi. She has a high regard for you. That's why I'm telling you this. She is struggling with her marriage. Can't have children, you know."

"If you say so," I replied.

"She longs for stimulation. She used to paint until the critics put her down. There was an article in the Sydney Herald saying that while she had a gift for expression with her brilliant colors, her themes are not equal to the technique. Quite a put-down, don't you think?"

"I don't know anything about painting."

Nadia rolled her eyes Naomi style and sighed.

"Do you know anything about anything; or are you another one of those big dumb Yanks that Colin likes to hire, like your friend Sam?"

"I'm a former Marine captain. I am also the one teacher at Woolooware High School that supported

Naomi when she was being trashed for her liberal views. By the way, I taught both ancient and modern history. That's hard work."

Her eyes softened. "Sorry if I was impertinent."

"Apology accepted."

"Naomi's one art show failed miserably. The critics claimed her work was concerned merely with colors and surfaces. They called her work too superficial, even decadent."

"Decadent? I'm not so sure. I've seen Naomi's paintings, and she paints herself mostly, in the style of Kirchner. That may be narcissistic. But to hear her work called decadent surprises me," I said.

"Narcissistic? Yes, but I believe that it is in her narcissism that her artistic felicity resides," Nadia said, the edge gone from her voice. "Too bad she has given up her painting."

"Like I said. I know nothing about art. You've lost me with all of this."

"But you understand Naomi. Her painting is much like she is. It has glamour. Don't you agree?"

"I suppose. You are a very interesting person. I wish I could respond more to your assessment."

"Be a friend to my sister. She may need your support to keep Sam Gatlin at a distance."

"I understand what you're trying to tell me."

"I hope so."

"What's in your urn? I saw you were carrying it around when I came in?"

"Oh, these are Quentin's ashes. Whizzer got them for me."

* * *

Nadia drifted off into the growing crowd. I walked over to the bar, which was separated from the balcony by a beaded curtain. Mr. Abodeely was sitting at the bar. He was wearing a blue-striped, seersucker suit, and with his white hair and ruddy face, he looked distinguished. We shook hands and he thanked me for being part of the team that brought his daughter back.

Mary was there also, dressed in a white summer dress, looking somewhat sad in the late afternoon light. She was leaning on the rail of the east balcony, the one that faced the Tasman Sea, and she waved when she saw me. I wondered what she knew about Reggie's apparent disappearance. Whizzer's guess was that Reggie was on his way back up to Queensland and the Eden Bay commune.

Down in Cronulla Park a group of surfers had gathered. They were jive-assing around, playing Bob Marley tunes on a big boom box, singing along with *I Shot The Sheriff*.

Colin busted my reverie, grabbing my arm. "I need to talk to you. Let's go to Bob's office. Bob and Dr. de Fillio are there. Something terrible has happened, something that will jeopardize the application for Vat Phou becoming a World Heritage Site," Colin said.

* * *

Bob was sitting in a high back chair with his feet up on a teak desk. Dr. de Fillio was sitting across from him on a sturdy teak coffee table. Next to him was the statue of the Devi. I recognized it at once.

"Dr. de Fillio tells me that when you recovered Karl's remains, Miss Swan asked you to load some statues," Colin said.

"That's true. Talk to Naomi about it. It was part of the deal," I replied.

"Was this Devi one of the statues?" Colin asked.

"Yes. What's the big deal?"

"Those statues were art treasures from Vietnam. That's the big deal, and it appears that Dr. von Zielke blew the whistle, so-to-speak. Interpol got involved, as did the Gimet Museum," Bob said.

"Bad news," I replied, my gut beginning to twist.

"That's not the half of it. Miss Swan's been implicated, as was this Captain Katay, who was involved with the recovery of Karl von Zielke's remains. He's already history, shot at sunrise by the Vietnamese," Bob said.

"The Vietnamese? They are involved?" I asked.

"They're all over southern Laos. Vietnam and Cambodia are in an undeclared border war. The Vietnamese intend on trying Miss Swan as a smuggler. That trial is to proceed next week. She is to be tried before a People's Court," Bob said.

"To avoid embarrassment to his portfolio, KV has denied any knowledge of what went down, but Dr. de Fillio tells me that this incident threatens Vat Phou's application to become a World Heritage Site," Colin continued, pacing the floor.

"What are you going to do?" I asked.

"For starters, Dr. de Fillio will be taking back the Devi to KV. KV will save face, presenting the recovered statue to his Vietnamese allies," Bob said.

"Miss Swan is now being held by two of Dub's men, former bodyguards," Dr. de Fillio added.

"Woody tells us that KV doesn't want anything to happen to Miss Swan," Colin said.

"And?" I asked.

"And we go get her, Dai 'ui," Bob said. "She

may be a smuggler, but she is also one of ours. Oh, come on Dai 'ui?" Bob said, thumping his forehead with the base of his hand. "You, Sam, and Graham make one more trip back to Laos. Woody's arranged things in Vientiane, slicked the proper palms, including KV's. He flies Dr. de Fillio and Naomi to KV. Graham flies you and Sam into the old compound. Dub's men have never met Graham so the ruse should work well."

"They think two rich Australians are coming in to buy rare animals for the black market. That deception will allow you and Sam to pick up Miss Swan. Woody will bribe everyone," Colin added.

"We stage tomorrow in Gamoowea. We go in armed this time, and backed up by some Hmong who are former members of the Special Guerilla Unit. You with us?" Bob asked.

"Yeah, I am, if Sam is," I reply.

"You said two Aussies? Who's the other stooge you found to do this?" I asked.

"Oh yes. Why, Whizzer, of course. Now I'm going to go find Sam and tell him about the project. And I'm going to tell him that you are part of it."

Bob and Dr. de Fillio left to find Sam. I was about to follow them when Colin motioned to me,

"A word. We need to talk further," Colin said.

I followed Colin into another room where a large Kirchner painting hung on the wall. It was one the Berlin scenes.

"Bob has a Kirchner," I said.

"Yes, a recent gift from Naomi and me."

"Nice! Very nice!" I replied.

"I need to take you into my confidence. What I am about to tell you should not be shared with either Sam or Naomi. Can I do that, one friend to another?" Colin said, solemnly.

"Sure," I said, wondering if he was going to ask me about Sam's indiscretion with Naomi.

"Miss Swan was doing exactly what I asked her to, by putting the Devi on Woody's plane. Therefore, now you and I must do what we can to bring her out of Laos," Colin said, lighting a Cuban cigar.

"I don't understand. You knew she was stealing art treasures?"

"Yes, I told her to arrange that. Our transporting the Devi was intended to save it from oblivion."

"I gather that Naomi wasn't clued in."

"No. She wasn't. And, ironically, neither was Bob," Colin said with a crafty smile. "Although Naomi would not agree with me on this, these new draconian national ownership laws on antiquities are crippling the acquisition process for the great cosmopolitan museums of the world," Colin said, smugly. "Vietnam doesn't own the legacy of those ancient Cham antiquities any more than the hard yakka drunks down at the Hotel Cecil. My view, and that of Dr. de Fillio, is that such cultural property belongs to the ages, to history, and needs to be studied in the large encyclopedic museums of France, Britain, Germany, and the United States."

"Apparently Dr. von Zielke doesn't share your viewpoint," I said.

"No. Unfortunately he does not. Like Naomi, he ascribes to the 1970 UNESCO convention, a supposed system of rules governing all cultural property, including the paintings in this room. They will both give you some rubbish about the exploitation of the West, about how the big museums and archaeology in general have plundered the cultural wealth and heritage of this or that Third World country."

"Clearly you don't agree with them," I said.

"I find their perspectives both misguided and naive. The legal question is who owns these antiquities. I happen to believe that they belong to humanity as a whole. I view art as a way of creating a new kind of world citizen, one who is more cosmopolitan and civilized. If Miss Swan had not taken the Devi, it would have rotted away, unappreciated in backwater Da Nang."

"But the Devi is still from Vietnam. Yet, you're telling me that it is not part of their heritage."

"Historically, ancient art was often viewed apart from its archaeological setting. The legal term is *cosa morta*, or a dead thing, to cite Italian law."

"And now that has changed?"

"Indeed it has. As a legal concept, cultural property can include almost any form of artistic or intellectual work deemed to be of national value to a particular nation. The Italians now forbid anyone from taking anything out of the country. There will be no end to this fiasco. If I hadn't acted when I did some years ago, our precious collection of Kirchner would still be in some insipid German archive! My God, Abodeely told me that the Greeks now want the British Museum to return the Elgin Marbles."

"Mr. Abodeely? He's part of this?"

Colin took a long draw from his cigar. His reply came through a cloud. "No. Well, yes. In a way he is. Abodeely made quite a bit of money importing antiquities from the former territories of the Ottoman Empire." Colin leaned forward to whisper. "He has a reliquary made in Fatimid Egypt, from the Topkapi Palace art collection of Mehmed II. It is exquisite, crafted of gilt silver around a translucent pink alabaster vessel. Now that's a real hedge against inflation."

"How ironic that Bob doesn't know your involvement with Miss Swan," I said.

"Yes, it is ironic. Bob is oblivious, and I want things to remain that way. You see Bob had this vision called Southeast Asia Company, and he came to our firm to see what could be done. But I am the one who made it all happen with my contacts at the London School of Economics. I got into Laos, not Bob. Miss Swan was one of his former agents, and, of course, they once were lovers. He cares about getting her back," Colin said, soberly. "And he would take exception to my engaging her as a smuggler. If a death sentence wasn't hanging over Miss Swan's head, this would all be quite amusing."

"I don't understand why Bob doesn't simply send in a CIA snatch team to get her."

"Not an option. Miss Swan has been kept on Bob's payroll without the knowledge of his superiors," Colin chuckled.

Colin then sat back and gazed out at the Tasman Sea. Down in Cronulla Park the surfers were still playing the Bob Marley tape. The crowd had grown and they were drinking big bottles of Toohey's Flag Ale. Someone, clearly drunk, was singing along with *No Woman, No Cry*.

"Bob has a big ego, is quite arrogant, actually, and not so clever as he thinks," Colin said, putting out his cigar. "Naomi tells me that Celia is fond of Kirchner, especially the paintings he did of those dancers. When your baby is born, we'd like to give her one of those as a gift," Colin said, smiling.

"That's very generous, Colin, extremely generous," I said, in disbelief.

"Well, you two have been very good friends."

It occurred to me then that Colin was the master of the skull game. He possessed both a gift and a method. His method was to manipulate people through his generosity and the granting of favors. His gift was the charismatic power to arouse intellectual enthusiasm for his own ideas. In many ways he reminded me of Prospero, the clever illusionist from *The Tempest*. I looked down at all the people walking along Ozone Street. The Café Ritz was full of even more people, beautiful people who, like Colin, considered themselves privileged, part of the elite. It was then we heard the screams.

"It's Mary Abodeely! She's jumped from the balcony,“ Nadia said, tears in her eyes.

* * *

Sam, Maggie, Naomi, and Celia, walked back with me to our apartment. Colin stayed behind to help Bob with the police. We sat out on the balcony for a long time, watching the sun go down and listening to the sounds down in Cronulla Park. Then Maggie broke the quiet.

"Sam, did it ever occur to you that if Dai 'ui here had taken time to talk to Mary when she came by looking for him, all this shit might not have happened? You dragged him off on one of your escapades, and a number of people who depended on him, including his lovely wife, have suffered as a result," Maggie said.

Sam stood and faced Maggie. "That escapade was at the request of your brother, or have you forgotten that I work for him?"

Then Maggie rose up, glaring at Sam. "Mary reached out for help from someone she trusted, and because of you that person wasn't there. Just like you're never here for me."

"Maggie, this last trip to Laos was really necessary. Colin insisted," Naomi said.

"Everything Colin wants is always necessary," Maggie snapped. "The only things he really cares about are feeding his face and trying to impress people with his art collection."

"But Sam…" Naomi tried to continue.

"And don't try to defend Sam. I know what's been going on between you two! Sam, plan on sleeping somewhere else tonight besides my apartment. You and I are done. I had hoped to change you. What a fool I was to try."

"I made of mess of things," Sam said humbly.

"That is an understatement!" Maggie was shouting now. "I should have known you couldn't live a life bound by a commitment to another. And you said that I was your one true love! What rubbish! I'll make arrangements to have your belongings delivered. Just send me an address!" She made a swift turn and was out the door.

Sam and Celia ran after Maggie, following her down the stairs. Naomi and I could hear Maggie shouting at Sam, the shouts growing hysterical.

"Why, Naomi?" I asked.

"Why? That should be obvious, even to a naïve Yank like you. Colin doesn't seem to have time for me anymore. And he lies to me. He thinks that I don't know about his little arrangements with Miss Swan. Colin is a fool. So why not indulge, a kind of sweet revenge? As my cousin Ian once said, what would the human heart be if it lived only in the dark, wanting for the moon's splendors?"

"You must be joking? This is about more than an indulgence. This is about betrayal."

"Who has betrayed whom? Think about it. You know, I have failed as a teacher, an artist, and now as a wife. And I can't have children. So, spare me any of your chauvinistic judgments."

"I just don't know what to say," I said, listening to the continued shouting in the stairwell.

Naomi gazed out at the Tasman Sea as she spoke. "Roger that, as Sam likes to say. He certainly was a more than willing partner."

It was clear that any further conversation was pointless. Naomi turned to view herself in the floor length mirror that hung on our wall. The mirror reflected the rising moon and the Dog Star, that brightest of celestial bodies seen as the gateway to the afterlife. I imagined Naomi's translucent form passing through that mirror as if it were a doorway to the infinite, to be reborn.

I was suddenly overcome with a great despair. Mary was gone. That one so beautiful and full of grace could have taken her own life, for whatever reason, left all of us stunned, in a state of profound disbelief. Along with the shocking deaths of Lotus and Quentin, so sudden and meaningless, I felt as if my equilibrium were gone, and that the disturbing events of the past few days would leave permanent scars on all involved.

Sam's search for the things that he had lost would go on, while others, including myself, would remain caught up in the mess that he and Naomi had created. Sam was like that Heavenly Wolf of Chinese myth who guarded the celestial bridge between heaven and hell. With one foot anchored in the past, his passing over that bridge to end his search was prevented until such time that his soul reached perfection. So Sam remained suspended in his own uncertainty, bewitched by his desire for

Naomi, and governed by a saturnine nature given to wild and impulsive behavior. There would be no bridge to ultimate happiness for him in this life.

* * *

Chapter Ten: Gamoowea

There wasn't much talk on the flight to Gamoowea. I was still in a state of shock over Mary's suicide. Colin remained in Sydney for the funeral while the team flew out. My wife was not at all happy with this trip, even though she liked the money I would earn. If Celia had understood the danger, she would have never let me go.

"Well, as they say back in Iowa, it's nut-cutting time," Sam said, examining his Remington 700 BDL sniper rifle. "Dai 'ui, this weapon has a four digit serial number. That means it was in service during the late Sixties in the Nam. The great Carlos Hathcock himself might have used this weapon."

"I met Hathcock on Hill 55 back in July of 1969," I said. "We were on an operation together."

"You never told me that before," Sam said.

"Lots of things I've never told you. Like, I can't believe I'm doing this. I got a kid due in six weeks. I should have my head examined," I said.

"Mary's death shook you up. I can tell," Sam said. "Dai 'ui, you saw all kinds of people wasted in the Nam. So I don't get it. You're not going to chicken-dick out on me, are you?"

Clearly Sam was back to his old callous self. The cynical, world-weary nihilist so relentless in the pursuit of his own purposes had returned, and he could be obnoxious. But Sam was my fellow Marine, and that bonded us in complex ways. There was something true and unambiguous about our friendship that transcended his poisonous behavior.

"No. It's just that I was so close to Mary. And having a KIA in Nam always shook me up."

"Time for a reality check, Dai 'ui. Here, this is your new weapon," Sam said, handing me an AK-

47. “I can’t believe I ate those goddamn mushrooms. I must have been nuts.”

“I tried to get you away from that Wolly Man. But you had a mind of your own,” I replied.

“My mind was in pussy lock over Lotus. It was all about Pussy, Dai ‘ui. Gets me in trouble every time. Maybe I’m the one needing a reality check.”

“Not to mention the blotter acid you ate,” I said.

“Yeah, I think that’s when my problems began.”

I looked out the window as we descended into Gamoowea. It was raining, and the wide yellow, grassy plain was now lush with new growth. To the south, where the great sandstone ridge marked the edge of grassy plain, the open woodlands were teeming with huge flocks of pink and gray Galahs.

Maggie’s study suggested that the Glossy Black Cockatoos living along that sandstone ridge were not stragglers wandering down from Queensland, but a rare breeding population taking advantage of the environment created by the seep and abundant growth of casuarinas. I recalled our visit to the seep, and how Naomi had encouraged Maggie to take that blotter acid. Only a weak hit, she had said, turning our little jaunt into one of Quentin’s reality-blurring events. Reality certainly became blurred that day, as the three of them shed what Naomi called their shallow bourgeois conventions. Sam was right. That was the day things began to fall apart.

* * *

Captain Graham reviewed our plan at least three times that hot, humid afternoon in Gamoowea, covering each person’s role and the steps in the process. We would fly to Laos in the Captain’s Pilatus Porter. After we were on the ground in

Champasak, the Captain and Whizzer would meet with Dub's men. Having been dropped off upriver, Sam and I would rendezvous with a couple of Hmong who would guide us to Miss Swan. While this task was being completed, the captain and Whizzer would purchase a pair of Binturongs, Whizzer having invented a story that Frank Sinatra wanted them for a Hollywood zoo.

* * *

Dinner was a simple meal of steak and baked potatoes, washed down with Foster's Ale. Whizzer raved about the steaks, and dominated the table conversation. Dr. de Fillio, Sam, and Captain Graham hardly spoke. For once Naomi didn't utter a word about what was served. She seemed deep in thought, and sat with Julia after the meal.

All the men withdrew to sit out on the front porch, smoking Cuban cigars, and cleaning their weapons. Graham gave Sam a Ruger .22 pistol with a silencer. Whizzer and I were given Smith & Wesson .38 Specials. Sam was to carry his Remington 700 BDL sniper rifle. Whizzer, Graham, and I carried Russian-made AK-47s, possibly the best assault rifle in the world.

We started swapping stories. Listening to Dr. de Fillio was like being on a page of history. He had shared so many of the great experiences of his time. He had served in World War One, but he didn't look that old. When it was my turn, I told the story of Long Daddy Green, the semi-albino crocodile Sam and I encountered in the Northern Territory. When I finished, Captain Graham yawned.

"Julia and Naomi have turned in for the night. I think I'm ready. You blokes can stay up if you want. By the way, there's a lunar eclipse tonight. You're welcome to drive out to that sandstone ridge by the seep. You'll get the best view there. Take one of the jeeps," Graham said.

Sam, Dr. de Fillio, Whizzer, and I packed into a World War Two vintage Willy's jeep and followed the track to the sandstone ridge. Sam drove, and it took us a half hour. On the way he pulled out a fifth of Jack Daniels.

"Dai 'ui, want a drink?"

"Yeah, why not," I said, passing the bottle to Dr. de Fillio.

The old man took a big pull on the bottle. He then passed it to Whizzer who likewise took a big swig. Sam laughed and shook his head.

* * *

We reached the seep and stepped up onto the series of sandstone ledges until we were on top of the ridge. The various night insects called to each other among the trees, snapping and clicking in the heat. I was amazed how nimble Dr. de Fillio was for such an old man. This was the highest ground around, and the open woodland stretched away in the full moonlight. Even with the moon, one could see the Southern Cross and several constellations.

"Good view of Orion and the Dog Star," Sam said, passing the fifth to Whizzer.

"I had enough, mate. I'm done for the night," Whizzer said, lying back to gaze up at the sky.

Dr. de Fillio took another big swig.

"When I was a young man I made the curious discovery that Sirius, the brightest star in the sky, had a small companion, a white dwarf, as they say.

So, even in its brightest illumination, the Dog Star is accompanied by a perpetual shadow," Dr. de Fillio said, handing the bottle to me.

I should have known better, but I took a swig.

"That's Sam's lucky star," I said.

"In the past the dwarf was more massive than its brother, Sirius. Now it has exhausted its nuclear fuel and faded into this unseen shadow star, an influencing force we have yet to fully understand."

"A unseen star that pulls at its brother," I said.

"Yes, that brings to mind the Devi. In the Shakti tradition of Hinduism, the Devi is the supreme godhead, the source of virtually everything, seen or unseen. She is considered to be the cosmos itself, simultaneously the unseen force and explanation of all creation as well as the energy that animates it, the divine feminine," Dr. de Fillio said.

"Naomi told me about this divine feminine," Sam said. "The worship of a single goddess under many names. That's what Naomi said, as I recall."

"Well Sam, whatever you or Naomi believe, it all ends with the grave," Dr de Fillio said, finishing the Jack Daniels. "All the planets and stars above us are pulled simultaneously in a multitude of directions by the gravitation of black holes we can't see. They are also in the grip of an invisible anti-matter, a kind of metaphorical Devi. Their destiny is to be spun into a flashing wheel of cosmic gas."

"Do you believe that everything is lost with death?" I asked.

"I do," Dr. de Fillio replied.

Whizzer piped up. "I can fucking relate to that,"

"I relate to Jack Daniels," Sam added, cynically.

"Here comes the eclipse!" Whizzer said, scrambling to his feet.

We stood watching the lunar shadow in the heavens. Looking down from my vantage point on the cliff, the pond formed by the seep lay still and deep. The shadow of the earth passed over the moon and the insects stopped their clicking. As the eclipse progressed, my intuition told me Dr. de Fillio was right, that we are all influenced by unseen forces in the cosmos we don't understand, each individual destiny governed by it's own metaphorical Devi.

Dr. de Fillio spoke with quiet intensity. "When you are at the end of your life like I am, and you have a moment such as this, the whole of your life can come flooding back."

"I think I understand," I said, steadying myself.

"What rubbish," Whizzer said quietly.

At the eclipse of the moon we were lucky that there were no clouds. Something was blooming among the trees, the heavy fragrance hanging in the air. As the eclipse ended, the rhythm of the night callers started again, snapping and clicking in the heat. Then a wild squawking began, interspersed with high-pitched shrieks.

"Them's bloody cockatoos," Whizzer said.

We walked along the sandstone ridge toward the direction of the sound. The shrieking grew louder, and when Whizzer shined his flashlight down the cliff face we could see a pair of Glossy Black Cockatoo parents defending a nest in an ancient hollow tree. Two half-grown chicks peered out of the recesses of the nest, stretching their skinny necks. A dark shape was climbing up the tree, the object of the parents' panic. Without hesitation Whizzer pulled his Smith & Wesson .38 Special and emptied it at the dark form.

"Feral cat! Missed the bugger. Make a good

yarn when we get back," he said.

"Whizzer, you can't hit shit," Sam said.

Hearing those Glossy Black Cockatoos shrieking in the night trees I had an uneasy feeling, as if what we were witnessing were a kind of sign, a warning. Dr. de Fillio came over and leaned on my shoulder. The old man was very tired, and I helped him down off the ridge. All the while the Glossy Black Cockatoos kept up with their screaming, their cries like that of a wounded Marine I remembered, calling for help from a distant hedgerow in the darkness. We took a squad to get that Marine, and he kept muttering how he thought we had abandoned him as we pulled him back. Maybe it was the excessive drinking, but that encounter with those Glossy Black Cockatoos was one of those events from my Australian experience that still comes back to haunt me, like the encounter with Long Daddy Green.

* * *

Naomi and Dr. de Fillio took an Air Siam flight to Vientenne to meet with KV. I couldn't help but recall how bribes are viewed as part of the *Les Regles de Jeu.* Naomi said what had happened during that last trip was all part of a previously written script. So now the story continued with Captain Graham and Whizzer posing as Aussie smugglers involved in the illegal animal trade. It was a credible story.

We flew up the Mekong beyond the town of Champasak and dropped into a recently cleared field. It was almost noon, and to the east several hundred acres of coffee trees stretched away toward the Bolovens Plateau. Sam and I jumped out of the plane and ran into the cover of the coffee trees, linking up with our two Hmong guides. Captain Graham spun the plane around and immediately took off for Colonel Dub's old airstrip. He wasn't on the ground more than a minute, at most.

Woody had recruited our two guides from the Ban Vinai Refugee Camp. The short one looked to be in his late forties, the tall one in his thirties. Both had grown up with conflict, fighting all their adult lives. The tall one had an elephant head tattooed on his right shoulder so we nicknamed him Elephant. He liked that. The short one became Shorty.

We were only a kilometer from Colonel Dub's compound. We followed the river to find Colonel Dub's large, sprawling plantation house hadn't changed since our last visit. According to Woody, Colonel Dub's old bodyguards had assumed control over his property.

* * *

Behind the plantation house was that long building that had once stored coffee. A single truck was parked in front of the warehouse, packed with crates of various sizes. A lone guard was standing outside the building to greet us.

Not much taller than Shorty, I guessed him to be in his fifties. He had a shock of gray hair under his Pathet Lao style rain hat, and had a big smile on his face. He beckoned us into the warehouse.

Miss Swan was waiting for us, having been freed from her locked quarters by the smiling Laotian who was supposed to guard her. All part of the *Les Regles de Jeu*, I thought to myself, along with the appropriate and well-placed bribes, of course.

* * *

We left immediately, and the Laotian guard came with us. His getting out of Laos was obviously part of the deal. Our timing proved to be excellent. For no sooner had we entered a cluster of coffee trees than Captain Graham and Whizzer appeared. Behind them were Colonel Dub's bodyguards, each carrying a cage containing a young Binturong.

Just as they were boarding the plane a truck drove up with a squad of Vietnamese soldiers in the back. Graham revved his engines and turned the plane down the strip. A Vietnamese officer jumped out of the truck, yelling and waving his arms. Graham ignored the officer and started down the strip. The officer ordered his men to shoot, pulling out his pistol and firing at the cockpit. I saw one of the rounds shatter the windscreen and hit Whizzer.

"Fucker shot Whizzer!" I said.

Sam dropped prone and sighted in on the officer with his Remington BDL. It was a mere hundred yard shot and the officer's head literally disappeared. Captain Graham must have seen the shot because he was down the strip and into the air, brushing the treetops.

"Dai 'ui, we got to take out that squad! All they have are bolt-action rifles. I'll pin them down while you and Shorty flank them!"

The Vietnamese were all young, unseasoned soldiers. Their uniforms appeared brand new and there was little wear on their web gear. Sam dropped two of them in a matter of seconds. The other two threw their weapons and tried to run. Shorty caught those two with a sustained burst from his AK-47. One brave Vietnamese soldier stood his ground and fired his rifle at Sam. The round went wide and struck our smiling Laotian guard square in the chest. Shorty's next burst cut the last Vietnamese in half. Then we were into the trees.

Five minutes later, we made radio contact with Captain Graham. Whizzer had taken a round through his cheek, a flesh wound, but he was in need of medical attention immediately. Graham was taking him back to Thailand. We were to proceed north and wait at our rendezvous site.

* * *

Chapter Eleven: Elephant And Shorty

A straight mud beach stretched along the east bank of the Mekong for about a mile in both directions. We recognized the stretch of beach on our map and proceeded, moving north to our rendezvous site. A thick, dark single-canopy forest grew down to the riverbank.

"Shorty, I think we should head down this beach. We can move fast and get a head start on any NVA patrol who may come looking for us," Sam said.

"No do! Numba Ten," Shorty said.

"We have to get some distance between us and any NVA, real quick-like," Sam said.

So, against the advice of Elephant and Shorty, we made our way along the beach. Elephant and Shorty were fearful of remaining so close to the Mekong, and kept asking to head inland. They wanted to travel across country to the safety of a friendly upland village.

I wanted to stay put and wait for dark. At night we could move with less fear of being observed from the river. But the Hmong were afraid of night movement so far from their home territory. Impatient with me, and as a precautionary measure, Sam wondered if we should split our team. Elephant knew of a cave in a karst outcropping just ahead. However, the cave was not big enough for all of us.

* * *

When we reached the far end of the mud beach, Miss Swan asked if she could rest. There was a bend in the Mekong at that spot that prevented us from continuing. At that point I was worried that Elephant and Shorty would abandon us. Miss Swan must have also sensed this because she told them in Laotian that Sam had been on the ground in Laos during his second tour in Southeast Asia, and that he had a sense of the terrain, having done some of his training in the area. When Elephant and Shorty heard this, they seemed to brighten up.

"Do you think these guys are going to bug out?" I asked Sam.

"I don't think so. They are both former members of the Special Guerrilla Unit, and it would shame their relatives back at the refugee camp if they abandoned us. Miss Swan is doing fine. My guess is that the NVA are tracking us, and it's only a matter of time before they catch up. She says we should head inland to this big karst. Maybe lay chilly for a while," Sam replied.

"Roger that. You know best."

"Maybe. If we have to separate, Elephant can take Miss Swan and me upriver to our rendezvous point. You and Shorty put a hurt on whoever's tracking us. I got a bag with two claymores and five toe-poppers. Take it and lay down some shit behind you that may slow them up."

"Shorty know how to get to this karst?"

"Affirmative, but it's also on the map. I'll show you. Between here and there we need to find a second rendezvous point, in case we split. Be on the lookout for that."

"Sounds like a good plan. I'm going to set a couple of these toe poppers right here. If we're being tracked, as you suspect, we'll hear something," I said.

* * *

Shorty scouted the edge of the single canopy forest for several hundred yards in either direction but could find no trails, only dark, endless forest stretching inland. Elephant said there was a large stream flowing into the Mekong a half a kilometer or so upriver. So we broke through the underbrush until we found that stream. It was fast flowing, with a gravel bottom, and offered us a way inland.

We pressed upstream as quickly as possible. Miss Swan, however, was not up to the pace, and had to rest. About that time we heard one of the toe-poppers go off.

"They're behind us," Sam said.

"Yeah, for sure," I replied, chambering a round into my AK-47.

About a quarter kilometer further on we came upon a wide area that had been timbered out, a maze of brush and huge stumps. There we found a sizeable lone tree that was hollow, and thus had been spared the timber pirates.

"Maybe I should climb that tree and have a look around," Sam said.

When Sam was about half-way up the trunk, he called down to me.

"We have about a hundred NVA walking on line about three hundred yards to our left. I'm going to help you set the rest of the toe-poppers."

A large group of NVA was attempting to make their way through the heavy brush. The new growth of bamboo and thorny tangles was making their progress difficult. We set the remaining toe-poppers, knowing that we had NVA behind us and to our left front.

"Time to split up, Dai 'ui. I'll take Miss Swan and Elephant. You and Shorty should head to this village off in that far ridgeline. Maybe draw the

NVA your way, what do you think?"

"It's worth a try. You keeping the radio?"

"I think I better. We'll hunker down. Give it a day or so. Then we rendezvous at this tree. We're less than a kilometer from our pick-up point. If you can't get back, hang out in that friendly ville. I'll know where to find you."

* * *

Shorty and I crossed the cutover area in front of the line of NVA, making for the tall forest on the far side. One of their scouts must have had sharp eyes. We were halfway across when we heard him shout. The NVA were two hundred yards from us when they opened up, spraying the area with a heavy volume of fire. A random AK-47 round struck Shorty in the hip, spinning him around once before he hit the dirt.

When I got to him I saw that he was gut shot, his blue and cream-colored innards spilling out of where the round made its exit from his body. The blood flow was slow, but I could see it in his eyes. He knew he was history. He was a tough little guy, and nodded to the far timber for me to go, biting his lip because of the pain. I was surprised when he handed me his wallet.

"Go my ville, go!" He said, pointing to a path that led toward higher ground. "Take money to my family. Go my ville. Go now!"

Then he pointed to the two grenades I was carrying on my belt, and I understood. I gave him the frags and slung his AK-47 over my shoulder.

A round cracked close, passing next to my ear, and I looked up to see that the NVA line was running toward us. A young NVA officer, a lieutenant with a new uniform, was leading the charge, his pistol in one hand, waving his men forward with the others. The fool was running in a straight line, directly at me. I drew down on his midsection and squeezed off a round. His pith helmet was still flying through the air when I looked up from my shot.

The advancing line of NVA dropped to the ground, realizing their mistake. It was too late. Their rash charge across the open area exposed them, even though they lay prone. Then I heard the Remington 700 BDL and saw an NVA head disappear in a red mist.

Through his Urthel scope Sam was close enough to read the lettering on the NVA uniforms. When an NVA senior Staff NCO tried to get to the wounded lieutenant, Sam put a round through his guts. As quickly as he could chamber a round, Sam was taking out NVA. As Woody would have said, this was a piece of cake. I counted seven hits and the NVA platoon was in chaos.

One of the wounded NVA was shrieking, and I couldn't help but recall those Glossy Black Cockatoos we had encountered in Gamoowea. Shorty poked me in the side and pointed to our right where several NVA were trying to flank me. I dropped one immediately and the others withdrew. But it was clear that my time with Shorty was up. The little guy again pointed to the forest, never uttering a word. I watched him pull the pins on the two grenades. Then he rolled over, feigning death, with the grenades placed next to his belly. I felt like such a coward, leaving him like that. But that's the way it went down, with him wanting to go out taking a couple of NVA. For a brief moment I listened to the terrible sobbing cries of the wounded

NVA, then I made for the edge of the forest.

* * *

As soon as I reached the forest I found some cover. A moment later I heard the frag grenades explode. These guys are rookies, I thought. After the frags went off a number of them ran up to what was left of Shorty. I watched them standing around while one of them appeared to be searching Shorty's body. My jaw dropped when I saw him hold in the air what I believed to be Shorty's quivering liver. It was still steaming. Back in the Nam I had heard the stories of those who ate the livers of their enemies. I was drawing down on the liver-eater when I saw his lower jaw disappear. Sam was still in the game, and the NVA dropped back, giving me more valuable time. At a mere two hundred yards, for a Marine like Sam, it was more like target practice.

* * *

On the far side of the forest I moved deeper in a thicket of tall dry cane. I continued to head away from the Mekong through these dense tangles, following a compass azimuth toward what my map told me was the friendly village. I could see a lot of high ground between the village marked on my map and me. But in the tall, dense thickets, I couldn't make out any landmark.

When I stumbled on a path through the cane I was tempted to follow it. The going would be easier but I knew that it was only a matter of time before the NVA trackers would come looking. They couldn't miss my trail through the cane break.

There was no way to cover my trail, or was there?

I remembered a story about the Viking King, Harald Hardrata, and of how he used fire to create a diversion, and thus escaped pursuit from a band of mounted knights. Kneeling, I checked the wind. It was blowing in the right direction. Then I gathered some grass and broken cane together, lighting the pile with my Zippo. Soon I had a fire blazing, with the wind taking the flames westward toward the Mekong, covering the ground from whence I came, consuming the trail I left behind.

* * *

Once out of the cane thickets, I passed through an area overgrown with scrub and mature bamboo. The ground started to rise. On either side of me, sharp, limestone karsts jutted up through distant trees. Then I entered a gigantic forest like no other I had ever seen, even in Vietnam. This was triple-canopy hardwood forest, where the trees soared, sometimes reaching a maximum diameter of six or seven feet, with branches starting at sixty feet. The height and spreading tops of the trees prevented the sun from penetrating to the ground. Under this dark canopy, further shaded by vines that ran up the massive trunks to spread out their foliage in the sunlight above, there was no underbrush. The forest floor was too dark. Only small, broad-leaved plants survived between the trees.

I could walk with ease among the great trunks. Moving up a slope, I found the terrain crisscrossed by game trails only a few inches wide, leaving just enough space for a runner, or a squad-sized patrol to pass in single file. The stillness was disconcerting. The forest was silent, but for the occasional sparrow-like call of a bird high up in the gloom of the trees. Every turn in the trail was a possible ambush.

* * *

The ground continued to get steeper, and I saw that I was at the foot of a steep cliff. For the better part of an hour, I scaled its face, being careful to keep within the cover of the vegetation. Once I reached the top the views were staggering, even in the late twilight. To the east, the undulating green of the impenetrable forest stretched away as far as I could see. To the north, tight ravines tumbled into rolling piedmont hills thick with that telltale light green of mature bamboo. To the west, a cloud of dense smoke rose, marking the spread of the fire that I started earlier.

Beyond the rising smoke, I could see the winding Mekong. Whichever way I turned my eye, I was confounded by a vast landscape broken by deep valleys and rugged karsts that jutted up above the green expanse of the forest. There was no way I was going to find Shorty's friendly village. It was out there somewhere, lost in the hazy distances, distances that melted away into the distant clouds on the horizon. I kept thinking back to how I had left Shorty. I took out his wallet and looked through it. There was a lot of money in American greenbacks as well as several family photos, including one of two twin girls in their teens. I began to shiver. I stood on that high place, feeling abandoned and totally alone.

* * *

Under a rock overhang I found some shelter. But a thunder crash brought me to my knees. It seemed as if the very earth shook with each thunderclap. Lightning flashed all around me, spearing the high ridges. Blasted by the cold wind, I crouched under a rock ledge for some protection from the icy rain. Eventually I was able to build a small fire from scattered brush and leaves.

I was disgusted with the turn of events, my running away from the NVA and leaving Shorty. How could I face any Hmong I encountered? What would I tell them, that I left one of their own, while I watched his quivering liver pulled from his body? I recalled that the Roman Stoic philosopher Seneca had something to say about death and honor. But I couldn't remember the exact phrase. Better to die than suffer dishonor, something like that. In the morning I would retrace my steps and find out what happened to Sam, maybe even avenge Shorty.

Thunder crashed again. In my mind's eye I could see Celia and her sister having coffee on the balcony of our condo. Fatigue was taking its effect. The vision of Celia drew closer and I reached out, but her image quickly spun away, rushing down the path toward the forest. Then I fell into an exhausted sleep.

* * *

The next morning when I awoke I could hear elephants calling in the jungle below me. I watched a Binturong robbing a bird's nest high up in the trees. Then I saw a giant hot pink millipede crawl from under the rock overhang where I had spent the night. It was the deadly poisonous Desmoxytes, yet to be fully described by science, according to Dr.

Carlton-Smythe. I froze, holding my breath. Two feet long and thick as an Aussie breakfast sausage, the millipede scurried over my boot and disappeared under the leaves.

I got up slowly and started to retrace my steps toward the Mekong, getting closer to the elephants. Once out of the triple-canopy forest, I found them feeding in the thick cane. Although they were clearly a wild herd, they didn't seem bothered by my presence in their territory.

My plan was to keep in the cover of the cane thickets that dominated what I now realized was a gradual slope down to the Mekong, a kind of savannah, with occasional thick patches of jungle. When I moved into another extended patch of triple canopy, I felt another presence among the huge trees soaring above me.

In the distance I could hear someone firing signal shots. My guess was NVA scouts were signaling back and forth to one another. I wound my way slowly downhill, using the massive trunks for cover. I reached a spot I remembered where two trails crossed. Although the trail was only a few feet wide, I could clearly read the sign. A group of men had passed this way in single file. In the gloom of the forest, where every turn in the trail was a possible ambush, I sat down to listen. NVA trail watchers could be waiting for me. I could smell smoke from what must have been a cooking fire, and realized that I must be closer to that friendly village than I thought. So I moved toward the smell of the smoke, still going downhill, but parallel to the trail.

* * *

I finally found the tiny hamlet, if one would call it that. There were only four structures, small log houses on stilts. A cooking fire smoldered, and to the right of the fire the bodies of two young men lay on the ground, shot execution style in the back of the head, hands bound behind their backs. Both had been gutted, their private parts removed and thrown in the dirt. A naked toddler wandered in a daze through the small clearing. Then I heard a woman sobbing. Two NVA rapists were taking turns with a pair of teen-age Hmong women.

Apparently an NVA patrol had found this Hmong hideaway. A third NVA, maybe eighteen years old, stood by guarding an older Hmong man who sat on the ground with his hands tied in front of him. The third NVA had brand new web gear, obviously a raw recruit, and he stared at the two rapists in shock, clearly distracted. I then noticed the two women looked alike. They were the twins in Shorty's photo. I could have walked away from that terrible scene. But I wouldn't have been able to live with myself. My AK-47 had one of those wicked, fold out bayonets. I unfolded it.

One of the rapists, clearly a senior staff NCO from the look of him, snickered, and then called to the recruit to join in. The recruit shook his head, turning just as I clubbed him in the head with my AK-47. The snickering one was on one knee, trying to pull his pistol when he took a full butt stroke to the face, knocking him back upon the second rapist who was tangled up and trying to withdraw. With one quick movement I brought my metal butt stock down on the second rapist's head.

The recruit rose to one knee, whimpering and spitting out teeth, blood pouring from his smashed nose. The old Hmong leaped to his feet, his hands still tied, and grabbed the recruit from behind in a deadly stranglehold. The staff NCO raised his hands as if to surrender but the woman he had raped already had his pistol in her hand. Before I could stop her she fired a round into the back of his head. A bright red stream sprayed out of his forehead like a fountain, covering the two women with blood. She then turned to the second rapist just as he was lifting his head. He blinked, his eyes wide in shock, as she pulled the trigger.

* * *

The old Hmong man gathered up the toddler and we were out of there, leaving the three dead NVA. The twins were indeed Shorty's daughters, the toddler his grandson, and the old man his brother. I gave them Shorty's wallet with the money and photos. They understood, and eventually took me down a trail back toward the Mekong. I watched them disappear into the forest, heading upland.

For the better part of an hour, I traveled downhill, staying just off the trail. The jungle changed to single canopy, with more patches of cane and clumps of tall bamboo. Just as I was about to enter one of the cane thickets I spotted three trail watchers. Only one was watching the trail, leaning against a tree and looking away from me. Two others were dozing before a small fire, their weapons bolt-action rifles. No automatic weapons!

For a moment I thought I might be able to slip by them but that was not the case. I failed to see that there was a fourth trail watcher in one of the trees above me, and he shouted to the others. I blew him out of the tree with a quick burst; then sprayed the others at point blank range. The last thing I recall was running among the massive trees, weaving and dodging downhill, plunging recklessly to reach cover in the thick cane.

* * *

I stayed off the trails, making my way through the burned-out area until I found my way back to the one sure landmark, the large hollow tree Sam had designated as our rendezvous. Once at the tree, I could see that bend in the Mekong with the straight muddy beach. I crouched down and waited in the twilight. Then from inside the hollow tree I heard a whisper.

"Dai 'ui, I thought you bought the farm," Sam whispered.

"Sam, you are safe," I whispered back.

"Quiet. The NVA are searching all around us. Elephant took Miss Swan to the strip where Woody flew them out. We're supposed to wait till nightfall, and head downriver along that long strand of muddy shore. Woody is sending a boat to pick us up. They will radio us when they are in position," Sam said. "Party is almost over," he added, smiling.

"Thanks for sticking around. You saved my bacon with that Remington," I said.

"There were too many NVA, or I would have followed your trail to see if you were still alive. I decided to hang around this tree, hoping that you would return," Sam said.

"I saw you get the liver-eater," I said

"Yeah, Want a shot of Jack Daniels?" Sam asked.

"Roger that. Big time!"

* * *

The boat pick-up went smoothly. When we returned to the Ban Vinai Refugee Camp, Naomi, Colin, and Woody were waiting for us. Colin said that Whizzer's wound was under control. However, the Thai police were looking for Miss Swan. Interpol had contacted the Thai authorities. Colin had asked Captain Graham to fly Miss Swan on to Hong Kong right away. Woody was to fly us back by way of Wat Tham Krabok Monastery. Naomi was taking more sick Hmong kids to the abbot.

The fact that Interpol was on Miss Swan's trail worried me. When he blew the whistle, Dr. von Zielke passed Miss Swan's photo on to Interpol. Interpol then sent her photo worldwide, and she was now on the global wanted list for the crimes of money-laundering and art theft.

* * *

Once again the abbot was there to meet us. This time he had about thirty monks with him. Naomi went to greet the abbot while Sam and I off-loaded the sick Hmong refugees. Per his role, Woody checked and re-checked the plane.

Colin stood apart, under the shade of a big tree, making notes in his little book. After we finished the off-loading, he motioned us over to him.

"I called you both over to let you know that this is our final mission. I'm shutting down the company for good, including the branch offices in Hong Kong and Jo-burg. Consider this a two-week notice," Colin said, coldly.

"What? Just like that?" Sam asked, surprised.

"Yes, just like that. Sam, you won't be traveling back to Australia with the rest of us. Woody will take us to Bangkok and then come back to fly you to Hong Kong. You can help close our Tower Centre office. Where you go from there is up to you."

"Then it's over," Sam replied.

"Indeed, in more ways than one. Nadia told me that she thought you and Naomi were involved. I told her that was rubbish, and that Naomi would never indulge in such an indiscretion, especially with a big dumb Yank who was nobody."

Colin's response surprised me. Clearly he was not prepared to walk away from his adored Naomi. Maybe the history they shared, the emotional dossier they carried, was too great for them to part. Yet, if there were any lessons learned from all this, they seemed to be irrelevant. I think it was Anais Nin, the French writer, who said that we don't see things as they are; we see things as we are.

"Well, Dai 'ui, look how Colin Musto has turned. You notice, come nut-cutting time, he never crossed the Mekong with us," Sam was talking to me, but glaring at Colin.

I was speechless, and just shook my head. Sam was just warming up.

"But that's okay. Colin would have been out of place with Captain Graham, you, me, even Whizzer. You know Colin, Naomi has a lot of sand. She's not afraid to do her part when called upon," Sam said.

"What was that Naomi told me this morning, something about the road to redemption being through good works? Think about that! Goodbye," Colin said, walking to the plane.

"You're a lot like your sister, Colin, overly controlling, self-righteous, and pumped-up by your own ideas. If you were ever in combat you'd be dead," Sam called after him.

Colin stopped, turned back toward us, and with a smile said. “That’s why Bob and I hired a fool like you. But I’ll take your thoughts under advisement.”

Colin continued toward the plane. Now Sam was loud enough for the monastery to hear.

“But you know what else Colin, you’re no fun! If Naomi didn’t organize your social life, you wouldn’t have any friends! And you surround yourself with a bunch of phonies who kiss your ass! You’re not a real Australian at all, are you?”

Colin stopped and turned.

“Sam, keep away from me! And say your goodbyes to Naomi when she kneels before the abbot to talk of her redemption. Maybe you should be kneeling there beside her.”

“You used me, Colin. Just like you use folks like Captain Graham and the Dai ‘ui here. You’re like that sneaky Emu-Man you told us about, the one who transformed himself into a snake.”

“Correction, the Emu-Man became a Rainbow Serpent, not a mere snake. Thank God my sister didn’t marry you,” Colin said, walking to the plane.

The sun dipped below the horizon as I boarded the Pilatus. A tree frog croaked in the dense bamboo, and the air had that pervasive, musky smell that came with the rainy season in Southeast Asia. The Hmong children and the monks were singing, smiling, waving to us as we lifted off in the twilight.

Sam and Naomi were in front of the crowd. Naomi stood with her arms folded and head down, and we could see that Sam had put his arm around her. From that distance Sam looked very sad.

Across the Mekong, that infamous river of bad memories, southern Laos was reeling under the impact of the Pathet Lao, but the warlord, Colonel

Dub, was dead. KV, the power broker, was continuing the advance of socialism. More technical professionals and educators would flee the country in the coming months. But Naomi Musto had made it her mission to help them, part of her unfinished business, what she was to call her personal road to redemption.

Later I learned from Woody what happened the next day. Woody witnessed the actual event where Naomi and Sam both knelt before the abbot. Given a generous donation left by Colin, the abbot was quite obliging. Chanting the good luck prayer, the abbot tied a red piece of braided yarn around each of their wrists, first Naomi, then Sam, kissing both on the cheek, and blessing the new path each was to take. An hour later Woody was in the air, whisking Sam off to Hong Kong, and leaving Naomi behind to pursue her new path.

* * *

Chapter Twelve: Old Trails

After we abandoned Sam in Thailand, I returned to Cronulla to hear that Reggie's body had been found floating in Gunnamatta Bay. The body had been in the water quite a while, and that made me wonder if Mary had known somehow, precipitating her jump from Bob's balcony. The authorities suspected foul play since drugs were found in the body. I called Whizzer for some answers. Whizzer met me at the Café Ritz, having done some checking.

"Reggie overdosed while skin-popping heroin for the first time," Whizzer said.

So Whizzer was right. Bryan and Malcolm had been dealing heroin in Cronulla.

"My guess is that Brian Hully slipped Reggie a high-speed dose, an act of retribution for our pulling him and Mary out during the raid at Wollumbin Falls. A real shame," Whizzer added.

Reggie's parents were having a memorial service. But I just couldn't bring myself to attend. Whizzer also mentioned that his wife and son had arrived safely in Sydney, and that Bob was leaving Australia, retiring to Las Vegas.

I heard from Woody that for a time Sam found security work in Hong Kong. Once back in the States, Sam sent us a letter saying he had no hard feelings, writing that Miss Swan was living in Hong Kong with a drug lord, and had refused to see him.

When we left Australia, Naomi gave Celia a small Kirchner painting. It was one of those that hung on their west wall depicting several couples dancing and embracing, very erotic. I would have preferred a painting from their south wall, one of those haunting scenes from a Berlin nightclub.

Celia likes what she calls the soul in Kirchner's work. Maybe that was an effect of all the absinth he drank.

That should have been a warning for me. After we left Australia, I picked up the habit of drinking three or four absinthes a day, preferably Absinth Mata Hari made in Austria, sixty per cent alcohol by volume, and a vivid emerald green. It is very dry on the palate, with faint aromas of lemon and lime.

After my third absinth I would hallucinate, traveling those old trails again. I never used to believe in things called ghosts. But I have learned there are things that return to haunt us, feeding our fears. I have also come to believe that there is a grand design, an interconnected framework infinite in its possibilities, one that we can know only inductively through the signs and the synchronous events that arise throughout our lives.

Lately I have been helping those less fortunate than myself get on their feet again, especially homeless veterans. Maybe the good Karma that results from that will lead me to some redemption. At the end of *The Searchers,* John Wayne seems to find the kind of deliverance where he is at peace with both his past and present. I wish I could do that with my life.

At times I will wake from a dream, troubled by a distant recollection, only to lay sleepless until daybreak, still hearing those high-pitched shrieks. When lying awake I draw comfort from playing old tunes. Whenever I play Bob Marley and the Wailers, especially *No Woman, No Cry,* I can see the surfers gathering in Cronulla Park, singing along to a boom box and messing around. Quentin is telling the tale of how he looked into the sullen eyes of that White Pointer in the clear green deep that bright day off North Cronulla Beach. Winsome Mary is also there, dressed in a sleeveless, white cotton dress. She is arm-and-arm with Reggie, and they are watching the full moon rise over Shark Island, out where the sky meets the water, the breeze lifting the fronds of the Washingtonian Palms ever so slightly.

Our family finally settled down in the mountains west of Denver, and for thirty years I've followed old trails used by the Mountain Utes, tracking wildlife through the snow, often at first light. Every spring I walk the high meadows to where the bull elk shed their antlers, the magpies scolding me through the scrub-oaks. While the weather is still cool, and before the snakes come out, I find the new paths along the Front Range where deer bed down to watch the lights stretching away across the plains. When the high country is swept by sudden rain, with Denver's office towers glinting in the distance, Southeast Asia seems no more than an abstraction, a history as cryptic as the rock pictures left by the ancients along the Arkansas River. Up here, for a time, a mind can leave behind what remains unresolved to find the kingfisher tunneling into a clay bank within a narrow canyon, and glimpse the otters on their muddy slick. Some habits are hard to break, and a natural inclination takes me down old trails, especially in the dark of the night. But I no longer believe that everything is lost with death.

* * *

Epilogue

Of all the tales from my in-county Australian experiences, the story of Long Daddy Green is the most hair-raising. But as I have learned since then, retelling the story of a traumatic event can have tremendous healing power; and over time, whenever I would tell the tale, the chronic pain in my leg seemed to lessen.

Woody wrote me that Colin was still telling the story of Long Daddy Green in 1984 when he placed third in the Australian Malt Whiskey Tasting Championships held at Bondi. Naomi had just returned from Thailand and her ongoing work with the Hmong children. After the tasting they continued on with their marathon drinking, opening a bottle of 1962 *Chateau D'Yquem,* which Colin liked to call one of the great wines of the century.

They dined that night at a fine restaurant in Crow's Nest, celebrating with perfect black winter Perigord truffles imported from France, the occasion warranting the best. The slow service brought out Naomi's belligerent streak. And perhaps Naomi's loud complaints angered the Rainbow Serpent. For Colin rolled over his vintage canary-yellow MG on the way back to Ozone Street, killing both himself and Naomi.

Years later, as Sam was lying in a hospital bed dying of Agent Orange-related cancer, I brought him up-to-date on Colin and Naomi. I also told him about a giant feral hog weighing 480 pounds that Woody shot out at the Pilbarra Cattle Station in Western Australia, and of how Whizzer met his sad end during rush hour in the middle of Sydney's Central Station, dropping dead of a heart attack at forty-eight.

Of course, we talked one last time about Long Daddy Green, and recalled how Colin had rambled on endlessly about the dreaming places, and of myths like the Emu Man and the Namarrgan Sisters. Sam even managed a brief chuckle, wondering if Colin, Naomi, and Long Daddy Green were waiting to greet him on the other side, in that common dream place where all our creation ancestors meet.

* * *

That day we left what was to become Kakadu National Park, Maggie felt compelled to report our encounter with Long Daddy Green to a couple of rangers. Further travel through his home area was banned; and eventually the rangers captured and relocated Long Daddy Green to preserve him from illegal hunters, going so far as to deny his existence to a reporter from the Sydney Morning Herald.

After Maggie and Sam finally parted company, Celia and I exchanged Christmas letters with her for some years. In 1987 she married a fellow teacher from the UK. Those two still live in Taree, and have three boys, all of whom play Rugby League. Colin would have been proud of that.

Maggie made a livelong study of the Glossy Black Cockatoos. With the help of Captain John Graham, Julia, and their two daughters, all of whom still live in Gamoowea, the area surrounding the seep has been made into a bird sanctuary.

My daughter, Inga, occasionally travels to Australia on business. She turned thirty on her last trip to Sydney, and took an extra day to visit Ozone Street. Many of the older buildings have been torn down, making way for more high-rise condos. But the bathing pool where I once found a tiny octopus remains along the promenade, and during the night

Ring Tail Possums still peer down from the Washingtonian Palms in Cronulla Park.

After all these years, when waxing through a sentimental reminiscence with my grandchildren, I like to share with them how it is with Aboriginal oral tradition, and the way stories are passed on, stories often expressing continuity between nature and what my wife, Celia, likes to call the imperishable realm of the eternal soul. Maybe passing on the story helps us transcend our own perishable bodies, and, in the telling, a spirit is enabled that lives on in the memories of those who heard the tale, and who will pass along the story once again. That process is truly a form of real and enduring immortality.

Upon being relocated, Long Daddy Green disappeared for a period, going back upriver to the dreaming places of the Namarrgarn Sisters, out of the reach of those seeking to take his photo or covet his hide. Maggie wrote that a longtime bushman and former buffalo hunter named Max reported seeing him a number of times in the past thirty years. Max claims Long Daddy Green is a grand eighteen footer now, living in an isolated backwater overhung by ancient red gums. There he waits, listening to the flies buzz, and to the squawks and whistles of the Glossy Black Cockatoos, careful not to disturb the Rainbow Serpent.

* * *

Historical Note

In the late 1950s, Southeast Asia, including Laos, became an important region with the fall of China to communism and the emerging communist rebellion in Vietnam. America sent its Green Berets to train Hmong guerrillas to oppose the Vietnamese and Pathet Lao. Then in the 1960s and 1970s, the Central Intelligence Agency of the United States supported and funded an army made up of members of the preliterate, aboriginal Hmong tribe who lived on the Plain of Jars and the area of the famed Ho Chi Minh trail in Laos. In 1961, General Vang Pao, with CIA assistance, organized an army of 9000 men. The word Hmong means "free man" and they proved to be extremely loyal and dedicated guerrilla freedom fighters for the Americans engaged in the Secret War in Laos. There they rescued downed pilots, and cut off supplies coming down the trail through the Annamese Cordillera mountain range in Laos that were destined for South Vietnam and the North Vietnamese Army (NVA). By 1963, the CIA increased this secret army to 20,000 to fight America's second war, the air war in Laos where by 1968 U.S. pilots battled thousands of communist troops and flew 300 sorties a day.

When South Vietnam fell in April 1975, the Hmong people were abandoned by U. S. politicians and suffered from a campaign of retribution by communists who still today hunt them down in the heavy jungles and imprison them in communist internment-refugee camps. A Vietnamese broadcast called for their complete extermination and evidence of chemical warfare against their villages was proven. Facing this obvious genocide the

United States began accepting Hmong refugees and by 1990 about 100,000 had entered and become citizens. Many have settled in California, Iowa, Minnesota, and Colorado.

The Hmong refugee exodus came in phases with the first lasting from 1975 to 1977. That phase, mostly soldiers from the secret army and their families, settled in Ban Vinai. Another phase occurred between 1978 and 1982, a period when both lowland and highland Laotians fled the compulsory farm collectivization enforced by the Lao communist government. As the exodus grew the United Nations set up additional camps, with most refugees living in squalid conditions. During the final phase, from 1982 to 1986, as persecution of the Hmong grew with the resistance movement, the numbers of Laotian refugees living in Thailand grew to about 75,000, of which about 54,000 were Hmong in Ban Vinai and Chiang Kham camps.

By the mid-1980s, the Ban Vinai camp had grown to over 45,000 people living on approximately 400 acres. Repression of the Hmong in Laos and declining economic conditions contributed to the steady flow of Hmong refugees into Thailand. Development assistance from the West was minimal, with refugees depending on camp rations from the UNHCR and other humanitarian organizations, such as Wat Tham Krabok Monastery, for survival.

In December 2003, the United States finally announced its intentions to consider for resettlement the Hmong at Wat Tham Krabok. That process has since moved forward. Yet, today many of the Hmong who are living in this country, and who fought as the loyal and brave warriors of the SGU (Special Guerrilla Unit) led by General Vang Pao have no access to benefits with our Veterans Administration. Just as Congress recognized the role of the Philippine Scouts who fought alongside our servicemen in World War II, granting them well-earned benefits, so too the Congress should grant similar rights to those Hmong of the SGU. They were responsible for saving many pilots, and many other American fighting men, measured in NVA soldiers and supplies that were stopped cold on the Ho Chi Minh Trail in Laos, and did not make it to the war effort in South Vietnam.

- Bob Fischer, Colonel USMC, (Ret), Former advisor to the Vietnamese Marine Corps, and Lecturer on Strategy and Tactics of the Insurgent, Naval War College

Replica of the Devi

Photo by Dave Scott

Hotel Cecil, Cronulla, NSW 1976

Photo by Author

Author on Ozone Street. Cronulla, NSW 1976

Photo by Author

About the Author

Dan Guenther was a captain in the U.S. Marine Corps. His first three novels, *China Wind*, (Ivy, 1990) (Redburn, 2007), *Dodge City Blues* (Redburn, 2007), and *Townsend's Solitaire* (Redburn, 2008), were based on his combat tours in Vietnam. Subsequent to leaving active duty with the Marine Corps, Guenther spent two years working in Australia and traveling throughout the South Pacific. Dan has also published poetry in several small magazines and anthologies, most recently in *Open Range: Poetry of the Reimagined West*, (Ghost Road Press, 2007). He has a BA in English from Coe College and a Masters of Fine Arts in English from the University of Iowa where he attended the Iowa Writers' Workshop. www.danguenther.com

About Redburn Press

This is the newest Redburn Press title. Redburn Press gets its name from the early Melville novel. In it, the autobiographical narrator goes to sea for the first time, excitedly. The ship is full of fascinating types, eccentric human nature in its motley richness. Wellingborough Redburn then encounters more "life and life only".

I want Redburn Press to be that ship in a bottle, so to speak. I will publish – and republish --- eclectic, various, good books full of life. Dan Guenther's *Glossy Black Cockatoos* is such a book.

China Wind, *Dodge City Blues*, and *Townsend's Solitaire*, the three books of the Dan Guenther's Lost Vietnam Trilogy, are still available from Redburn Press online or through your local bookstore.

Mark Kohut
Publisher
November 2009

Photo of Cronulla Park off Ozone Street with large, Washingtonian Palms and Cronulla Beach in the background, and sea gulls and a Sulfur-Crested Cockatoo in the foreground, NSW 1976

Photo by Author

www.ingramcontent.com/pod-product-compliance
Lightning Source LLC
LaVergne TN
LVHW091046080826
845145LV00002B/642

* 9 7 8 1 9 3 3 7 0 4 0 4 3 *